Hamlin Garland

A spoil of office

a story of the modern West

Hamlin Garland

A spoil of office
a story of the modern West

ISBN/EAN: 9783744745406

Printed in Europe, USA, Canada, Australia, Japan

Cover: Foto ©Andreas Hilbeck / pixelio.de

More available books at **www.hansebooks.com**

A SPOIL OF OFFICE.

A STORY OF

THE MODERN WEST.

BY

HAMLIN GARLAND,

AUTHOR OF
"MAIN-TRAVELLED ROADS," "JASON EDWARDS," "A MEMBER OF
THE THIRD HOUSE," "A LITTLE NORSK," ETC.

BOSTON, MASS.:
ARENA PUBLISHING COMPANY,
COPLEY SQUARE.
1892.

To William Dean Howells, the foremost historian of our common lives and the most vital figure in our literature, I dedicate this study of the great middle West, its contemporary life and landscape.

CONTENTS.

A SPOIL OF OFFICE.

A STORY OF THE MODERN WEST.

BY HAMLIN GARLAND.

I.

THE GRANGE PICNIC.

EARLY in the cool hush of a June morning in the seventies, a curious vehicle left Farmer Councill's door, loaded with a merry group of young people. It was a huge omnibus, constructed out of a heavy farm wagon and a hay rack, and was drawn by six horses. The driver was Councill's hired man, Bradley Talcott. Council himself held between his vast knees the staff of a mighty flag in which they all took immense pride. The girls of the grange had made it for the day.

Laughter and scraps of song and rude witticisms made the huge wagon a bouquet of smiling faces. Everybody laughed, except Bradley, who sat with intent eyes and steady lips, his sinewy brown hand holding the excited horses in place. This intentness and self-mastery lent a sort of majesty to his rough-hewn face.

"Let 'em out a little, Brad," said Councill. "We're a little late."

Behind them came teams, before them were teams, along every lane of the beautiful upland prairie, teams were rolling rapidly, all toward the south. The day was perfect summer; it made the heart of reticent Bradley Talcott ache with the beauty of it every time his thoughts went up to the blue sky. The larks, and bobolinks, and red-wings made every meadow riotous with song, and the ever-alert king-birds and flickers flew along from post to post as if to have a part in the celebration.

On every side stretched fields of wheat, green as emerald and soft as velvet. Some of it was high enough already to ripple in the soft winds. The corn fields showed their yellow-green rows of timid shoots, and cattle on the pastures luxuriated in the fullness of the June grass; the whole land was at its fairest and liberalest, and it seemed peculiarly fitting that the farmers should go on a picnic this day of all days.

At the four corners below stood scores of other wagons, loaded to the rim with men, women and children. Up and down the line rode Milton Jennings, the marshal of the day, exalted by the baton he held and the gay red sash looped across his shoulders. Everywhere were merry shouts, and far away at the head of the procession the Burr Oak band was playing. All waited for the flag whose beautiful folds flamed afar in the bright sunlight.

Every member of the grange wore its quaint regalia, apron, sash, and pouch of white, orange, buff and red. Each grange was headed by banners, worked in silk by the patient fingers of the women. Counting the banners there were three Granges there — Liberty Grange, Meadow Grange, and Burr Oak Grange at the lead with the band. The marshal of the leading grange came charging back along the line, riding magnificently his fiery little horse.

"Are we all ready?" he shouted like a field officer.

"Yaas!"

"All ready, Tom?"

"Ready when you are," came the fusillade of replies.

He consulted a moment with Milton, the two horses prancing with unwonted excitement that transformed them into fiery chargers of romance, in the eyes of the boys and girls, just as the sash and baton transfigured Milton into something martial.

"All ready there!" shouted the marshals with grandiloquent gestures of their be-ribboned rods, the band blared out again and the teams began to move toward the west. The men stood up to look ahead, while the boys in the back end of the wagons craned perilously over the edge of the box to see how long the line was. It seemed enormous to them, and their admiration of the marshals broke forth in shrill cries of primitive wildness.

Many of the young fellows had hired at ruinous expense the carriages in which they sat with their girls, wearing a quiet air of aristocratic reserve which did not allow them to shout sarcasms at Milton, when his horse broke into a trot and jounced him up and down till his hat flew off. But mainly the young people were in huge bowered lumber wagons in wildly hilarious groups. The girls in their simple white dresses tied with blue ribbon at the waist, and the boys in their thick woolen suits which did all-round duty for best wear.

As they moved off across the prairie toward the dim blue belt of timber which marked the banks of Rock River, other processions joined them with banner, and bands, and choirs, all making a peaceful and significant parade, an army of reapers of grain, not reapers of men. Some came singing "John Brown," or "Hail, Columbia." Everywhere was a voiced excitement which told how tremendous the occasion seemed. In every wagon hid in cool deeps of fresh-cut grass, were unimaginable quantities of good things which the boys never for a moment forgot even in their great excitement.

On the procession moved, with gay flags and flashing banners. The dust rolled up, the cattle stared across the fences, the colts ran snorting away, tails waving like flags, and unlucky toilers in the fields stopped to wave their hats and gaze wistfully till the caravan passed. The men shouted jovial words to them, and the boys waved their hats in ready sympathy.

At ten o'clock they entered the magnificent grove of oaks, where a speaker's stand had been erected, and where enterprising salesmen from Rock River had erected soda water and candy stands, with an eye to business.

There was already a stupendous crowd, at least so it seemed to the farmers' boys. Two or three bands were whanging away somewhere in the grove; children were shouting and laughing, and boys were racing to and fro, playing ball or wrestling; babies were screaming, and the marshals were shouting directions to the entering teams, in voices that rang through the vaulted foliage with thrilling effect, and the harsh bray of the ice cream and candy sellers completed the confusion.

Bradley's skill as a horseman came out as he swung into the narrow winding road which led through threatening stumps into the heart of the wood past the speaker's stand. Councill furled his great flag and trailed it over the heads of those behind, and Flora and Ceres, and all the other deities of the grange upheld the staff with smiling good-will. And so they drew up to the grand stand, the most imposing turn-out of the day. They sprang out and mingled with the merry crowd, while Bradley drove away. After he had taken care of the team he came back towards the grand stand and wandered about alone. He was not a native of the country and knew very few of the people. He stood about with a timid expression on his face that made him seem more awkward than he really was. He was tall, and strong, and graceful when not conscious of himself as he was now. He felt a little bitter at being ignored — that is, he felt it in a vague and wordless way.

Lovers passed him in pairs, eating peanuts or hot candy which they bit off from a huge triangular mass still hot from the kettle. He had never seen any candy just like that, and wondered if he had better try a piece. The speaking on the stand attracted and held his attention, however. Oratory always had a powerful attraction for him. He moved forward and stood leaning against a tree.

Seats had been arranged in a semi-circle around the stand, on which the speakers of the day, the band, and the singers were already grouped. All around, leaning against the trees, twined in the branches of the oaks, or ranked against the railing, were the banners and mottoes of the various granges. No. 10, Liberty Grange, "Justice is our Plea." Meadow Grange, "United We Stand, Divided We Fall." Bethel Grange, "Fraternity." Other mottoes were "Through Difficulties to the Stars"; "Equal Rights to All, Special Privileges to None." A small organ sat upon the stand surrounded with the singers. Milton, resplendent in his sash and his white vest and black coat, sat beside the organist Eileen, the daughter of Osmond Deering.

The choir arose to sing, accompanied by the organ, and their voices rolled out under the vaulted aisles of foliage, with that thrilling, far-away effect of the singing voice in the midst of illimitable spaces. This was followed by prayer, and then Mr. Deering, the president, called upon everybody to join in singing the national anthem, after which he made the opening address.

He spoke of the marvellous growth of the order, how it had sprung up from the soil at the need of the farmer; it was the first great movement of the farmer in history, and it was something to be proud of. The farmer had been oppressed. He had been helpless and would continue helpless till he asked and demanded his rights. After a dignified and earnest speech he said: —"I will now introduce as the next speaker Mr. Isaac Hobkirk."

Mr. Hobkirk, a large man with a very bad voice, made a fiery speech. "Down with the middlemen," he cried, and was applauded vigorously. "They are the blood-suckers that's takin' the life out of us farmers. What we want is to deal right with the manufacturers, an' cut off these white-handed fellers in Rock River who git all we raise. Speechifyin' and picnickin' is all well an' good, but what we want is *agents*. We want agents f'r machinery, wheat buyers, agents f'r groceries, that's what we want ; that's what we're here for ; that's what the grange was got together for.   Down with the middlemen !"

This brought out vigorous applause and showed that a very large number agreed with him.   Bradley sat silently through it all.   It didn't mean very much to him, and he wished they'd sing again.

The chairman again came forward.   "Napoleon said 'Old men for counsel, but young men for war.'   But our young men have listened patiently to us old fellows for years, and mebbe they don't think much of our counsel.   I'm going to call on Milton Jennings, one of our rising young men."

Milton, a handsome young fellow with yellow hair and smiling lips, arose and came forward to the rail, feeling furtively in his coat-tail pocket to see that his handkerchief was all right.   He was a student at the seminary, and was considered a fine young orator.   This was his first attempt before so large an audience.

"Ladies and gentlemen," he began after clearing his throat.   "Brothers and sisters of the Order : I feel highly honored by the president by being thus called upon to address you.   Old men for counsel is all right, if they counsel what we young men want, but I'm for war ; I'm for a fight in the interests of the farmer. Not merely a defensive warfare but an offensive warfare.

"How? By the ballot. Mr. President, I know you don't agree with me. I know it's a rule of the Order to keep politics out of it, but I don't know of a better place to discuss the interests of the farmer. It's a mistake. We've got to unite at the ballot box; what's the use of our order if we don't? We must be represented at the State legislature, and we can't do that unless we make the grange a political factor.

"You may talk about legislative corruption, Mr. President, and about county rings, to come near home. (Cheers and cries, "Now you're getting at it," "That's right," etc.) But the only way to get 'em out is to vote 'em out. ("That's a fact.") You m'say we can talk it over outside the order. Yes, but I tell you, Mr. President, the order's the place for it. If it's an educational thing, then I say it ought to educate and educate in politics, Mr. President.

"I tell you, I'm for war! Let's go in to win! When the fall's work is done, in fact, from this time on, Mr. President, the farmers of this county ought to organize for the campaign. Cut and dry our tickets, cut and dry our plans. If we begin early and work together we can strangle the anacondy that is crushing us, and the eagle of victory will perch on our banners on the third of November, and the blood-suckers trouble us no more forever."

With this remarkable peroration, spoken in a high monotonous key, after the fashion of the political orator, Milton sat down mopping his face, while his admirers cheered.

The chairman, who had been nervously twisting in his chair, hastened to explain.

"Fellow-Citizens: I'm not to be held responsible for anything anybody else speaks on this platform. I do not believe with our young brother. I think that politics will destroy the grange. To make it a debating school on political questions would bring discord and wrangling into it. I hope I shall never see the day. I now ask Brother Jennings to say a few words."

Mr. Jennings, a fat and jolly farmer, came to the front looking very hot. His collar had long since melted.

"I aint very much of a speech-maker, Mr. President, brothers and sisters. Fact is, I sent my boy down to the seminary to learn how to talk, so't I wouldn't haf to. I guess he represents my idees purty well, though, all except this political idee. I don't know about that. I aint quite made up my mind on that point. I guess I'd better leave the floor for somebody else."

"Glad you left the floor," whispered Milton to his father as he sat down by his side. Milton was a merciless joker, especially upon his father.

"We have with us to-day," said the chairman, in the tone of one who announces the coming in of the dessert, "one of the most eloquent speakers in the State, one whose name all grangers know, our State lecturer, Miss Ida Wilbur."

The assembly rose to its feet with applause as a slender young woman stepped forth, and waited, with easy dignity to begin her speech. There was something significant in her manner, which was grave and dignified, and a splendid stillness fell upon the audience as she began in a clear, penetrating contralto:

"Brothers and sisters in the Order: While I have been sitting here listening to your speakers, I have been looking at the mottoes on your banners, and I have been trying to find out by those expressions what your conception of this movement is. I wonder whether its majesty appears to you as it does to me." She paused for an instant. "We are in danger of losing sight of its larger meaning.

" Primarily, the object of the grange has been the education of the farmers. It has been a great social educator, and I am glad, my friends and neighbors, when I can look out upon such an assembly as this. I see in it the rise of the idea of union, and intelligent union ; but principally I see in it the meeting together of the farmers who live too much apart from the rest of the world.

"I believe," she cried with lifted hand, "I believe this is the greatest movement of the farmer in the history of the world. It is a movement against unjust discrimination, no doubt, but it has another side to me, a poetic side, I call it. The farmer is a free citizen of a great republic, it is true ; but he is a *Solitary* free citizen. He lives alone too much. He meets his fellow-men too little. His dull life, his hard work, make it almost impossible to keep his better nature uppermost. The work of the grange is a social work." She was supported by generous applause.

"It is not to antagonize town and country. The work of the grange to me is not political. Keep politics out of it, or it will destroy you. Use it to bring yourselves together. Let it furnish you with pleasant hours. Establish your agencies, if you can, but I care more for meetings

like this.   I care more for the poetry there is in
having Flora, and Ceres, and Pomona brought
into the farmer's home."

Her great brown eyes glowed as she spoke and
her lifted head thrilled those who sat near enough
to see the emotion that was in the lines of her
face.   The sun struck through the trees, that
swayed in masses overhead, dappling the up-
turned faces with light and shade.   The leaves
under the tread of the wind rustled softly, and
the soaring hawk looked down curiously as he
drifted above the grove, like a fleck of cloud.

On Bradley, standing there alone, there fell
something mysterious, like a light.   Something
whiter and more penetrating than the sunlight.
As he listened, something stirred within him, a
vast longing, a hopeless ambition, nameless as it
was strange.   His bronzed face paled and he
breathed heavily.   His eyes absorbed every detail
of the girl's face and figure.   There was wonder
in his eyes at her girlish face, and something like
awe at her powerful diction and her impersonal
emotion.   She stood there like an incarnation of
the great dream-world that lay beyond his horizon,
the world of poets and singers in the far realms
of light and luxury.

"I have a dream of what is coming," she said

in conclusion, and her voice had a prophetic ring.
"I see a time when the farmer will not need to
live in a cabin on a lonely farm. I see the
farmers coming together in groups. I see them
with time to read, and time to visit with their fellows. I see them enjoying lectures in beautiful
halls, erected in every village. I see them gather
like the Saxons of old upon the green at evening
to sing and dance. I see cities rising near them
with schools, and churches, and concert halls, and
theatres. I see a day when the farmer will no
longer be a drudge and his wife a bond slave, but
happy men and women who will go singing to
their pleasant tasks upon their fruitful farms."
The audience did not cheer, it sat as if in church.
The girl seemed to be speaking prophecy.

"When the boys and girls will not go West nor
to the city; when life will be worth living. In
that day the moon will be brighter and the stars
more glad, and pleasure, and poetry, and love of
life come back to the man who tills the soil."

The people broke into wild applause when she
finished. All were deeply stirred. Tears were
streaming down many faces, and when Deering
arose to announce a song by the choir his voice
shook and he made no secret of his deep emotion.
After the song, he said: "Neighbors, we don't

want to spoil that splendid speech with another
this day.   The best thing we can do is to try to
think that good time is here and eat our dinner
with the resolution to bring that good time as
soon as possible."

Bradley stood there after the others had risen.
The dazzling pictures called up by the speaker's
words were still moving confusedly in his brain.
They faded at last and he moved with a sigh and
went out to feed the horses their oats.

II.

THE DINNER UNDER THE OAKS.

THE dinner made a beautiful scene, the most idyllic in the farmer's life. The sun, now high noon, fell through the leaves in patches of quivering light upon the white table-cloth, spread out upon the planks, and it fell upon the fair hair of girls, and upon the hard knotted fingers of men and women grown old in toil. The rattle of dishes, the harsh-keyed, unwonted laughter of the women, and the sounding invitations to dinner given and taken filled the air. The long plank seats placed together made capital tables, and eager children squatted about wistfully watching the display of each new delicacy. The crude abundance of the Iowa farm had been brought out to make it a great dinner. The boys could hardly be restrained from clutching at each new dish.

The Councills and the Burns families took dinner together. Mrs. Burns, fretful and worn, cuffed the children back from the table while bringing out her biscuit and roast chicken. Some sat stolidly silent, but big-voiced Councill joked in his heavy way with everyone within earshot.

"Well, the Lord is on our side, neighbor Jennings, to-day, anyhow," he roared across the space of two or three tables.

"He's always on our side, brother Councill," smiled Jennings.

"Wal, I'd know about that. Sometimes I'm a leettle in doubt."

"Got something good to eat?" inquired Jennings of Mrs. Councill.

"Land sakes, no! We never have anything fit to eat since Jane's gone to havin' beaux; my cookin' aint fit for a hawg to eat."

"I aint a-goin' to eat it, then," roared Councill in vast delight at his joke on himself. "I'll go over and eat with Marm Jennings." They all roared at this.

"Tell us so't we c'n laff," called Mrs. Smith, coming over to see what they did have.

"Where's Brad?" said Mrs. Councill, looking about her. "Aint he comin' to dinner?"

"I don't see him around anywheres. Mebbe he's out feed'n the horses," replied Councill, without concern.

"Say! that was a great speech that girl made," put in Brother Smith, coming over with a chicken leg in one hand and a buttered biscuit in the other.   "But what we want is free trade "—

"What we want is a home market," said Milton, some distance away.

"Oh, go to — Texas with y'r home market!"

"Tut, tut, tut, no politics, brethren," interrupted Jennings.

Bradley, ignored by everybody, was standing over by the trunk of a large oak tree, watching from afar the young girl who had so stirred him. She was eating dinner with Deering, his wife, and daughter, and Milton, who was there, looking very bright and handsome, or at least he appeared so to Eileen Deering, a graceful little girl, his classmate at the seminary.

Miss Wilbur sat beside Deering, who was a large man with a type of face somewhat resembling Lincoln's. She was smiling brightly, but her smile had something thoughtful in it, and her eyes had unknown deeps like a leaf-bottomed woodland pool across which the sun fell. She was feeling yet the stress of emotion she had felt in speaking, and was a little conscious of the admiring glances of the people.

She saw once or twice a tall, roughly dressed young farmer, who seemed to be looking at her steadily, and there was something in his glance, a timid worshipful expression, that touched her and made her observe him more closely. He was very farmer-like, she noticed; his cheap coat fitted him badly, and his hat was old and shapeless. Yet there was something natively fine and chivalrous in his admiration. She felt that.

"You're a farmer's daughter yourself," said Deering, as if they had been speaking of somebody else who was.

"Yes, my father was a farmer. I'm a teacher. I only began a little while ago to speak in the interest of the farmer. It seems to me that everybody is looking out for himself except the farmer, and I want to help him to help himself. I expect to speak in every county in the State this winter."

Bradley crept nearer. He was eager to hear what she was saying. He grew furtive in his manner, when she observed him, and he felt as if he were doing something criminal. He saw Miss Wilbur say something to Mr. Deering, who looked up a moment later and said to Bradley, whom he did not know, "Why, certainly, come and have some dinner, plenty of it."

Bradley flushed hot with shame and indignation, and moved away deeply humiliated. They had taken him for a poor, friendless, lonely tramp, and there was just enough truth in his loneliness to make it sting.

"Say, Brad, don't you want some grub?" called Councill, catching sight of him.

"Quick, 'r'y lose it," said Burns.

He sat down and fell upon the dinner silently, but there was a hot flush still upon his face. He was not a beau. It had always been difficult for him to address a marriageable woman, and a joke on that subject threw him into dumb confusion. He had lived a dozen tender dreams of which no one knew a word. Indeed, he never acknowledged them to himself. He had admired in this way Eileen Deering whom he had seen with Milton a few times during the year. He now envied Milton his easy air of calm self-possession in the presence of two such beautiful girls. There was a bitter feeling of rebellion in his heart.

Miss Wilbur had stirred his unexplored self. Down where ambitions are born; where aspirations rise like sun-shot mists, her words and the light of her face had gone. Already there was something sacred and ineffably sweet about her voice and face. She had come to him as the right woman comes sometimes to a man, and thereafter his whole life is changed.

He walked away from the few people he knew,

and tried to interest himself in the games they were playing but he could not. He drifted back to the grand stand and sought about till he could see Miss Wilbur once more. She was so pure, so beautiful to him.

The hour or two after dinner was spent in visiting and getting acquainted, and the time seemed all too short. Each granger took this opportunity of inquiring after the health of the other grangers of the county. The young people wandered in laughing, romping groups about the grounds, buying peanuts and sugar candy, and drinking the soda water and lemonade which the venders called with strenuous enterprise.

On the shadowed side of the stand the leading men of the grange gathered, consulting about plans and measures.

"Now, it seems to me that we're going on all right now," said Deering. "We're getting our goods cheap and we're cuttin' off the middleman."

"And we're getting hold of the railways."

"Yes, but it don't amount to nothin' compared to what ought to be done. We ought 'o oust them infernal blood-suckers that's in our court-house, and we want to do it as a grange."

"No," said Jennings in his placid way, "we can do that better. I've got a plan."

"What we want," said Hobkirk, "is a party, a ticket of our own, then we can "—

"No, we can't do that. It won't be right to do that. We must stand by the party that has given us our railway legislation."

Milton and several of the younger farmers drew off one side and talked earnestly about the fall campaign.

"They'll beat us again unless we go in together," Milton said with emphatic gesticulation. Milton was a natural politician. His words found quick response in the erratic Hobkirk, who had good ideas but whose temperament made all his words jagged shot. He irritated where he meant to convince.

Bradley listened to it all without feeling that he had any part in it. It didn't seem to him that politics had anything to do with the beautiful words of the girl. On the stand the choir began to sing again and he walked toward them. They sang on and the people listened while they packed away the dishes. They sang "Auld Lang Syne," and "We'll Meet Beyond the River," with that characteristic attraction of the common people for wistful, sorrowful cadences which is a paradox not easily explained.

"All aboard!" called Councill from his wagon

as Bradley drove the team up to the band stand. While the merry young people clambered in and paired off along the seats he was seeing Miss Wilbur shaking hands with the people who paused to say good-by. His heart ached for a glance of her brown eyes and a word, but he held the reins in his great hands and his face showed only his usual impassive reticence. He was only Councill's herdman.

The banners were taken up, the children loaded in, the boys looking back wistfully to the games and the candy-stands. Councill unfurled his flag to the wind, and Bradley swung the eager horses into the lane. On all sides the farmers' teams were getting out into the road; the work of the marshals was done. Each man went his own gait.

The young people behind Bradley began to sing:—

> "Out on an ocean all boundless we ride,
> We're homeward bound,
> Homeward bound."

And so along each lane through the red sunset the farmers rolled home. Home through lanes bordered with velvet green wheat, across which the sunlight streamed in dazzling yellow floods.

Home through wild prairies, where the birds nested and the gophers whistled. The dust rose up, transformed into gold by the light of the setting sun. The children fell asleep in their tired mothers' arms. The men shouted to each other from team to team, discussing the speakers and the crops.

Smiles were few as each wagon turned into its gateway and rolled up to the silent house. The sombre shadow of the farm's drudgery had fallen again on faces unused to smiling.

Only the lovers lingering on the road till the moon rose and the witchery of night came to make the girlish eyes more brilliant, softening their gayety into a wistful tenderness, only to these did the close of the day seem as sweet and momentous as the morning. While the trusty horse jogged on, impatient of the slow pace set by his driver, the lovers sat with little to say, but with hearts lit by the light that can glorify for a few moons, at least, even the life of ceaseless toil.

III.

BRADLEY RESOLVES TO GO TO SCHOOL.

A FARM is a good place to think in, if a man has sufficient self-sustaining force — that is, if work does not dominate him and force him to think in petty or degrading circles.

It is a lonely life. Especially lonely on a large farm in the West. The life of a hired man like Bradley Talcott is spent mainly with the horses and cattle. In the spring he works day after day with a drag or seeder, moving to and fro an animate speck across a dull brown expanse of soil. Even when he has a companion there is little talk, for there is little to say, and the extra exertion of speaking against the wind, or across distances, soon forces them both into silence.

True, there is the glory of the vast sweep of sky, the wild note of the crane, the flight of geese, the multitudinous twitter of sparrows, and the subtle exalting smell of the fresh, brown earth ; but these things do not compensate for human society. Nature palls upon the normal man when he is alone with her constantly. The monotone of the wind and the monochrome of the sky oppress him. His heart remains empty.

The rustle of flashing, blade-like corn leaves, the vast clean-cut mountainous clouds of June, the shade of shimmering popple trees, the whistle of plover and the sailing hawk do not satisfy the man who follows the corn-plow with the hot sun beating down all day upon his bent head and dusty shoulders. His point of view is not that from the hammock. He is not out on a summer vacation. If he thinks, he thinks bitter things, and when he speaks his words are apt to be oaths.

Still a man has time to think and occasionally a man dominates his work and refuses to be hardened and distorted. Many farmers swear at the team or the plow and everything that bothers them. Some whistle vacantly and mechanically all day, or sing in endless succession the few gloomy songs they know. Bradley thought.

He thought all summer long. He was a powerful man physically and turned off his work with a ready knack which left him free to think. All day as he moved to and fro in the rustling corn rows, he thought, and with his thinking, his powers expanded. He had the mysterious power of self-development.

The centre of his thinking was that slender young woman and the words she had uttered. He repeated her prophetic words as nearly as he could a hundred times. He repeated them aloud as he plowed day after day, through the dreamful September mist. He began to look ahead and wonder what he should do or could do. Must he be a farmer's hired man or a renter all his life? His mind moved slowly from point to point, but it never returned to its old dumb patience. His mind, like his body, had unknown latent forces. He was one of those natures whose delicacy and strength are alike hidden.

"Brad don't know his strength," Councill was accustomed to say. "If he should ever get mad enough to fight, the other feller'd better go a-visitin'." And a person who knew his mind might have said, "If Bradley makes up his mind to do a thing he'll do it." But no one knew his mind. He did not know its resources himself.

His mind seized upon every hint, and bit by bit his resolution was formed. Milton, going by one Monday morning on his way to the seminary, stopped beside the fence where Brad was plowing and waited for him to come up. He had a real interest in Bradley.

"Hello, Brad," he called cheerily.

"Hello, Milt."

"How's business?"

"Oh, so so. Pretty cold."

The wind was blowing cold and cuttingly from the north-west. Milton, rosy with his walk, dropped down beside the hedge of weeds in the sun and Brad climbed over the fence and joined him. It was warm and cosy there, and the crickets were cheeping feebly in the russet grass where the sunlight fell. The wind whistled through the weeds with a wild, mournful sound. Bradley did not speak for some time. He listened to Milton. At last he said abruptly —

"Say, Milt, what does it cost to go to school down there?"

"Depends on who goes. Cost me 'bout forty dollars a term. Shep an' I room it and cook our own grub."

"What's the tuition?"

"Eight dollars a term."

"Feller could go to the public school for nauthin', couldn't he?"

"Yes, and that'd be all it 'ud be worth," said Milton with fine scorn at an inferior institution.

"What does a room cost?" Brad pursued after a silence.

"Well, ours cost 'bout three dollars a month,

but we have two rooms. You could get one for fifty cents a week."

He looked up at Brad with a laugh in his eyes. "Don't think of starting in right off, do you?"

"Well, I don't know but I might if I had money enough to carry me through."

"What y' think o' doin', study law?"

"No, but I'd kind o' like to be able to speak in public. Seems t' me a feller ought 'o know how to speak at a school meetin' when he's called on. I couldn't say three words to save m' soul. They teach that down there, don't they?"

"Yes, we have Friday exercises and then there are two debating clubs. They're boss for practice. That's where I put in most o' my time. I'm goin' into politics," he ended with a note of exalted purpose as if going into politics were really something fine. "Are you?"

"Well, there's no tellin' what minit a feller's liable to be called on and I'd kinder like to"—He fell off into silence again.

Milton jumped up. "Well, hold on, this won't do f'r me; I must mosey along. Good-by," he said, and set off down the road.

"When does the next term begin?" called Bradley.

" November 15th," Milton replied, looking about for an instant. " Better try it."

Bradley threw the lines over his shoulder and, bending his head, fell into deep calculation. Milton's clear tenor was heard ringing across the fields, fitfully dying away. Milton made the most of everything, and besides he was on his way to see Eileen. He could afford to be gay.

Bradley thought, even while he husked the corn, one of the bitterest of all farm tasks when the cold winds of November began to blow. Councill had a large field of corn and every morning in the cold and frosty light Ike and Bradley were out in the field, each with a team. Beautiful mornings, if one could have looked upon it from a window in a comfortable home. There were mornings when the glittering purple and orange domes of the oaks and maples swam in the mist dreamfully, so beautiful the eyes lingered upon them wistfully. Mornings when the dim lines of the woods were a royal purple, and gray-blue shadows streamed from the trees upon the yellow-green grass.

Husking was the last of the fall work and the last day of husking found Bradley desperately undecided. They had been working desperately all the week to finish the field on Saturday. It

was a bitter cold morning. As they leaped into
the frost-rimmed wagon-box and caught up the
reins, the half-frozen team sprang away with desperate energy, making the wagon bound over the
frozen ground with a thunderous clatter.

In every field the sound of similar wagons getting out to work could be heard. It was not yet
light. A leaden-gray dome of cloud had closed in
over the morning sky and the feeling of snow was
in the air. There was only a dull flush of red in
the east to show the night had been frostily clear.

Ike raised a great shout to let his neighbors
know he was in the field. Councill, with a fork
over his shoulder, was on his way down the lane
to help a neighbor thresh. Ike jovially shook the
reins above his colts and Bradley followed close
behind, and the two wagons went crashing
through the forest of corn. The race started the
blood of the drivers as well as that of the teams.
The cold wind cut the face like a knife and the
crackling corn-stalks flew through the air as the
wagons swept over them. Reaching the farther
side they turned in and faced toward the house,
the horses blowing white clouds of breath.

"Jee Whitaker!" shouted Ike, as he crouched
on the leeward side of his wagon, and threshed
his arms around his chest, after having finished

blanketing his team to protect them against the ferocious wind. "I'm thunderin' glad this is the last day of this kind o' thing."

He looked like a grizzly bear in bad repair. He had an old fur cap on his head that concealed his ears and most of his face. He wore a ragged coat that was generally gray, but had white lines along the seams. Under this he wore another coat still more ragged, and the whole was belted at the waist with an old surcingle. Like his father, he was possessed of vast physical strength, and took pride in his powers of endurance.

"Wal, here goes," he said, stripping off his outside coat. "It's tough, but it aint no use dreadin' it."

Bradley smiled back at him in his wordless way, and caught hold of the first ear. It sent a shiver of pain through him. His fingers, worn to the quick, protruded from his stiff, ragged gloves, and the motions of clasping and stripping the ear were like the rasp of a file on a naked nerve. He shivered and swore, but his oath was like a groan.

The horses, humped and shivering, looked black and fuzzy, by reason of their erected hair. They tore at the corn-stalks hungrily. Their tails streamed sidewise with the force of the wind, which had a wild and lonesome sound, as it swept across the sear stretches of the corn. The stalks towered far above the heads of the huskers, but did little to temper the onslaught of the blast.

Occasional flocks of geese drifted by in the grasp of the inexorable gale, their necks out-thrust as if they had already caught the gleam of their warm southern lagoons. Clouds of ducks, more adventurous, were seen in irregular flight, rising and falling from the lonely fields with wild clap-ping of wings. Only the sparrows seemed indif-ferent to the cold.

There was immensity in the dome of the unbroken, seamless, gray threatening sky. There was majesty in the dim plain, across which the morning light slowly fell. The plain, with its dark blue groves, from which thin lines of smoke rose and hastened away, and majesty in the wind that came from the illimitable and desolate north. But the lonely huskers had no time to feel, much less to think, upon these things.

They bent down to their work and snatched the red and yellow ears bare of their frosty husks with marvelous dexterity. The first plunge over, Bradley found as usual that the sharpest pain was over. The wind cut his face, and an occasional driving flake of snow struck and clung to his face and stung. His coat collar chafed his chin, and the frost wet his gloves through and through. But he warmed to it and at last almost forgot it. He fell into thought again, so deep that his work became absolutely mechanical.

"Say, Brad, let's go to that dance over at Davis's," shouted Ike, after an hour of silence.

"I guess not."

"Why not?"

"Because I aint invited."

"Oh, that's all right; Ed, he told me to bring anyone I felt like."

"I aint going, all the same. I may be in Rock River by next Wednesday."

"They aint no danger o' you're going to Rock River."

Bradley fell once more into the circle of his plans and went the round again. He had saved two hundred dollars. It was enough to take him to school a year, but what then? That was the recurring question. It was the most momentous day in his life. Should he spend his money in this way? Every dollar of it represented toil, long days of lonely plowing or dragging, long days under the burning harvest sun. It was all he had, all he had to show for his life. Was it right to spend it for schooling?

"What good'll it do yeh?" Ike asked one day

when Bradley was feeling out for a little helpful sympathy. "Better buy a team with it and rent a piece of land. What y' goan to do after you spent the money?"

"I don't know," Bradley had replied in his honest way.

"Wal, I'd think of it a dum long spell 'fore I'd do it," was Ike's reply, and Councill had agreed with it.

Bradley fell behind Ike, for he wanted to be alone. He had grown into the habit of accounting to *Her* for his actions, and when he wished to consult with *Her*, he wanted to be alone. There was something sacred, even in the thought of *Her*, and he shrank from having his thoughts broken in upon by any careless or jesting word.

As he pondered, his hands grew slower in their action and, at last, he stopped and leaned against the wagon-box. Something came into his heart that shook him, a feeling of unknown power, a certainty of faith in himself. He shivered with an electric thrill that made his hair stir.

He lifted his face to the sky and his eyes saw a crane sailing with stately grace, in measureless circle, a mere speck against the unbroken gray of the sky. There seemed something prophetic; something mystic in its harsh, wild cry that fell, like the scream of the eagle, a defiant note against wind and storm.

"I'll do it," he said, and his hands clinched. At the sound of his voice he shivered again, as if the wind had suddenly penetrated his clothing. His dress made him grotesque. The spaces around him made him pathetic, but in his golden-brown eyes was something that made him sublime.

The thought which he dared not utter, but which lay deep under every resolution and action he made, was the hope, undefined and unacknowledged to himself, that sometime he might meet her and have her approve his action.

IV.

BRADLEY'S TRIALS AT. SCHOOL.

THE morning on which Bradley was to begin his term at the seminary was a clear, crisp day in later November. He had rented a room in the basement of a queer old building, known as the Park Hotel, a crazy mansard-roofed structure which held at regular intervals some rash men attempting to run it as a hotel.

Bradley had rented this cellar because it was the cheapest place he could find. He agreed to pay two dollars a month for it, and the use of the two chairs, and cooking stove, which made up its furnishing. He had purchased a skillet and two or three dishes, Mrs. Councill had lent him a bed, and he seemed reasonably secure against hunger and cold.

He looked forward to his entrance into the school with dread. All that Monday morning he stood about his door watching for Milton and seeing the merry students in procession up the walk. The girls seemed so bright and so beautiful, he wondered how the boys could walk beside them with such calm unconcern. Their laughter, their mutual greetings threw him into a profound self-pity and disgust. When he joined Milton and Shepard, and went up the walk under the bare-limbed maple trees, he shivered with fear. They all seemed perfectly at home, with the exception of himself.

Milton knowing what to expect smuggled him into the chapel in the midst of a crowd of five or six others, and thus he escaped the derisive applause with which the pupils were accustomed to greet each new-comer at the opening of a term. He gave one quick glance at the rows of faces, and shambled awkwardly along to his seat beside Milton, his eyes downcast. He found courage to look around and study his fellow-students after a little and discovered that several of them were quite as awkward, quite as ill at ease as himself.

Milton, old pupil as he was (that is to say, this was his second term), sat beside him and indicated the seniors as they came in, and among the rest pointed out Radbourn.

"He's the high mucky-muck o' this shebang," Shep whispered.

"Why so?" asked Bradley, looking carefully at the big, smooth-faced, rather gloomy-looking young fellow.

Shep hit his own head with his fist in a comically significant gesture. "Brains! What d' ye call 'em, Milt? Correscations of the serry beltum."

Shepard was a short youth with thick yellow hair, and a comically serious quality in the twist of his long upper lip.

Milton grinned. "Convolutions of the cerebrum, I s'pose you're driving at. Shep comes to school to have fun," Milton explained to Bradley.

"Chuss," said Shep, by which he meant yes; "an' I have it, too, betyerneck. I enter no plea, me lord" —

There came a burst of applause as a tall and attractive girl came in with her arms laden down with books. Her intellectual face lit up with a smile at the applause, and a pink flush came into her pale cheek. "That's Miss Graham," whispered Shepard; "she's all bent up on Radbourn."

The teachers came in, the choir rose to sing, and the exercises of the morning began. Bradley thought Miss Graham, with her heavy-lidded, velvety-brown eyes, looked like Miss Wilbur. Her eyes were darker, he decided, and she was taller and paler; in fact, the resemblance was mainly in her manner which had the same dignity and repose.

At Milton's suggestion Bradley remained in his seat after the rest of the pupils had marched out to the sound of the organ. Then Milton introduced him to the principal, who took him by the hand so cordially that his embarrassment was gone in a moment. "Come and see me at eleven," he said. After a short talk with him in his room a couple hours later, his work was assigned.

"You'll be in the preparatory department, Mr. Talcott, but if you care to do extra work we may get you into the junior class. Jennings, look after him a little, won't you?"

The principal was a kind man, but he had two hundred of these rude, awkward farmer-boys, and he could not be expected to study each one closely enough to discover their latent powers. Bradley went away down town to buy his books, with a feeling that the smile of the principal was not genuine, and he felt also that Milton was a little ashamed of him here in the town. Everything seemed to be going hard with him. But his hardest trial came when he entered the class-room at one o'clock.

He knew no one, of course, and the long, narrow room was filled with riotous boys and girls all much younger than himself. All the desks seemed to be occupied and he was obliged to run the gauntlet of the entire class in his search for a seat. As he walked down the room so close to the wall that he brushed the chalk of the blackboard off upon his shoulder, he made a really ludicrous figure. All of his fine, free, unconscious grace was gone and his strength of limb only added to his awkwardness.

The girls were of that age where they find the keenest delight in annoying a bashful fellow such as they perceived this new-comer to be. His hair had been badly barbered by Councill and his suit of cotton diagonal, originally too small and never a fit, was now yellow on the shoulders where the sun had faded the analine dye, and his trousers were so tight that they clung to the tops of his great boots, exposing his huge feet in all their enormity of shapeless housing. His large hands protruded from his sleeves and were made still more noticeable by his evident loss of their control.

"Picked too soon," said Nettie Russell, with a vacant stare into space, whereat the rest shrieked with laughter. A great hot wave of blood rushed up over Bradley, making him dizzy. He knew that joke all too well. He looked around blindly for a seat. As he stood there helpless, Nettie hit him with a piece of chalk and someone threw the eraser at his boots.

"Number twelves," said young Brown.

"When did it get loose?"

"Does your mother know you're out?"

"Put your hat over it," came from all sides.

He saw an empty chair and started to sit down, but Nettie slipped into it before him. He started for her seat and her brother Claude got there apparently by mere accident just before him. Bradley stood again indecisively, not daring to look up, burning with rage and shame. Again someone hit him with a piece of chalk, making a resounding whack, and the entire class roared again in concert.

"Why, its head is *wood!*" said Claude, in apparent astonishment at his own discovery.

Bradley raised his head for the first time. There came into his eyes a look that made Claude Russell tremble. He again approached an empty chair and was again forestalled by young Brown. With a bitter curse he swung his great open palm around and laid his tormenter flat on the floor, stunned and breathless. A silence fell on the group. It was as if a lion had awakened with a roar of wrath.

"Come on, all o' ye!" he snarled through his set teeth, facing them all. As he stood thus the absurdity of his own attitude came upon him. They were only children, after all. Reeking with the sweat of shame and anger which burst from his burning skin, he reached for a chair.

Nettie, like the little dare-devil that she was, pulled the chair from under him, and he saved himself from falling only by wildly clutching the desk before him. As it was, he fell almost into her lap and everybody shrieked with uncontrollable laughter. In the midst of it, Miss Clayson, the teacher, came hurrying in to silence the tumult, and Bradley rushed from the room like a bull from the arena, maddened with the spears of the toreador. He snatched his hat and coat from the rack and hardly looked up till he reached the haven of his little cellar.

He threw his cap on the floor and for a half hour raged up and down the floor, his mortification and shame and rage finding vent in a fit of cursing such as he had never had in his life before. All awkwardness was gone now. His great limbs, supple and swift, clenched, doubled, and thrust out against the air in unconscious lightning-swift gestures that showed how terrible he could be when roused.

At last he grew calm enough to sit down, and then his mood changed to the deepest dejection. He sank into a measureless despair. A terrible ache came into his throat.

They were right, he was a great hulking fool. He never could be anything but a clod-hopper, anyway. He looked down at his great hand, at his short trousers, and the indecent ugliness of his horrible boots, and studied himself without mercy to himself. He acknowledged that they were hideous, but he couldn't help it.

Then his mind took another turn and he went over the history of that suit. He didn't want it when he bought it, but he found himself like wax, moulded by the soft, white, confidential hands of the Jew salesman, who offered it to him as a special favor below cost. In common with other young men of his sort he always felt under obligation to buy if he went into a store, even if there was nothing there that suited him. He knew when he bought the suit and paid eleven dollars for it that he would always be sorry, and its cheapness now appalled him.

He always swore at himself for this weakness before the salesman, and yet, year by year he had been cheated in the same way. For the first time, however, he saw his clothing in all its hideousness. Those cruel girls and grinning boys had shown him that clothes made the man, even in a western school. The worst part of it was that he had been humiliated by a girl and there was no redress. His strength of limb was useless here.

He sat there till darkness came into his room. He did not replenish the coal in the stove that leered at him from the two broken doors in front, and seemed to face him with a crazy, drunken reel on its mis-matched legs. He was hungry, but he sat there enjoying in a morbid way the pang of hunger. It helped him someway to bear the sting of his defeat.

It was the darkest hour of his life. He swore never to go back again to that room. He couldn't face that crowd of grinning faces. He turned hot and cold by turns as he thought of his folly. He was a cursed fool for ever thinking of trying to do anything but just dig away on a farm. He might have known how it would be; he'd got behind and had to be classed in with the children ; there was no help for it ; he'd never go back.

The thought of *Her* came in again and again,

but the thought couldn't help him. *Her* face drove the last of his curses from his lips, but it threw him into a fathomless despair, where he no longer defined his thoughts into words. *Her* face shone like a star, but it stood over a bottomless rift in the earth and showed how impassable its yawning barrier was.

There came a whoop outside and a scramble at the door and somebody tumbled into the room.

"Anybody here?"

"Hello, where are you, Brad?"

He recognized Milton's voice. "Yes, I'm here; but wait a minute."

"Cæsar, I *guess* we'll wait! Break our necks if we don't," said the other shadow whom he now recognized as Shep Watson. "Always live in the dark?"

They waited while he lighted the dim little kerosene lamp on the table. "O conspiracy, shamest thou to show thy dangerous brow by night," quoted Shep in the interim.

"Been 'sleep?" asked Milton.

"No. Se' down, anywheres," he added on second thought, as he realized that chairs were limited.

"Say, Brad, come on; let's go over t' the society."

"I guess not," said Brad sullenly.

"Why not?" asked Milton, recognizing something bitter in his voice.

"Because, I aint got any right to go. I aint goin' t' school ag'in. I'm goin' west."

"Why, what's up?"

"I aint a-goin', that's all. I can't never ketch up with the rest of you fellers." His voice broke a little, "an' it aint much fun havin' to go in with a whole raft o' little boys and girls."

"Oh, say now, Brad, I wouldn't mind 'em if I was you," said Milton, after a pause. He had the delicacy not to say he had heard the details of Bradley's experience. "We all have to go through 'bout the same row o' stumps, don't we, Shep? The way to do with 'em is to jest pay no 'tention to 'em."

But the good-will and sympathy of the boys could not prevail upon Bradley to go with them. He persisted in his determination to leave school. And the boys finally went out leaving him alone. Their influence had been good, however; he was distinctly less bitter after they left him and his thoughts went back to Miss Wilbur. What would she think of him if he gave up all his plans the first day, simply because some mischievous girls and boys had made him absurd? When he thought of her he felt strong enough to go back, but when he thought of his tormentors and what he would be obliged to endure from them, he shivered and shrank back into despondency.

He was still fighting his battle, when a slow step came down the stairs ending in a sharp rap upon the door. He said, "Come in," and Radbourn, the most powerful and most popular senior, entered the room. He was a good deal of an autocrat in the town and in the school, and took pleasure in exercising his power on behalf of some poor devil like Bradley Talcott.

"Jennings tells me you're going to give it up," he said, without preliminary conversation.

Bradley nodded sullenly. "What's the use, anyhow? I might as well. I'm too old, anyhow."

Radbourn looked at him a moment in silence. "Put on your hat and let's go outside," he said at length, and there was something in his voice that Bradley obeyed.

Once on the outside Radbourn took his arm and they walked on up the street in silence for some distance. It was still, and clear, and frosty, and the stars burned overhead with many-colored brilliancy.

"Now I know all about it, Talcott, and I know

just about how you feel. But all the same you must go back there to-morrow morning."

"It aint no use talkin', I can't do it."

"Yes, you can. You think you can't, but you can. A man can do anything if he only thinks he can and tries hard. You can't afford to let a little thing like that upset your plans. I understand your position exactly. You're at a disadvantage," he changed his pace suddenly, stopping Bradley. "Now, Talcott, you're at a disadvantage with that suit. It makes you look like a gawk, when you're not. You're a stalwart fellow, and if you'll invest in a new suit of clothes as Jennings did, it'll make all the difference in the world."

"I can't afford it."

"No, that's a mistake, you can't afford *not* to have it. A good suit of clothes will do more to put you on an equality with the boys than anything else you can do for yourself. Now let's drop in here to see my friend, who keeps what you need, and to-morrow I'll call for you and take you into the class and introduce you to Miss Clayson, and you'll be all right. You didn't start right."

When he walked in with Radbourn the next morning and was introduced to the teacher, Nettie Russell stared in breathless astonishmemt. He was barbered and wore a suit which showed his splendid length and strength of limb.

"Well said! Aint we a big sunflower! My sakes! aint we a-coming out!" "No moon last night." "Must 'a ben a fire." "He got them with a basket and a club," were some of the remarks he heard.

Bradley felt the difference in the atmosphere, and he walked to his seat with a self-possession that astonished himself. And from that time he was master of the situation. The girls pelted him with chalk and marked figures on his back, but he kept at his work. He had a firm grip on the plow-handles now, and he didn't look back. They grew to respect him, at length, and some of the girls distinctly showed their admiration. Brown came over to get help on a sum and so did Nettie, and when he sat down beside her she winked in triumph at the other girls while Bradley patiently tried to explain the problem in algebra which was his own terror.

He certainly was a handsome fellow in a rough-angled way, and when the boys found he could jump eleven feet and eight inches at a standing jump, they no longer drew any distinctions between his attainments in algebra and their own. Neither did his poverty count against him with them.   He sawed wood in every spare hour with desperate energy to make up for the sinful extravagance of his new fifteen dollar suit of clothes.

He was sawing wood in an alley one Saturday morning where he could hear a girl singing in a bird-like way that was very charming. He was tremendously hungry, for he had been at work since the first faint gray light, and the smell of breakfast that came to his senses was tantalizing.

He heard the girl's rapid feet moving about in the kitchen and her voice rising and falling, pausing and beginning again as if she were working rapidly. Then she fell silent, and he knew she was at breakfast.

At last she opened the door and came out along the walk with a tablecloth. She shook her cloth, and then her singing ceased and Bradley went on with his work.

"Hello, Brad!" called a sudden voice.

He looked up and saw Nettie Russell's roguish face peering over the board fence.

"Hello," he replied, and stood an instant in wordless surprise. "I didn't know you lived there."

"Well, I do. Aint tickled to death to find it

out, I s'pose? Say, you aint so very mad at me, are yeh?" she added insinuatingly.

He didn't know what to say, so he kept silent. He noticed for the first time how childishly round her face was!

She took a new turn. "Say, aint you hungry?"

Bradley admitted that he had eaten an early breakfast. He did not say it was composed of fried pork and potatoes and baker's bread, without tea, coffee, or milk.

The girl seemed delighted to think he was hungry.

"You wait a minute," she commanded, and her smiling face disappeared from the top of the fence. Brad went to work to keep from catching cold, wondering what she was going to do. She reappeared soon with a fat home-made sausage and a couple of warm biscuits which she insisted upon his taking.

"They're all buttered and — they've got sugar on 'em," she whispered significantly.

"Say, you eat now, while I saw," she commanded, coming around through the gate.

She had put on her fascinator hood, but her hands and wrists were bare. She struggled away on a log, putting her knee on it in a comically resolute style.

"The saw always goes crooked," she said in despair. Bradley laughed at her heartily.

"Say, do you do this for fun?" she asked, stopping to puff, her cheeks a beautiful pink.

"No, I don't. I do it because I'm obliged to."

She threw down the saw. "Well, that beats me; I can't saw, but I can cook. I made them biscuits." She challenged his opinion, as he well knew.

"They're first rate," he admitted, and they were friends. She watched him eat with apparent satisfaction.

"Say, I can't stay here, I'll freeze. Are yeh going to be here till noon?"

"Yes."

"Well, when I whistle you come in and get some grub, will yeh?" Bradley smiled back at her laughing face.

"This ain't your folks' wood pile."

"What's the difference?" she replied. "You jest come in, will yeh?"

"Yes, I'll come."

"Like fun you will! Honest?" she persisted.

"Hope to die," he said solemnly.

"That's the checker," she said, and disappeared with a click of the tongue.

Bradley worked away in a glow of cheerfulness.

It was astonishing how much this little victory over a roguish girl meant to him. He had changed one person's ridicule to friendship, and it seemed to be prophetic of other victories.

The time seemed very short that forenoon. Once or twice Nettie came out to bring some news about the cooking.

"Say, I'm making an apple pie. I'm a dandy on pies and cakes."

"I guess they would be 'pizen' cakes."

She threw an imaginary club at him.

"Well, if that ain't the sickest old joke! You'll go without any pie if you get off such a thing again."

But as dinner-time drew on he felt more and more unwilling to go into the kitchen.

He heard her whistle, but he remained at the saw-horse. It would do in the country, but not here. He had no right to go in there and eat.

There was a note of impatience in her voice when she looked over the fence and said, "Why don't you come?"

"I dassant!"

"Oh, bother! What y' 'fraid of?"

"What business have I got to eat your dinner? This aint your wood-pile."

"Say, if you don't come in I'll — I dunno what !"

"Bring it out here, it's warm."

"I won't do it ; you've got to come in ; the old man's gone up town and mother won't throw you out.   There isn't anybody in the kitchen.   Come on now," she pleaded.

Bradley followed her into the house, feeling a good deal like a very large dog, very hungry, who had followed a child's invitation into the parlor, and felt out of place.

He sat down by the fire, and silently ate what she placed before him, while she chattered away in high glee.   When Mrs. Russell came in, Nettie did not take the trouble to introduce him to her mother, who moved about the room in a wordless way, smiling a little about the eyes.   She was entirely subject to her daughter.   She heard them discussing lessons and concluded they were classmates.

Bradley went back to his wood-sawing and soon finished the job.   As he shouldered his saw and saw-buck, Nettie came out and peered over the fence again.

"Say, goin' to attend the social Monday ?"

"Guess not.   I ain't much on such things."

"It's lots o' fun ; we spin the platter and all

kinds o' things. I'm goin'," she looked archly inviting.

Bradley colored. He was not astute, but hints like this were not far from kicks. He looked down at his saw as he said, "I guess I won't go, I've got to study."

"Well, good-by," she said without mortification. She was so much of a child yet that she could be jilted without keen pain. "See y' Monday," she said as she ran into the house.

Someway Bradley's life was lightened by that day's experience. He went home to his bleak little room in a resolute mood. He sat down at his table upon which lay his algebra, determined to prepare Monday's lessons, but the pencil fell from his hand, his head sank down and lay upon the open page before him. Woodsawing had worn him down and algebra had made him sleep.

V.

BRADLEY RISES TO ADDRESS THE CARTHAGINIANS.

HE was now facing another terror, the Friday afternoon recitals, in which alternate sections of the pupils were obliged to appear before the public in the chapel to recite or read an essay. It was an ordeal that tried the souls of the bravest of them all.

Unquestionably it kept many pupils away. Nothing could be more terrible to a shrinking awkward boy or girl from a farm than this requirement, to stand upon a raised platform with nothing to break the effect of sheer crucifixion. It was appalling. It was a pillory, a stake, a burning, and yet there was a fearful fascination about it, and it was doubtful if a majority of the students would have voted for its abolition. The preps and juniors saw the seniors winning electrical applause from the audience and fancied the same prize was within their reach. There was no surer or more instant success to be won than that which followed a splendid oratorical effort on the platform. It was worth the cost.

Each new-comer dreaded it for weeks and talked about it constantly. Bradley, like all the rest before him, could not eat a thing on the morning preceding his trial, and in fact had suffered a distinct loss of oppetite from the middle of the week.

Mary Barber, a tall, awkward, badly-dressed girl, met him as he was going up the steps after the first bell.

"Say, how you feelin'! I've shook all the mornin'. I don't know what I'm goin' to do. I'm just sick."

"Why don't you say so an' get off?" Bradley suggested.

"Because that's what I did last time, and it won't work any more." The poor girl's teeth were chattering with her fright. She laughed at herself in an hysterical way, and wrung her hands, as if with cold, and dropped back into the broadest kind of dialect. "Oh, I feel 'sif my stomach was all gone."

Nettie Russell regarded it all as merely another disagreeable duty to be shirked. Nothing troubled her very much. "You just wait and see how I get out of it," she said, as she passed by. At two o'clock the principal came in, and removed even the small pulpit, so that nothing should stand between the shrinking young orators and the keen derisive eyes below.

The chapel was a very imposing structure to Bradley. It was square and papered in grey-white with fluted columns of the Corinthian order of architecture, and that touch of history and romance did not fail of its effect on the country boys fresh from the barn-yard and the corn-rows. It added to their fear and self-abasement, as they rolled their slow eyes around and upward. The audience consisted mainly of. the pupils arranged according to classes, the girls on the left and the boys on the right. In addition, some of the towns-people, who loved oratory, or were specially interested in the speakers of the day, were often oresent to add to the terror of the occasion.

Radbourn came in with Lily Graham, talking earnestly. He was in the same section with Bradley, a fact which did not cheer Bradley at all. Jack Carver came in with a jaunty air. His cuffs and collar were linen, and his trousers were tailor-made, which was distinction enough for him. He had no scruples, therefore, in shirking the speaking with the same indifference Nettie Rus-sell showed.

Milton, who came in the first section, was jok-ing the rest upon their nervousness.

"Say, when did you eat y'r last meal?" he whispered to Bradley.

"Yesterday morning," Bradley replied, unable to smile.

All the week the members of the last section had been prancing up and down the various rooms in boarding-houses, to the deep disgust of their fellow students, who mixed harsh comments throughout their practice, as they shouted in thunder tones :

"I came not here to talk. ('Then why don't you shut up?') You know too well the story of our thraldom. ('You bet we do, we've heard it all the week.') The beams of the setting sun fall upon a slave. ('Would a beam of some sort would fall on you.') O Rome! Rome!"—("Oh, go roam the wild wood.')"

All the week the boarding-house mistresses had pounded on the stove-pipe to bring the appeal of "Spartacus to the Romans" down to a key that would not also include all the people in the block. All to no purpose. Spartacus was aroused, and nothing but a glaive or a battle-axe could bring him to silence and submission. The first section now sat smiling grimly. Their revenge was coming.

After the choir had sung, the principal of oratory, note-book in hand, came down among the pupils, and began the fateful roll-call.

The first name called was Alice Masters, an ambitious, but terribly plain and awkward girl, She had not eaten anything since· the middle of the week, and was weak and nervous with fright. She sprang out of her seat, white as a dead person, and rushed up the aisle. As she stepped upon the platform she struck her toe and nearly fell. The rest laughed, some hysterically, the most of them in thoughtless derision. The blood rushed into her face and when she turned, she seemed to be masked in scarlet. She began, stammeringly, her fingers playing nervously with the seams of her dress.

"Beside his block the sculptor —

"Beside his block—

"Beside, the sculptor stood beside"—

She could not think of another word, not one, and she fell into a horrible silence, wringing her hands piteously. It was impossible for her to go on, and impossible for her to leave the floor till the word of release came.

"That will do," said the principal in calm unconcern, and she rushed from the room, and the
next name was called. At length Nettie Russell
faced the audience, a saucy smile on her lips, and
a defiant tilt to her nose. She spoke a verse of
"Twinkle, twinkle, little star," to the vast delight
of the preps, who had dared her to do it. The
principal scowled darkly, and put a very emphatic
black mark opposite her name.

As name after name was called, Bradley's chill
deepened, and the cold sweat broke out upon his
body. There was a terrible weakness and nausea
at his stomach, and he drew long, shivering inspi-
rations like a man facing an icy river, into which
he must plunge. His hands shook till he was
forced to grasp the desk to hide his tremor.

He was saved from utter flight by Radbourn,
who came before him. Whatever nervousness
the big senior had ever felt, he was well over
now, for he walked calmly up the aisle, and took
his place with easy dignity. He scorned to
address the Romans, or the men of England.
He was always contemporaneous. He usually
gave orations on political topics, or astounded his
teachers by giving a revolutionary opinion of
some classic. No matter what subject he dealt
with, he interested and held his audience. His

earnest face and deep-set eyes had something compelling in them, and his dignity and self-possession in themselves fascinated the poor fellows, who sat there in deathly sickness, shaking with terror.

Bradley felt again the fascination of an orator, and again his heart glowed with a secret feeling that he, too, could be an orator like that. He felt strong, and cool, and hopeful, while Radbourn was speaking, but afterward that horrible, weakening fear came back upon him.

He couldn't look at poor Harry Stillman, who came on a few names further. Harry had pounded away all the week on Webster's reply to Hayne, and he now stood forth in piteous contrast to his ponderous theme. His thin, shaking legs toed-in like an Indian's, and his trousers were tight, and short, and checked, which seemed to increase the tightness and shortness. He had narrow shoulders and thin, long arms, which he used like a jumping jack, each gesture being curiously unrelated to his facial expression, which was mainly appealing and apprehensive. As Shep Watson said, "He looked as if he expected a barn to fall on him."

At last Bradley's name was spoken, and he rose in a mist. The windows had disappeared,

They were mere blurs of light.   As he walked up the aisle the floor fell away from the soles of his feet.   He no longer walked, he was a brain floating in space.   He made his way to the stage without accident, for he had rehearsed it all so many times in his mind that unconscious cerebration attended to the necessary motions.   When he faced the assembly, he seemed facing a boundless sea of faces.   They in their turn were awed by something they saw in his eyes.   His face was white and his eyes burned with a singular light. A mysterious power emanated from him as from the born orator.

Like all the rest he had taken a theme that was far beyond his apparent powers, and the apparent comprehension of his audience; but they had been fed so long upon William Tell, Rienzi, Marc Antony and Spartacus, that every line was familiar.   Nothing was too ponderous, too lofty, too peak-addressing for them.

He mispronounced the words, his gestures were awkward and spasmodic, but lofty emotion exalted him and vibrated in his voice.   He thrilled every heart.   He had opened somewhere, somehow, a vast reservoir of power.   A great calm fell upon him.   A wild joy of new-found strength that awed and thrilled his own heart.   It seemed as if a new spirit had taken his flesh. As he went on he grew more dignified and graceful. His great arms seemed to be gigantic, as he thundered against the Carthaginians. Everybody forgot his dress, his freckled face, and when he closed, the applause was instant and generous.

As he walked back to his seat, the exultant light went out of his eyes, his limbs relaxed, the windows and the sunlight cleared to vulgar day, and his face flushed with timidity. He sat down with a feeling of melancholy in his heart, as if something divine had faded out of his life.

But Radbourn reached out his hand in the face of the whole school and said, "First rate!" The pupils had the western love for oratory, and several of them crowded about to congratulate him on his speech.

Bradley did not feel at all sure of his success. He had been something alien to himself in that speech, and he could not remember what he had said or done. He was not at all sure that he had done the right thing or the best thing. He was suspicious of his power because he no longer felt it. He was like a man who had dreamed of flying and woke to find himself paralyzed. After his triumph he was the same great, awkward, country hired-man.

"Say, look here, Talcott," said Radbourn, as they met at the door of the chapel going out, "I'm going to propose you as a member of the Delta; come up Monday, and I'll put you through."

"Oh, they don't want me."

"Don't be so modest. They're in need of just such men. You'll be in demand now, no fear about that."

There was a struggle now to get him into the societies, which were, as usual, bitter rivals. He was secretly anxious to be one of the debaters. In fact he had counted more on that than upon all the rest of the advantages of the school. He thought it would please *Her* better.

He joined the Delta, over which Radbourn presided, and wore the society pin with genuine pride. He sat for several meetings silently in his seat, awed by the excessive formality of proceedings, and the strictness of the parliamentary rules. It was a curious thing to see the meeting come to order out of a chaos of wrestling, shouting, singing members whose excess of life filled the room like a crowd of prize-fighters.

Rap! Rap! And the sound of the gavel stilled the noise as if each man had received a blow on his head.

They took their seats while the stern president remained standing. One final rap, and the room was perfectly quiet, and every member an inexorable parliamentarian, ready to question decisions, or rise to points of order at the slightest infraction of Cushing's manual. Radbourn ruled with a gavel of iron, but they all enjoyed it the more. Half the fun and probably half the benefit of the society would have been lost with the loss of order.

This strenuous dignity awed Bradley for a time. His fellows seemed transformed into something quite other than their usual selves, into grave law-makers. This strangeness wore away after a time and he grew more at ease. He began to study Cushing along with the rest. It laid the foundation for a thorough knowledge of the methods of conducting a meeting, which was afterward of so much value to him.

His first attempt at debating was upon the question, "Should farmers be free traders?" a question which was introduced by Milton, who was always attempting to introduce questions which would strike fire. Nothing pleased his fun-loving nature more than to take part in a "live debate."

As real free traders were scarce, Mason, a brilliant young Democrat, requested Radbourn to take the side of free trade, and he consented. Milton formed the third part of the free trade cohort. He liked the fun of trying to debate on the opposite side, a thing which would have been impossible to Bradley's more intense and simple-hearted nature. What he believed he fought for.

Mason led off with a discussion of the theory of free exchange and made a passionate plea, florid and declamatory, which gave Fergusson, a cool, pointed, scholarly Norwegian, an excellent chance to raise a laugh. He called the attention of the house to the "copperhead Democracy," which the gentleman of the opposition was preaching. He asked what the practical application would mean. Plainly it meant cheap goods.

"That's what we want," interrupted Mason, and was silenced savagely by the chairman.

"England would flood us with cheap goods."

"Let 'em flood," said somebody unknown, and the chairman was helpless.

Fergusson worked away steadily and was called down at last.

He was distinguished as one of the few men who always talked out his ten minutes.

Radbourn astonished them all by saying with absolute sincerity: "Free trade as a theory is right. Considered as a question of ethics, as a question of the trend of things, it's right. The right to trade is as much my right, as my right to produce. The one question is whether it ought to be put into operation at once. There is no reason why the farmer should uphold protection."

From this on his remarks had a mysterious quality. "I'm a free trader, but I'm not a Democrat. Tariff tinkering is not free trade, and I don't believe the Democrats would do any more than the Republicans, but that aint the question. The question is whether the farmers should be free traders."

After the discussion along familiar lines had taken place, Radbourn resumed the chair and called on any one in the room to volunteer a word on either side. "We would like to hear from Talcott," he said.

"Talcott, Talcott," called the rest.

Bradley rose, as if impelled by some irresistible power within himself. He began stammeringly. He had but one line of thought at his command, and that was the line of thought indicated by Miss Wilbur in her speech at the picnic, the Home Market idea, upon which he had spent a great deal of thought. "Mr. Chairman, I don't believe in free trade. I believe if we had free trade it would make us all farmers for England. It aint what we ought t' do. We've got gold in our hills, an' coal an' timber to manufacture. What we want t' do is to build up our industries; make a home market."

As he went on with these stock phrases, he seemed to get hold of things which before had seemed out of his reach, scraps of speeches, newspaper comments, an astonishing flood of arguments, or at least what he took for arguments, came rushing into his mind. He reached out his hands and grasped and used phrases not his own as if they were bludgeons. He assaulted the opposition blindly, but with immense power.

He sat down amid loud applause, and young Mason arose to close the affirmative. He was sarcastic to the point of offence.

"He has said 'em all," he began, alluding to Bradley, "all the regulation arguments of Republican newspapers. And as for the leader of the opposition, he has got off the usual sneer at copperhead Democracy. This debate wouldn't have been complete without that remark from my esteemed leader of the opposition. Where argument fails, misrepresentations and sneers may do service with the injudicious. I trust the judges will remember that the argument has been on our side, and the innuendoes on the side of the opposition."

The verdict of the judges was in favor of the free traders, but the decision of the judges had less effect on Bradley than the surprising revelation of Radbourn's thought. There were phrases whose reach and significance he did not realize to the full, but their effect was not lost. He never forgot such things.

He was thinking how diametrically opposite Miss Wilbur's ideas were, when Radbourn came up, and said with a significant smile:

"Well, Talcott, you *did* get hold of all the regulation stock material. The Home Market idea is a great field for you. You think a city is of itself a good thing? You think a city means civilization. Well, I want to tell you, and maybe you won't believe me, cities mean vice, and crime, and poverty, and vast wealth for the few, and as for the Home Market idea, how would it do to let the farmer buy in the same market in which he sells? He sells in the world's market, but you'd force him to buy in a protected market."

Radbourn went off with a peculiar smile, which left Bradley uncertain whether he was laughing at him or not. He began from that moment to overhaul his stock of phrases, to see if they were really shopworn and worthless. He was growing marvellously, his whole nature was now awake. He thought, as he sawed wood in the back alleys of the town, and at night he toiled at his books. Those were great days. New powers were swiftly burgeoning.

Radbourn spoke to several of the politicians of the town about Bradley.

"There is a good deal in that man Talcott. Of course he's just beginning, but you'll hear from him on the stump. He is an orator that reaches people. He has the advantage of most of us; he's in dead earnest when he's advocating Republicanism."

Radbourn had times of saying things like this when his hearers didn't know what to make of him.

"It's just his way," some one usually said, and the rest sat in silence. They didn't enjoy it, but as Radbourn was not running for any office and was known to be a powerful thinker, they thought it best not to antagonize him.

"I wonder if he intends the law?" asked Judge Brown.

"I see what the Judge is driving at," Radbourn said quickly, "he thinks he can make a Democrat of him."

The group laughed. Democrats were in a hopeless minority, but the judge and Colonel Peavey never lost their proselyting zeal.

"The Judge is always on hand like a sore thumb," said Amos.

"The Judge'll be on the right side of the tariff one of these fine days, and have the laugh on the lot of yeh."

"What y' idee about that, Rad?"

"Good heavens! You don't expect to have protection always, do yeh?" was his only reply.

A day or two later he said to Bradley —

"Talcott, Brown wants to see you. He wants to make you a 'lawyer's hack'! Now I'd say to most men, don't do it, but if he offers to give you a place take it. It won't be worse than sawing wood thirty hours a week."

Following Radbourn's direction he passed up a narrow, incredibly grimy stairway, and knocked at a door at the end of a hall, whose only light came through the letter-slit in the door.

"Come in!" yelled a snarling voice.

Bradley entered timidly, for the voice was not at all cordial. The Judge, in his own den, was a different man from the Judge at Robie's grocery, and this day he was in bad humor. He sat with his heels on a revolving book-case, a law-book spread out on his legs, a long pipe in his hand.

If he uttered any words of greeting they were lost in the crescendo growl of a fat bull-dog, that lay in supple shining length at his feet.

"Down with yeh!" he snarled at the dog, who ceased his growling, but ran lightly and with ferocious suggestiveness toward Bradley and clung sniffing about his heels.

"Si' down!" the judge said, indicating a chair with his pipe, which he held by the bowl. He didn't otherwise make a motion.

Bradley sat down. This greeting drove him back into his usual stubborn silence. He waited for developments, his eyes on the dog.

"Well, young man, what can I do for you?" asked the lawyer after a long silence, during which he laid down one book, and read a page in another.

"Nothin', I guess."

"Well, what the devil did yeh come in here for?" he inquired, with a glare of astonishment. "Want 'o buy a dog?"

Bradley was mad. "I came because Radbourn sent me. I c'n git out agin, mighty quick."

The judge took down his heels. "Oh, you're that young orator. Why didn't yer say so, you damned young Indian?" He now rose and walked over to the spittoon before going on. Bradley knew that this rough tone was entirely different from the first. It was a sort of affectionate blackguardism. "I heard you speak last Friday. All you need, young man, is a chance to swing y'r elbows. You want room according to y'r strength, but you never'd find it in the Republican party. It's struck with the palsy."

The judge had been talking this for two presidential campaigns and didn't take himself at all seriously.

"What are you going to do?"

"I don't know, yet."

"Do you want 'o study law?"

"I don't know, sir. Do you think I can be a lawyer?"

"If you're not too damned honest. If you want 'o try it, I'll make an arrangement with you, that will be better than sawing wood anyhow, this winter, and you can keep right on with your studies. We'll see what can be done next year."

The old man had taken a liking to Bradley on account of his oratory, and the possibilities of making him a Democratic leader had really taken possession of him. He had no son of his own, and he took a deep interest in young men of the stamp of Milton and Bradley.

After he reached home that night, Bradley extended his ambitions. He dared to hope that he might be a lawyer, and an orator, which meant also a successful politician to him. Politics to him, as to most western men, was the greatest concern of life, and the city of Washington the Mecca whose shining dome lured from afar. To go to Washington was equivalent to being born again. "A man can do anything if he thinks so and tries hard," he thought, following Radbourn's words.

He bustled about cheerily, cooking his fried pototoes and scraps of meat, and boiling his tea. The dim light made his large face softer and more thoughtful than it had appeared before, and his cheerfulness over his lonely meal typed forth the sublime audacity, profound ignorance, and pathetic faith with which such a man faces the world's millions and dares to hope for success.

VI.

BRADLEY ATTENDS A CONVENTION.

ON a dreamful September day of the following year, Bradley was helping Milton Jennings to dig potatoes. It was nearly time for his return to school and to Judge Brown's office, and the two young men were full of plans. Milton was intending to go back for another year, and Bradley intended to keep up with his studies if possible, and retain his place with Brown also.

"Say," broke out Milton suddenly, "we ought to attend this convention."

"What convention?"

"Why, the nominating convention at Rock. Father's going this afternoon. I never've been. Let's go with him."

"That won't dig taters," smiled Bradley in his slow way.

"Darn the taters. If we're goin' into politics we want 'o know all about things."

" That's so. I would like to go if your father'll let us off on the taters."

Mr. Jennings made no objection "It'll be a farce, though, the whole thing."

" Why so ? "

" I'll tell you on the way down. Git the team ready and we'll take neighbor Councill in."

Bradley listened to Mr. Jennings' explanation with an interest born of his expanding ambition. His marvellously retentive mind absorbed every detail and the situation cleared in his mind.

For sixteen years the affairs of the country had been managed by a group of persuasive, well-dressed citizens of Rock River, who played into each other's hands and juggled with the county's money with such adroitness and address that their reign seemed hopelessly permanent to the discontented and suspicious farmers of the county. Year after year they saw these gentlemen building new houses, opening banks, and buying in farm mortgages "all out of the county," many grangers asserted.

Year after year the convention assembled, and year after year the delegates from the rural townships came down to find their duties purely perfunctory, simply to fill up the seats. They always found the slate made up and fine speakers ready to put it through with a rush of ready applause, before which the slower-spoken, disorganized farmers were well-nigh helpless. It was a case of perfect organization against disorganization and mutual distrust. Banded officialism fighting to keep its place against the demands of a disorganized righteous mob of citizens. Office is always a trained command. The intrenched minority is capable of a sort of rock-like resistance.

Rock River and its neighboring village of Cedarville, by pooling together could tie the convention, and in addition to these towns they always controlled several of the outlying townships by judicious flattery of their self-constituted managers, who were given small favors, put on the central committee, and otherwise made to feel that they were leading men in the township; and it was beginning to be stated that the county treasurer had regularly bribed other influential whippers-in, by an amiable remission of taxes.

"Why don't you fight 'em?" asked Milton, after Mr. Jennings had covered the whole ground thoroughly.

Councill laughed. "We've been a-fightin' um; suppose you try."

"Give us a chance, and we'll do our part. Won't we, Brad?"

Bradley nodded, and so committed himself to the fight. He was fated to begin his political career as an Independent Republican.

On the street they met other leading grangers of the county, and it became evident that there was a deep feeling of resentment present. They gathered in knots on the sidewalks that led up under the splendid maples that lined the sidewalks leading toward the court-house.

The court-house was of the usual pseudo-classic style of architecture, that is to say, it was a brick building with an ambitious facade of four wooden fluted columns. Its halls echoed to the voices and footsteps of the crowd that passed up its broad, worn and grimy steps into the court-room itself, which was grimier and more hopelessly filthy than the staircase with its stratified accumulations of cigar stubs and foul sawdust. Its seats were benches hacked and carved like the desks of a country schoolhouse. Nothing could be more barren, more desolate. It had nothing to relieve it save the beautiful stains of color that seemed thrown upon the windows by the crimson and orange maples which stood in the yard.

They found the room full of delegates, among whom there was going on a great deal of excited conversation. From a side room near the Judge's bench there issued, from time to time, messengers who came out among the general mob, and invited certain flattered and useful delegates to come in and meet with the central committee. There was plainly a division in the house.

"The rusty cusses are on their ears to-day," said Milton, "and there's going to be fun." His blue eyes were beaming with laughter, and his quick wit kept those who were within hearing on the broad grin."

"Goin' to down 'em t' day?" he asked of Councill.

"We're goin' t' try."

In one dishonest way or another the ring had kept its hold upon the county, notwithstanding all criticism, and now came to the struggle with smiling confidence. They secured the chairman by the ready-made quick vote, by acclamation for re-election. The president then appointed the committee upon credentials and upon nominations, and the work of the convention was opened.

The committee on nominations, in due course presented its slate as usual, but here the real battle began. Bradley suddenly found himself tense with interest. His ancestry must have been a race of orators and politicians, for the atmosphere of the convention roused him till it transformed him.

Here was the real thing. No mere debate, but a fight. There was battle in the air, now blue with smoke and rank with the reek of tobacco. There was fight in the poise of the grizzled heads and rusty, yellow shoulders of the farmers who had now fallen into perfect silence. In looking over them one might have been reminded of a field of yellow-gray boulders.

Colonel Russell moved the election of the entire slate, as presented by the nominating committee, in whom, he said, the convention had the utmost confidence. Four or five farmers sprang to their feet instantly and Osmond Deering got the floor. When he began speaking the loafers in the gallery stopped their chewing in excess of interest. He was one of the most influential men in the county.

"Mr. President," he began in his mild way, "I don't want to seem captious about this matter, but I want to remind this convention that this is the eighth-year that almost the same identical slate has been presented to the farmers of Rock County and passed against our wishes. It isn't right that it should pass again. It sha'n't pass without my protest." Applause. "This convention has been robbed of its right to nominate every year, and every year we've gone home feeling we've been made cat's paws of, for the benefit of a few citizens of Rock River. I protest against the slate. I claim the right to nominate my man. I don't intend to have a committee empowered to take away my rights to "—

The opposition raised a clamor, "Question! Question!" attempting to force a vote, but the old man, carried out of himself by his excitement, shook his broad flat hand in the air, and cried: "I have the floor, gentlemen, and I propose to keep it." The farmers applauded. "I say to this convention, vote down this motion and set down on the old-fashioned slate-making committee business. It aint just, it aint right, and I protest against it."

He sat down to wild excitement, his supporters trying to speak, the opposition crying, "Question, Question." Several fiery speeches were made by leading grangers, but they were met by a cool, smooth persuasive speech from the chairman of the nominating committee, who argued that it was not to be supposed that this committee chosen by this convention would bring in a slate which would not be a credit and honor to the country. True, they were mainly from Rock River and

Cedarville; but it must be remembered that the population of the county was mainly in these towns, and that no ticket could succeed which did not give a proper proportion of representation to these towns. These men could not be surpassed in business ability. They were old in their office, it was true, but the affairs of the county were passing through a critical period in their history, and it was an old and well-tried saying: "Never swap horses in the midst of a stream," anyhow, he was content to leave the matter to the vote of this convention.

The vote carried the slate through by a small majority, leaving the farmers again stunned and helpless, and the further business of the convention was to restore peace and good-will, as far as possible among the members. It was amazing to Bradley to find how easily he could be swayed by the plausible speeches of the gentlemanly chairman of the nominating committee. It was a great lesson to him in the power of oratory. The slate was put through simply by the address of the chairman of the committee.

On the way out they met Councill and Jennings walking out with Chairman Russell, who had his hand on a shoulder of each, and was saying, with beautiful candor and joviality: "Well, we beat you again. It's all fair in politics, you know."

"Yes, but it's the last time," said Jennings, who refused to smile. "We can't give this the go-by."

"Oh, well, now, neighbor Jennings, you mustn't take it too hard; you know these men are good capable men."

"They are capable enough," put in Deering, "but we want a change."

"Then make it," laughed Russell, good-naturedly defiant.

"We will make it, bet y'r boots," said Amos Ridings.

"Let's see yeh," was Russell's parting word, delivered with a jaunty wave of his hand.

The farmers rode home full of smoldering wrath. They were in fighting humor, and only needed an organizer to become a dangerous force.

VII.

THE FARMERS OUST THE RING.

THE following Saturday Bradley, who was still at work with Milton, saw Amos Ridings gallop up and dismount at the gate, and call Jennings out, and during the next two hours, every time he looked up he saw them in deep discussion out by the pig pen. Part of the time Jennings faced Amos, who leaned against the fence and whittled a stick, and part of the time he talked to Jennings who leaned back against the fence on his elbows, and studied Amos whittling the rail. Mrs. Jennings at last called them all to dinner, and still the question remained apparently unsolved, though they changed the conversation to crops and the price of wheat.

"Brad, set down here and make a lot o' copies of this call. Milt, you help him."

The call read :

"A NEW DEAL. REFORM IN COUNTY POLITICS."

"A mass convention of the citizens of Rock County will be held at Rock Creek Grove on September 28th, for the purpose of nominating a people's ticket. All who favor reform in politics and rebel against the ring-rule of our county officers are invited to be present.   Per order,

     AMOS RIDINGS,
     JOHN JENNINGS,
     WILLIAM COUNCILL,

         People's Committee.

"What's all this?" asked Milton of his father.

"We're going to have a convention of our own."

"We're on the war path," said Amos grimly. "We'll make them fellers think hell's t' pay and no pitch hot."

After dinner Amos took a roll of the copies of the call and rode away to the north, and Jennings hitched up his team and drove away to the south. Milton and Bradley went back to their corn-husking, feeling that they were "small petaters."

"They don't intend to let us into it, that's dead sure," said Milton. "All the samee, I know the scheme. They're going to bolt the convention, and there'll be fun in the air."

The county woke up the next morning to find its schoolhouse doors proclaiming a revolt of the farmers, and the new deal was the talk of the county. It was the grange that had made this revolt possible. This general intelligence and self-cognizance was the direct result of the work of the grange. It had brought the farmers together, and had made them acquainted with their own men, their own leaders, and when they came together a few days later, under the open sky, like the Saxon thanes of old, there was a spirit of rebellion in the air that made every man look his neighbor in the face with exultation.

It was a perfectly Democratic meeting. They came together that beautiful September day, under the great oaks, a witenagemote of serious, liberty-loving men, ready to follow wherever their leaders pointed.

Amos Ridings was the chairman, tall, grim-lipped and earnest-eyed. His curt speech carried the convention with him. His platform was a wagon box, and he stood there with his hat off, the sun falling upon his shock of close-clipped stiff hair, making a powerful and resolute figure with a touch of poetry in his face.

"Fellow-citizens, we've come together here to-day to organize to oust the ring that has held our county affairs in their hands so long. We can oust them if we'll stand together. If we don't, we can't. I believe we will stand together,

The grange has learned us something.   It's made us better acquainted with each other.   An' the time has come f'r a fight.   The first thing is a permanent chairman.   Who'll y' have for chairman?"

"I nominate Amos Ridings."

"Second the motion," cried two voices in quick succession.

The chairman's grim visage did not relax.   He had no time for false delicacy.   "Are y' ready f'r the question?"

"Yes, yes," shouted the crowd.

"All in favor, say 'Aye'."

There was a vast shout of approval.

Contrary minds 'No!   It's a vote."

The other officers were elected in the same way.   They were there for business.   They passed immediately to the nominations, and there was the same unanimity all down the ticket until the nominations for the county auditor began.

A small man lifted his hand and cried, "I nominate James McGann of Rock for auditor."

There was a little silence followed by murmurs of disapproval.   The first false note had been struck.   Someone seconded the motion.   The chairman's gavel fell.

"I want to ask the secretary to take the chair

for a few minutes," he said, and there was something in his voice that meant business. Something ominous. The delegates pressed closer. The secretary took the chair. "I've got something to say right here," Ridings began.

"Fellow-citizens, we're here in a big fight. We can't afford t' make any mistake. We can't afford to be tolled off the track by a bag of anise seed. Who is the man makin' this motion? Does anybody know him? I do. He's a spy. He's sent here f'r a purpose. Suppose he'd nominated a better man? His motion would have been out of place. His nomination of Jim McGann was a trick. Jim McGann can't git a pound o' sugar on credit in his own town. He never had any credit n'r influence. Why was he nominated? Simply to make us ridiculous — a laughin' stock. I want to put you on your guard. If we win it's got t' be in a straight fight. That's all I've got t' say. Recognize no nomination that don't come from a man y' know."

The convention clamored its approval, and the small spy and trickster slunk away and disappeared. There was a certain majesty in the action of this group of roused farmers. Nominations were seconded and ratified with shouts, even down through the most important officers in the county and town. It was magnificent to see how deep was the harmony of action.

Deering was forced to accept the nomination for treasurer by this feeling of the unanimity and genuineness which pervaded each succeeding action, and when the vote was called, and the men thrust their hands in the air and shouted, they had something of the same feeling that lay at the heart of the men of Uri, and Unterwalden, and Schwyz when they shouted their votes together in the valley with the mighty cordon of guarding mountains around them.

The grange had made this convention and its magnificent action possible. Each leading member of the grange, through its festivals, and picnics, and institutes, had become known to the rest, and they were able to choose their leaders instantly. The ticket as it stood was very strong. Deering as treasurer and Councill as sheriff, insured success so far as these officers were concerned.

On the way home Councill shouted back at the young men riding with Jennings: "Now's a good time for you young chaps t' take the field and lectioneer while we nominees wear biled collars, and set in the parlor winder."

"What you want to do is stay at home and dig

taters," shouted Milton. "A biled collar would defeat any one of yeh, dead sure."

This was, in fact, the plan of the campaign.

Amos Ridings assumed practical direction of it.

"Now we don't want a candidate to go out — not once. Every man stay at home and not open his head. We'll do the work. You tend your knittin' and we'll elect yeh."

The boys went out on Friday nights, to electioneer for the Granger ticket, as it was called.

"It's boss fun," Milton said to his father. "It's ahead o' husking corn. It does tickle me to see the future sheriff of the county diggin' pertaters while I'm ridin' around in my best clo'es makin' speeches."

"We'll have the whip-row on you when we get into office," replied Mr. Jennings.

"Don't crow till y'r out o' the woods," laughed Milton.

The boys really aroused considerable enthusiasm, and each had stanch admirers, though they were entirely opposed in style. Milton told a great many funny stories, and went off on what he considered to be the most approved oratorical flights. He called on the farmers to stand together. He asked them whether it was fair that the town should have all the offices. In short, he made very taking political harangues.

Bradley always arose in the same slow way. He was a little heavy in getting started. His deep voice was thick and husky at beginning, but cleared as he went on. His words came slowly, as if each were an iron weight. He dealt in facts — or what he believed to be facts. He had carefully collated certain charges which had been made against the officials of the county, and in his perfectly fearless way of stating them, there was immense power.

VIII.

BRADLEY OFFENDS NETTIE'S FATHER.

It was a singular thing to see the farmers suddenly begin to ask themselves why they should stand quietly by while the townsmen monopolized all the offices and defied the farmers to make a change. They laughed at the charges of chicanery in office, and openly said that "no man with corns on his hands and hayseed in his hair can be elected to office in the county." This speech was of the greatest value to the young champions. It became their text.

The speech that made Bradley famous among the farmers came about the middle of October. It was an open-air meeting in the Cottonwood township, one Saturday afternoon. He and Milton drove out to their appointment in a carriage which Milton had borrowed. It was a superb Indian summer day, and they were both very happy. Each had his individual way of showing it. Milton put his heels on the dash-board, and sung or whistled all the way out, stopping only occasionally to say :

"Aint this boss? This is what I call doin' a thing up brown. Wish I could do this for a stiddy business."

Bradley smiled at his companion's fun. He felt the pride and glory of it all, but he couldn't express it as Milton did. It was such a magnificent thing to be thus selected to push on a campaign. The mere idea of the crowd waiting out there for their arrival had something royal in it. And then this riding away into a practically unknown part of the county to speak before perfect strangers had an epic quality. Great things seemed coming to him.

They found quite an assembly of farmers, notwithstanding the busy season. It showed how deep was the interest in the campaign, and Milton commented upon it in beginning his speech.

"If a farmer ever gets his share of things, he's got to take time to turn out to caucuses and meetings, and especially he's got to stop work and vote."

Bradley arose after Milton's speech, which pleased the farmers with its shrewdness and drollery, feeling at a great disadvantage.

"My colleague," he began (preserving the formality of the Delta Society debates), "has told you of the ring that has controlled the officers of this county for so long, but he hasn't told you of the inside facts. I aint fightin' in this campaign to put the town people out and the farmers in; I'm fightin' to put thieves out and honest men in."

This was a blow straight out from the shoulder and was followed by great applause. But a few voices cried :

"Take that back !"

" I won't take anything back that I know is the truth."

"Yes, you will! That's a lie, an' you know it!" shouted an excited man a short distance away.

"Let me tell you a story," Bradley went on slowly. "Last session of court a friend of mine was on the jury. When court adjourned, he took his order on the county to the treasurer and asked for his pay. The treasurer said, 'I'm sorry, but they aint any funds left for the jurors' fees.'"

"'Can't you give me some out of some other fund ?'"

"' No, that won't do — can't do that.'

"' Well, when will yeh have some money in ?'

"'Well, it's hard tellin'—in two or three months, probably.'

"'Well, I'd like the money on this order. I need it. Can't I git somebody to cash it for me?'

"'Well, I dunno. I guess they'll take it at the store. My brother John might cash it—possibly, as an accommodation.'

"Well, my friend goes over to Brother John's bank, and Brother John cashes the order, and gives him eight dollars for it. Brother John then turns in the order to the treasurer and gets twelve dollars for it, and then they 'divvy' on the thing. Now, how's that for a nice game?"

"It's a damn lie!" shouted an excited man in the foreground. He had his sleeves rolled up and kept up a continual muttering growl.

"It's the truth," repeated Bradley. There was a strong Russell contingent in the meeting, and they were full of fight. The angry man in front repeated his shout:

"That's a lie! Take it back, or I'll yank yeh off'n that wagon box."

"Come and try it," said Bradley, throwing off his coat.

The excitement had reached the point where blows begin. Several irresponsible fellows were urging their companion on.

"Jump 'im! Jump 'im, Hank! We'll see fair play."

"Stand yer ground, Brad!" shouted the friends of the speaker. "We'll see they come one at a time."

"Oh, see here! No fightin'," shouted others. The man Hank was not to be silenced. He pushed his way to the wagon-wheel and shook his extended fist at the speaker.

"Take that back, you" —

Bradley caught him by his uplifted wrist, and bracing himself against the wheel, jerked his assailant into the wagon-box, and tumbled him out in a disjointed heap on the other side before he could collect his scattered wits.

Then Bradley stood up in his splendid height and breadth. "I say it's the truth; and if there are any more rowdies who want 'o try yankin' me out o' this wagon, now's your time. You never'll have a better chance." Nobody seemed anxious. The cheers of the crowd and the young orator's determined attitude discouraged them. "Now I'll tell yeh who the man was who presented that order. It was William Bacon; mebbe some o' you fellers want to tell him *he* lies."

He finished his speech without any marked interruption, and was roundly congratulated by the farmers. On the way back to Rock River, however, he seemed very much depressed, while Milton exulted over it all.

"Gosh! I wish I had your muscle, old man! I ain't worth a cent in things like that. Cæsar! But you snatched him bald-headed."

"Makes me feel sick," Bradley said. "I ain't had but one squabble before since I was a boy. It makes me feel like a plug-ugly."

Milton was delighted with it all. It made such a capital story to tell! "Say Brad, do you know what I thought of when you was yankin' that feller over the wheel? Scaldin' hogs! You pulled on him just as if he was a three-hundred pound shote. It was funny as all time!"

But Bradley had trouble in going to sleep that night, thinking about it. He was wondering what *She* would have thought of him in that disgraceful row. He tried to remember whether he swore or not. He felt, even in the darkness, her grave, sweet eyes fixed upon him in a sorrowful, disappointed way, and it made him groan and turn his face to the wall, to escape the picture of himself standing there in the wagon, with his coat off, shouting back at a band of rowdies.

But the story spread, and it pleased the farmers immensely. The boldness of the charge and the magnificent muscle that backed it up took hold of the people's imagination strongly, and added very greatly to his fame.

When the story reached Judge Brown, he was deeply amused. On the following Monday morning, as Brad was writing away busily, the Judge entered the room.

"Well, Brad, they say you called the Russells thieves."

"I guess perhaps I did."

"Well, aint that goin' to embarrass you a little when — when you're calling on Nettie?"

"I aint a-goin' to call there any more."

"Oh, I see! Expect the colonel to call on you, eh?"

"I don't care what he does," Bradley cried, turning and facing his employer. "I said what I know to be the truth. I call it thieving, and if they don't like it, they can hate it. I aint a-goin' to back down an inch, as long as I know what I know."

"That's right!" chuckled the Judge. As a Democrat, he rejoiced to see a Republican ring assaulted. "Go ahead, I'll stand by you, if they try the law."

IX.

THOUGH Bradley had called a good many times at the Russell house, to accompany Nettie to parties or home from school, yet he had never had any conversation to speak of with Russell, who was a large and somewhat pompous man. He knew his place, as a Western father, and never interfered with his daughter's love affairs. He knew Bradley as a likely and creditable young fellow, and besides, his experience with his two older daughters had taught him the perfect uselessness of trying to marry them to suit himself or his wife.

He was annoyed at this attack of Bradley upon him and his brother, the treasurer. It was really carrying things too far. Accustomed to all sorts of epithets and charges on the part of opposing candidates, he ought not to have been so sensitive

to Bradley's charge, but the case was peculiar.
It was exactly true, in the first place, and then it
came from a young man whom his daughter had
brought into the family, and whom he had begun
to think of as a probable son-in-law.

On Tuesday morning, just as Bradley was tum-
bling his dishes into a pan of hot water ("their
weekly bath," Milton called it), there came a
sharp knock on the door, and a girl's voice called
out clearly:

"Hello, Brad! Can I come in?"

"Yes, come in."

Nettie came in, her cheeks radiant with color,
her eyes shining. "Oh, washing your dishes?
Wait a minute, I'll help." She flung off her
coat in a helter-skelter way, and rolled up her
sleeves.

Bradley expostulated: "No, no! Don't do that!
I'll have 'em done in a jiffy. They aint but a
few."

"I'll wipe 'em, anyway," she replied. "Oh,
fun! What a towel!" she held up the side of a
flour-sack, on which was a firm-name in brown
letters. She laughed in high glee. There was a
delicious suggestion in the fact that she was
standing by his side helping him in his household
affairs.

Bradley was embarrassed, but she chattered away, oblivious of space and time. Her regard for him had grown absolutely outspoken and without shame. There was something primitive and savage in her frank confession of her feelings. She had come to make all the advances herself, in a confidence that was at once beautiful and pathetic. She met him in the morning on the way to school, and clung to him at night, and made him walk home with her. She came afternoons with a team, to take him out driving. The presence of the whole town really made no difference to her. She took his arm just the same, proud and happy that he permitted it.

"Oh, say," she broke off suddenly, "pa wants to see you about something. He wanted me to tell you to come down to-night." She was dusting the floor at the moment, while he was moving the furniture. "I wonder what he wants?" she asked.

"I don't know," he replied, evasively.

"Something about politics, I suppose." She came over and stood beside him in silence. She was very girlish, in spite of her assumption of a young lady's dress and airs, and she loved him devouringly She stood so close to him that she could put her hand on his, as it lay on the table.

Her clear, sweet eyes gazed at him with the confidence and purity of a child.

It was a relief to Bradley to hear the last bell ring. She withdrew her hand and threw down the broom which she had been holding in her left hand. "Oh, that's the last bell. Help me on with my cloak, quick!" He put her cloak on for her. She stamped her foot impatiently. "Pull my hair outside!"

He took her luxuriant hair in both his hands, and pulled it outside the cloak, and fitted the collar about her neck. She caught both his hands in hers, and looking up, laughed gleefully.

"You dassent kiss me now!"

He stooped and kissed her cheek, and blushed with shame. On the way up the walk to the chapel, he suffered an agony of remorse. He felt dimly that he had done his ideal an irreparable wrong. Nettie talked on, not minding his silence, looking up into his face in innocent glee, planning some new party or moonlit drive.

All that morning he was too deep in thought to give attention to his classes, and at noon he avoided Nettie, and went home to think, but try as he might, something prevented him from getting hold of the real facts in the case.

He was fond of Nettie. She stood near him,

an embodied passion. His love for Miss Wilbur, which he had no idea of calling love, was a vague and massive feeling of adoration, entirely disassociated from the flesh. She stood for him as the embodiment of a world of longings and aspirations undeveloped and undefined.

One thought was clear. He ought not to allow — that is the way it took shape in his mind — he ought not to allow Nettie to be seen with him so much, unless he intended to marry her, and he had never thought of her as a possible wife.

He didn't know how to meet Russell, so put off going down to his house, as he had promised. He excused himself by saying he was busy moving, anyway. He had determined upon taking a boarding-place somewhere in correspondence with his change of fortunes and when he had spoken of it, the Judge had said :

"Why not come up to my house? Mrs. Brown and I get kind of lonesome sometimes, and then I hate to milk an' curry horses, an' split kindlings, always did. Come up and try living with us."

Bradley had accepted the offer with the greatest delight. It meant a great deal to him. It took him out of a cellar and put him into one of the finest houses in town — albeit it was a cold and gloomy house. It was large, and white, and square, with sharp gables, and its blinds were always closed. He went up to dinner that day with the judge, to meet Mrs. Brown, whom he had never seen ; nobody saw her, for she was a perfect recluse.

She looked at her husband through her glasses in a calm surprise, as he introduced Bradley, and stated he had invited him to dinner.

"Well, Mr. Brown, if you will do such things, you must expect your company to take every-day fare."

"Maybe our every-day fare, Mrs. Brown, will be Sunday fare for this young man."

They sat down at the table, which Mrs. Brown waited upon herself, rising from her place for the tea or the biscuits. She said very little thereafter, but Bradley caught the gleam of her glasses fixed upon him several times. She had a beautiful mouth, but the line of her lips seemed to indicate sadness and a determined silence.

"Mrs. Brown, I wish you'd take care of this young man for a few weeks. He's my clerk, and I — ahem ! — I — suppose he's going to milk the cow and split the kindlings for me, to pay for his board in that useful way."

She looked at him again in silence, and the line of her lips got a little straighter, as she waited for the Judge to go on.

"This young man is going to study law with me, and I hope to make a great man of him, Mrs. Brown."

" Mr. Brown, I wish you'd consult with me once in a while," she said without anger.

"Mrs. Brown, it was a case of necessity. I was on the point of giving up the milking of that cow, and my back got a crick in it every time I split the kindlings. I consider I've done you a benefit and myself a favor, Mrs. Brown."

She turned her glasses upon Bradley again, and studied him in silence. She was a very dignified woman of fifty. Her hair was like wavy masses of molasses candy, and her brow cold and placid. Her eyes could not be seen, but her mouth and chin were almost girlish in their beauty.

The Judge felt that he had done a hazardous thing. He took a new tone, his reminiscent tone. "Mrs. Brown, do you remember the first time you saw me? Well, I was 'pirating' through Oberlin — (chopping wood, you remember we didn't saw it in those days) and living in a cellar, just like this young man. He's been cookin' his own grub, just as I did then, because he hasn't any money to pay for board. Now I think we ought to give him a lift. Don't you think so, Mrs. Brown?"

Her mouth relaxed a little. The glasses turned upon Bradley again, and looked upon him so steadily that he was able to see her gray eyes.

"Mr. Brown is always doing things without consulting me," she explained to Bradley, "but you are welcome, sir, if our lonesome house aint worse than your cellar. Mr. Brown very seldom takes the trouble to explain what he wants to do, but I'll try to make you feel at home, sir."

They ate the rest of the meal in silence. The Judge was evidently thinking over old times, and it would be very difficult to say what his wife was thinking of. At last he rose saying:

"Now if you'll come out, I'll show you the well and the cow." As he went by his wife's chair, he stopped a moment, and said gently, "He'll do us two lonely old fossils good, Elizabeth." His hand lay on her shoulder an instant as he passed, and when Bradley went out of the room, he saw her wiping her eyes upon her handkerchief, her glasses in her hand.

The Judge coughed a little. "We never had but one child — a boy. He was killed while out hunting" — he broke off quickly. "Now here's the meal for the cow. I give her about a panful twice a day — when I don't forget it."

Somehow, Mrs. Brown didn't seem so hard when he met her again at supper. The line of her mouth was softer. In his room he found many little touches of her motherly hand — a clean, sweet bed, and little hand-made things upon the wall, that made him think of his own mother, who had been dead since his sixteenth year. He had never had such a room as this. It appeared to him as something very fine. Its frigid atmosphere and lack of grace and charm did not appear to his eyes. It was nothing short of princely after his cellar.

His knowledge of the inner life of the common Western homes made him feel that this rigid coldness between the Judge and his wife was only their way. The touch of the Judge's hand on her shoulder meant more than a thousand worn phrases spoken every day. Under that silence and reserve there was a deep of tenderness and wistful longing which they could not utter, and dared not acknowledge, even to themselves. Their lonely house had grown intolerable, and Bradley came into it bringing youth and sunlight.

X.

A COUNTRY POLLING PLACE.

THE suffering of the county papers was acute. They had supported the "incumbents" for so long, and had derived a reciprocal support so long, that they could not bring themselves to a decision. The Democratic paper, the *Call*, was too feeble to be anything distinctive at this stage of its career Chard Foster had not yet assumed control of it. It lent a half-hearted support to the Independent movement, and justified its action on the ground that it was really a Democratic movement leading toward reform, and it assumed to be the only paper advocating reform. The other paper, unequivocally Republican, supported the regular ticket with that single-heartedness of enmity, born of bribery, or that ignorance which shuts out any admission that the other side has a case.

The Oak Grove schoolhouse was the real storm·

centre of the election, and there was a great crowd there all day. It was a cold, raw day. The men and boys all came in their overcoats and stood about on the leeward side of the school-house — where a pale sunlight fell — and scuffled, and told stories, and bet cookies and apples on the election.

Some of the boys made up fires out in the woods near by, to which they ran whooping whenever the cold became intolerable. They crouched around the flames with a weird return of ancestral barbarism and laughed when the smoke puffed out into their faces. They made occasional forages in company with boys who lived near, after eggs, and apples, and popcorn, which they placed before the fire and ate spiced with ashes.

Horsemen galloped up at intervals, bringing encouraging news of other voting places. Teams clattered up filled with roughly-dressed farmers, who greeted the other voters with loud and hearty shouts. They tumbled out of the wagons, voted riotously, and then clattered back into the corn-fields to their work, with wild hurrahs for the granger ticket.

The schoolhouse itself roared with laughter and excited talk, and the big stove in the centre devoured its huge chunks of wood, making the heat oppressive near it. No presidential election had ever brought out such throngs of voters, or produced such interested discussion.

Bradley had been made clerk. His capital handwriting and knowledge of book-keeping made him a valuable man for that work. He sat behind his desk with the books before him, and impassively performed his duties, but it was his first public appointment, and he was really deeply gratified. He felt paid for all his year's hard study.

About two o'clock, when the voters were thickest at the polls, a man galloped up with an excited air, and reining in his foaming horse, yelled:

"Deering has withdrawn in favor of Russell!" The crowd swarmed out.

"What's the matter?"

"Who spoke?"

"Deering has withdrawn in favor of Russell. Cast your votes for Russell," repeated the man, and plunged off up the road.

The farmers looked at each other. "What the hell's all this?" said Smith.

"Who was it?"

"I don't know."

"He's a liar, whoever he is," said Councill. "Where've I seen him before?"

"I know — it's Deering's hired man."

"You don't say so!" This seemed like the truth.

"I know who it is — it's Sam Harding," shouted Milton. "But that aint Deering's horse. It's a Republican trick. Jump y'r horse there, Councill." He was carried out of himself by his excitement and anger. The men leaped upon their horses.

"Some o' you fellers take his back trail," shouted Councill. "He come from Shell-rock and Hell's Corner."

The men saw the whole trick. This man had been sent out to the most populous of the county voting places to spread a lying report, trusting to the surprise of the announcement to carry a few indecisive votes for Russell.

Other men leaped their horses and rode off on Harding's back trail, while Councill, Milton, and old man Bacon rode away after him. Bacon growled as he rode:

"I'm agin you fellers, but by God! I b'lieve in a square game. If I kin git my paw on that houn'" —

They rode furiously in the hope of overtaking him before he reached the next polling-place. Milton was in the lead on his gray colt, a magnificent creature. He was light and a fine rider, and forged ahead of the elder men. But the "spy" was also riding a fine horse, and was riding very fast.

When they reached the next polling-place he was just passing out of sight beyond. They dashed up, scattering the wondering crowd.

"It's a lie! It's a trick!" shouted Milton. "Deering wouldn't withdraw. Cast every vote for Deering. It's all done to fool yeh!"

The others came thundering up. "It's a lie!" they shouted.

"Come on!" cried Milton, dropping the rein on Mark's neck, and darting away on the trail of the false courier.

The young fellows caught the excitement, and every one who had a horse leaped into the saddle and clattered after, with whoop and halloo, as if they were chasing a wolf.

The rider ahead suddenly discovered that he was being followed, and he urged his horse to a more desperate pace along the lane which skirted the woods' edge for a mile, and then turned sharply and led across the river.

Along the lane is the chase led. There was something in the grim silence with which Milton and Bacon rode in the lead that startled the spy's guilty heart.   He pushed his horse unmercifully, hoping to discourage his pursuers.

Milton's blood was up now, and bringing the flat of his hand down on the proud neck of his colt — the first blow he ever struck him, he shouted —

"Get out o' this, Mark!"

The magnificent animal threw out his chin, his ears laid flat back, he seemed to lower and lengthen, his eyes took on a wild glare.   The air whizzed by Milton's ears.   A wild exultation rose in his heart.   All the stories of rides and desperate men he had ever read came back in a vague mass to make his heart thrill.

Mark's terrific pace steadily ate up the inter-vening distance, and Milton turned the corner and thundered down the decline at the very heels of the fugitive.

"Hey!   Hold on there!" Milton shouted, as he drew alongside and passed the fellow.   "Hold on there!"

"Git out o' my way!" was the savage answer.

"Stop right here!" commanded Milton, rein ing Mark in the way of the other horse.

The fellow struck Mark.   "Git out o' my way!" he yelled.

Milton seized the bit of the other horse and

held it. The fellow raised his arm and struck him twice before Bacon came thundering up.

"H'yare! Damn yeh — none o' that!"

He leaped from his horse, and running up, tore the rider from his saddle in one swift effort. The fellow struggled fiercely.

"Let go o' me, 'r I'll kill yeh!"

Bacon growled something inarticulate .as he cuffed the man from side to side, shook him like a rag, and threw him to the ground. He lay there dazed and scared, while Bacon caught his horse and tied it to a tree.

He came back to the fellow as he was rising, and again laid his bear-like clutch upon him.

"Who paid you to do this?" he demanded, as Councill and the others came straggling up, their horses panting with fatigue.

The fellow struck him in the face. The old man lifted him in the air and dashed him to the ground with a snarling cry. His gesture was like that of one who slams a biting cat upon the floor. The man did not rise.

"You've killed him!" cried Milton.

"Damn 'im — I don't care!"

The man was about thirty-five years of age, a slender, thin-faced man with tobacco-stained whiskers. The fellows knew him for a sneaking fellow, but they plead for him.

"Don't hit 'im agin, Bacon. He's got enough."

The fellow sat up and looked around. The blood was streaming from his nose and from a wound in his head. He had a savage and hunted look. He was unsubdued, but was too much dazed to be able to do anything more than swear at them all.

"What a' yuh chasen' me fur, y' damn cowards? Six on one!"

"What're you do-un ridin' across the country like this fur?"

"None o' your business, you low-lived" —

Bacon brought the doubled leading-strap which he held in his hand down over the fellow's shoulders with a sounding slap.

"What you need is a sound· tannun," he said. He plied the strap in perfect silence upon the writhing man, who swore and yelled, but dared not rise.

"Give him enough of it!" yelled the crowd.

"Give the fool enough!"

Bacon worked away with a curious air of taking a job. The strap fell across the man's upheld hands and over his shoulders, penetrating even the thick coat he wore — but it was not the blows that quelled him, it was the look in Bacon's eyes. He saw that the old man would stand there till sunset and ply that strap.

"Hold on! Dam yeh — y' want 'o kill me?"

"Got 'nough?"

"Yes, yes! My God, yes!"

"Climb onto that horse there."

He climbed upon his horse, and with Bacon leading it, rode back along the road he had come, covered with blood.

"Now I want you to say with y'r own tongue ye lied," Bacon said, as they came to the last polling-place he had passed.

The crowd came rushing out with excited questions.

"What y' got there, Bacon?"

"A liar. Come, what ye goun't' say?" he asked the captive.

"I lied — Deering aint withdrawn."

They rode on, Councill and Milton following Bacon and his prisoner. At the Oak Grove schoolhouse a great crowd had gathered, and they came out in a swarm as the cavalcade rode up. Bradley left his book and came out to see the poor prisoner, who reeled in his saddle, covered with blood and dirt.

They rode on to the next polling-place, relentlessly forcing the man to undo as much of his villainy as possible. Milton remained with Bradley. "That shows how desperate they are," he said as they went back into the schoolhouse. "They see we mean business this time."

All was quiet, even gloomy, when Bradley and Milton reached Rock River. The streets were deserted, and only an occasional opening door at some favorite haunt, like the drug-store or Robie's grocery, showed that a living soul was interested in the outcome of the election. There were no bonfires, no marching of boys through the street with tin pans and horns.

Some reckless fellows tried it out of devilment, but were promptly put down by the strong hand of the city marshal, whose sympathies were with the broken "ring." It had been evident at an early hour of the day that the town of Rock River itself was divided. Amos Ridings and Robie had carried a strong following over into the camp of the farmers. A general feeling had developed which demanded a change.

Milton was wild with excitement. He realized more of the significance of the victory than Bradley. He had been in politics longer. For the first time in the history of the county, the farmers had asserted themselves. For the first time in the history of the farmers of Iowa, had they felt the power of their own mass.

For the first time in the history of the American farmer there had come a feeling of solidarity. They perceived, for a moment at least, their community of interests and their power to preserve themselves against the combined forces of the political pensioners of the small towns. They made the mistake of supposing the interests of the merchant, artisan, and mechanic were also inimicable.

They saw the smaller circle first. They had not yet risen to the perception of the solidarity of all productive interests. That was sure to follow.

XI.

STUDYING WITH THE JUDGE.

AFTER this campaign Bradley went back to his studies at the seminary and to his work in Brown's office. Milton did not go back. Deering made him his assistant in the treasurer's office, and he confided to Bradley his approaching marriage with Eileen.

In talking about Milton's affairs to Bradley, Mr. Jennings said sadly: "Well, that leaves me alone. He'll never come back to the farm. When he was at school I didn't miss him so much, because he was always coming back on a Saturday, but now — well, it's no use making a fuss over it, I s'pose, but it's going to be lonesome work for us out there."

"Mebbe he'll come back after his term of office is up."

Mr. Jennings shook his head. "No, town life

and office'll spoil 'im — and then he'll get married. You'll never go back on the farm. Nobody ever does that gets away from it and learns how to get a livin' anywhere else."

This melancholy sat strangely upon Mr. Jennings, who usually took things as they came with smiling resignation. It affected Bradley deeply to see him so gloomy.

Bradley found a quiet and comfortable home with Judge Brown and his odd old wife, who manifested her growing regard for him by little touches of adornment in his room, and by infrequent confidences. As for the Judge, he took an immense delight in the young fellow, he made such a capital listener. Between Bradley and the grocery he really found opportunity to tell all his old stories and philosophize upon every conceivable subject. He talked a deal of politics, quoting Jefferson and Jackson. He criticised members of Congress, and told what he would have done in their places. He criticised, also, the grange movement, from what he considered to be a lofty plane.

"They profess to have for a motto 'equal rights to all and special privileges to none,' and then they go off into class legislation. It's easy to talk that principle, but it means business when you stand by it. I haint got the sand to stand by that principle myself. It goes too deep for me, but it's something you young politicians ought to study on. One o' these days that principle will get life into it, and when it does things will tumble. The Democratic party used to be a party that meant that, and if it ever succeeds again it must head that way. That's the reason I want to get you young fellows into it."

These talks didn't mean as much to Bradley as they should have done. He was usually at work at something and only half listened while the Judge wandered on, his heels in the air, his cheek full of tobacco. Old Colonel Peavy dropped in occasionally, and Dr. Carver, and then the air was full of good, old-time Democratic phrases. At such times the Judge even went so far as to quote Calhoun.

"As a matter of fact, Calhoun was on the right track. If he hadn't got his States' Rights doctrine mixed up with slavery, he'd 'a' been all right. What he really stood for was local government as opposed to centralized government. We're just comin' around back to a part of Calhoun's position."

This statement of the Judge stuck in Bradley's mind; months afterward it kept coming up and becoming more significant each time that he talked upon it.

He thought less often of Miss Wilbur now, and he could hear her name mentioned without flushing. She had become a vaguer but no less massive power in his life. That beautiful place in his soul where she was he had a strange reverence for. He loved to have it there. It was an inspiration to him, and yet he did not distinctly look forward to ever seeing her, much less to meeting her.

Indefinite as this feeling was, it saved him from the mistake of marrying Nettie. Poor girl! She was in the grasp of her first great passion, and was as helpless as a broken-winged bird in the current of a river. She was feverishly happy and unaccountably sad by turns. The commands of her father not to see Bradley only roused her antagonism, and her mother's timid entreaties made no impression upon her. Not even Bradley's unresponsiveness seemed to have a decided discouraging effect.

Her classmates laughed at her, as they did at three or four other pairs in the school who proclaimed their devouring love for each other by walking to and from the chapel with locked arms, or who sat side by side in their classes with

clasped hands, indifferent to any rude jest, repri-
mand from the teacher, or slyly flung eraser.
The principal gave it up in despair, calling it a
"sort of measles which they'll outgrow."

It was really pitiful to the comprehending
observer. There was so much that was pain
mixed with this pleasure. There were so many
keen and benumbing disappointments, like that
of waiting about the door of the office for Bradley
to come down, and then to see him appear in
company with some client of Judge Brown. Not
that the client made so much difference, but the
cold glance of Bradley's eyes did. At such times
she turned away with quivering lip and choking
throat.

She had lost much of her pertness and bright-
ness. She talked very little at home, and it was
only when with Bradley that she seemed at all
like her old bird-like self. Then she chattered
away in a wild delight, if he happened to be in
a responsive mood, or feverishly and with a
forced quality of gayety if he were cold and
unresponsive.

Bradley knew he ought to decide one way or
the other, and often he promised himself that he
would refuse to walk or ride with her, but the
next time she came he weakly relented at sight of

her eager face. It took so little to make her happy, that the temptation was very great to yield, and so their lives went along. He took her to the parties and sleigh-rides with the young people, but on his return he refused to enter the house. He met her at the gate, and left her there upon his return.

The colonel had met him shortly after the election, and had threatened to whip him for his charges against him as an office-holder. He concluded not to try it, however, and contented himself by saying, "Don't you never darken my door again, young man."

But in general Bradley's life moved on uneventfully. He applied himself studiously to his work in the office. He was getting hold of some common law, and a great deal of common sense, for the Judge was strong on both these points.

"Young man," said the Judge one day, after Bradley had returned from a sleigh-ride with Nettie, "I see that the woman-question is before you. Now don't make a mistake. Be sure you are right. In nine cases out of ten, back out and you'll be right."

Bradley remained silent over by the rickety red-hot stove, warming his stiffened fingers. The Judge went on in a speculative way:

"I believe I notice a tendency in the times that makes it harder for a married man to succeed than it used to be. I think, on the whole, my advice would be to keep out of it altogether. More men fail on that account, I observe, than upon any other. You see it's so infernally hard to tell what kind of a woman your girl is going to turn out."

"You needn't worry about me," said Bradley a little sullenly.

"That's what Mrs. Brown said. I just thought I'd say a word or two, anyway. If I've gone too far, you may kick my dog over there."

Bradley looked at the sleeping dog, and back at the meditative Judge, and smiled. He sat down at his work and said no more upon the subject.

XII.

THE JUDGE ADVISES BRADLEY.

IT was at the Judge's advice that he decided to take a year at the law-school at Iowa City. He had been in the office over a year and a half, and though he had not been converted to Democracy, the Judge was still hopeful.

"Oh, you'll have to come into the Democratic camp," he often said. "You see, it's like this: the Republicans are so damn proud of their record, they're going to ossify, with their faces turned backward. They have a past, but no future. Now the Democratic party has no past that it cares particularly to look back at, and so it's got to look into the future. You progressive young fellows can't afford to stand in a party where everything is all done, because that leaves nothing for you to do but to admire some dead man. You'll be forced into the party of ideas, sure. I aint disposed to hurry you, you'll come out all right when the time comes."

Bradley never argued with him. He had simply shut his lips and his mind to it all. Democracy had lost some of its evil associations in his mind, however, and Free Trade and Secession no longer meant practically the same thing, as it used to do.

"Now people are damn fools — excepting you an' me, of course," yawned the Judge, one day in midsummer. "What you want to do is to take a couple of years at Iowa City and then come back here and jump right into the political arena and toot your horn. They'll elect you twice as quick if you come back here with a high collar and a plug-hat, even these grangers. They distrust a man in 'hodden gray' — no sort of doubt of it. Now you take my advice. People like to be pollygoggled by a sleek suit of clothes. And then, there is nothing that impresses people with a man's immense accumulation of learning and dignity like a judicious spell of absence."

It was very warm, and they both sat with coats and vests laid aside. The fat old bull-dog was panting convulsively from the exertion of having just climbed the stairs. The Judge went on, after looking affectionately at the dog:

"Ah, we're a gittin' old together, Bull an' me. We like the shady side of the street. Now you could make a good run in the county to-day, as you are, but your election would be doubtful, and we can't afford to take any chances. There are a lot o' fellers who'd say you hadn't had experience enough — too young, an' all that kind o' thing. We'll suppose you could be elected auditor. It wouldn't pay. It would only stand in the way of bigger things. Now you take my advice."

"I'd like to, but I can't afford it, Judge."

"How much you got on hand?"

"Oh, couple of hundred dollars or so."

The Judge ruminated a bit, scratching his chin. "Well, now, I'll tell yeh, Mrs. Brown and I had a little talk about the matter last night, and she thinks I ought to lend you the money, and — she thinks you ought to take it. So pack up y'r duds in September and start in."

Bradley's first impulse, of course, was to refuse, because he felt he had no claim upon the Judge's charity. It took hold of his imagination, however, and he talked it all over thoroughly during the intervening weeks, and the Judge put it this way:

"Now, there's no charity about this thing — I simply expect to get three hundred per cent. on my money, so you go right along and when you

come back we'll have a new shingle painted—
'Brown & Talcott.' We aint anxious to lose yeh.
As a matter of fact, Mrs. Brown and I'll be pretty
lonesome for the first few weeks after you go
away—and what I'll do about that cussed cow
and kindling-wood I really don't know. Mrs.
Brown suggested we'd better take in another
homeless boy, and I guess that's what we'll do."

A couple of nights later, while Bradley was sit
ting before his trunk, which he had begun to pacl
like the inexperienced traveller he was, severa
days in advance, Mrs. Brown came to the stairway
to tell him Nettie was below and wanted to see
him.

The poor girl had just heard that he was going
away and she met him with a white, scared face.
He sat down without speaking, for he had no
defence, except silence, for things of that nature.
The girl's fury of grief appalled him. She came
over and flung herself sobbing upon his lap, her
arms about his neck.

"Oh, Brad! Is it true? Are you going away?"

"I expect to," he replied coldly.

"You mustn't! You sha'n't! I won't let
you!" she cried, tightening her arms about him,
as if that would detain him. From that on, there
was nothing but sobs on her side, and expla-

nations on his — explanations to which her love,
direct and selfish, would not listen for a moment.
The unreserve and unreason of her passion at last
disgusted him.   His tone grew sharper.

"I can't stay here," he said.   "You've no business to ask me to.   I can't always be a lawyer's
hack.   I want to study and go higher.   I've got
to leave this town, if I ever amount to anything in
the world."

"Then take me with you!" she cried.

"I can't do that!   I can't any more'n make a
livin' for myself.   Besides, I've got to study."

"I'll make father give you some money," she
said.

He closed his lips sternly, and said nothing further.   Her agony wore itself out after a time, and
she was content to sit up and look at him and
listen to him at last while he explained.   And her
suppressed sobs and the tears that stood in her
big childish eyes moved him more than her unre-
strained sorrow.   It was thus she conquered him.

He promised her he would come home often,
and he promised to write every day, and by impli-
cation, though not in words, he promised to marry
her — that is to say, he acquiesced in her plans
for housekeeping when he returned and was established in the office.   He ended it all by walking

home with her and promising to see her every day
before he went, and as he kissed her good-night
at the gate, she was smiling again and quite
happy, although a little catching of the breath
(even in her laughter) showed that she was not
yet out of the ground-swell of her emotion.

Mrs. Brown was waiting for him when he
returned, and as he sat down in the sitting-room,
where she was busy at her sewing, she looked at
him in her slow way, and at last arose and came
over near his chair.

"Have you promised her anything, Bradley?"
she asked, laying her thimbled hand upon his
shoulder, as his own mother might have done.
Bradley lifted his gloomy eyes and colored a little.

"I don't know what I've said," he answered,
from the depth of his swift reaction. "More'n I
had any business to say, probably."

"I thought likely. You can't afford to marry
a girl out of pity for her, Bradley — it won't do.
I've seen how things stood for some time, but I
thought I wouldn't say anything." She paused
and considered a moment, standing there by his
side. "It's a good thing for both of you that
you're going away. You hadn't ought to have
let it go on so long."

"I couldn't help it," he replied with more

sharpness in his voice than he had ever used in speaking to her.

Her hand dropped from his shoulder. "No, I don't s'pose you could. It aint natural for young people to stop an' think about these things. I don't suppose you knew y'rself just where it was all leading to. Well, now, don't worry, and don't let it interfere with your plans. She'll outgrow it. Girls often go through two or three such attacks. Just go on with your studies, and when you come back, if you find her unmarried, why, then decide what to do."

Her touch of cynicism was accounted for, perhaps, by the fact that she had never had a daughter.

XIII.

BRADLEY SEES IDA AGAIN.

BRADLEY felt that the world was widening for him, as he took the train for Iowa City a few days later. He was now very nearly thirty years of age, and was maturing more rapidly than his friends and neighbors knew, for the processes of his mind, like those of an intricate coil of machinery, were hidden deep away from the casual acquaintance.

He had secured, in the two years at the seminary, a fairly good groundwork of the common English branches, and his occasional reading, and especially his attendance upon law-suits, had given him a really creditable understanding of common law. The Judge always insisted that law was simple, but it wasn't as profitable as — chicanery.

"Any man, from his fund of common sense,

can settle nine tenths of all law-suits, but that
aint what we're here for. A successful lawyer is
the fellow who tangles things up and keeps common law and common sense subordinated to chicanery and precedent. Damn precedent, anyway.
It means referring to a past that didn't know, and
didn't want to know, what justice was."

In the atmosphere of lectures like these, Bradley had unconsciously absorbed a great deal of
radical thought about law-codes, and now went
about the study of the history of enactments and
change of statutes without any servile awe of the
past. The Judge's irreverence had its uses, for it
put a law on its merits before the young student.

He found the law-school a very congenial place
to study. He passed the examinations quite
decently.

His life there was quiet and studious, for he
felt that he had less time than the younger men.
His age seemed excessive to him, by contrast.
He was very generally respected as a quiet,
decent fellow, who might be a fine consulting
lawyer, but not a good man in the courts. They
changed this opinion very suddenly upon hearing
him present his first plea.

His life consisted for the most part of passing
to and fro from his boarding-place to his recitation-

room, or to long hours of digging in the library. He saw from time to time notices of Miss Wilbur's lectures in the interests of the grange and upon literary topics. He determined to hear her if she came into any neighboring city. There was no one to spy upon him, if he made an expedition of that sort.

One beautiful winter day he read in the weekly paper of the town that she was about to appear at the Congregational church in a lecture entitled, "The Real Woman-question." He had an impulse to sing, which he wisely repressed, for he couldn't sing — that is, nothing which the hearer would recognize as singing. The Fates seemed working in his favor.

He had preserved a marked sweetness and purity of thought through all his hard life that made him a good type of man. His clear, steady eyes never gave offence to any woman, for nothing but sympathy and admiration ever looked out of them. The very thought that she was coming so near brought a curious numbness into his muscles and a tremor into his hands. He looked forward now to the evening of the lecture with the keenest interest he had ever felt.

The dazzling winter day seemed more radiant than ever before, when he heard some ladies in the post-office say Ida was in town. The blue shadows lay on the new-fallen snow vivid as steel. The warm sun showered down through the clear air a peculiar warmth that made the eaves begin to drop in the early morning. Sleighs were moving to and fro in the streets, and bright bits of color on the girls' hoods and in the broad knit scarfs which the young men wore, formed pleasing reliefs from the dazzling blue and white. Bells filled the air with jocund music.

Bradley walked straight away into the country. He wanted to be alone. It seemed so strange and sweet to be thus shaken by the coming of a woman. In the first few minutes he gave himself up to the thought that she was near and that he was going to hear her speak again. It made his hand shake and his heart beat quick.

He wondered if she would be changed. She would be older a little, but she would look just the same. He saw her stand again under the waving branches of the oaks, the flickering shadow on her brown hair, speaking again the words which had become the measure of his ambition, the prophecy of a social condition :

"I want to have everything I do to help us all on toward that time when the country will be filled with happy young people, and hale and hearty old people, when the moon will be **brighter**, and the stars thicker in the skies."

This was his thought. He had not **risen yet** to the conception of the real barrenness and squalor of the life he had lived.

His studies had made him a little more self-analytical, but there were inner deeps where he did not penetrate and there was one inner place which he dared not enter. A whirl of thought confused him, but out of it all he returned constantly to the thought that he should hear her speak again.

That evening he dressed himself with as much care as if he were to call upon her alone, and he dressed very well now. His clothes were substantial and fitted him well. His year's immunity from hard work had left his large hands supple and delicate of touch, and his face had attained refinement and mobility. His eyes had become more introspective and had lost entirely the ox-like roll of the country-born man. He was a handsome and dignified young man. His bearing on the street was noticeably manly and unaffected.

The lecture was in the church and the seats were all filled. It gratified him, at the same time that it hopelessly abased him to observe all this evidence of her power. As he waited for her to appear that tremor came into his hands again, and that breathlessness, and curiously enough he felt that horrible familiar sinking of the heart that he always felt just before he himself rose to speak.

Somebody started to clap hands, and the rest joined in, as two or three ladies entered the back part of the church and passed up the aisle. He looked up as they went by him, and caught a glimpse of a stately head of brown hair, modestly bent in acknowledgment of the applause, and he caught a whiff of the delicate odor of violets. His eyes followed the strong, firm steps of the young woman who walked between the two older women. There was something fine and dignified in her walk, and the odor of her dress as she passed lingered with him, but he did not feel that she was the same woman, till she turned and faced him on the platform.

He sat impassively, but his pulse leaped when her clear brown eyes running calmly over the audience seemed to fall upon him. She was the same woman, his ideal and more. She was fuller of form and the poise of her head was more womanly, but she was the same spirit that had come to be such a power and inspiration in his life.

As a matter of fact she had grown also. If

she had not, she would have seemed girlish to him
now; growing as he grew, she seemed the same
distance beyond him. Her self-possession in the
face of the audience appealed to him strongly.
Something in her manner of dress pleased him, it
was so individual, so like her simple, dignified,
beautiful self in every line.

She spoke more quietly, more conversation-
ally than when he heard her before, but her voice
made him shudder with associated emotions. Its
cadences reached deep, and the words she spoke
opened long vistas in his mind. She was defend-
ing the right of women to live as human beings,
to act as human beings, and to develop as freely
as men.

"I claim the right to be an individual human
being first and a woman afterward. Why should
the accident of my sex surround me with conven-
tional and arbitrary limitations? I claim the same
right to find out what I can do and can't do that
a man has. Who is to determine what my sphere
is— men and men's laws or my own nature?
These are vital questions. I deny the right of
any man to mark out the path in which I shall
walk. I claim the same right to life, liberty, and
the pursuit of happiness that men are demanding.

"It is not a question of suffrage merely—

suffrage is the smaller part of the woman-question — it is a question of equal rights. It is a question of whether the law of liberty applies to humanity or to men only. Absolute liberty bounded only by the equal liberties of the rest of humanity is the real goal of the race — not of man only, but woman too."

The ladies dimly feeling that liberty was a safe thing to cheer, clapped their hands softly under the cover of the nosier clapping of a few radicals who knew what the speaker was really saying. Bradley did not cheer — he was thinking too deeply.

" The woman question is not a political one merely, it is an economic one. The real problem is the wage problem, the industrial problem. The real question is woman's dependence upon man as the bread-winner. As long as that dependence exists there will be weakness. No individual can stand at their strongest and best while leaning upon some other. I believe with Browning and Ruskin that the development of personality is the goal of the race."

The ladies took it for granted that this was true as it was bolstered by two great names. A few, however, sat with wrinkled brows scenting something heretical in all that.

"The time is surely coming when women can no longer bear to be dependent, to be pitied or abused by men. They will want to stand upright and independent by their husbands, claiming the same rights to freedom of action, and demanding equal pay for equal work. She must be able to earn her own living in an *honorable* way at a moment's notice. Then she will be a free woman even if she never leaves her kitchen."

It was trite enough to a few of the audience, but, to others, it was new, and to many it was revolutionary. She was destined to again set a stake in Bradley's mental horizon. The woman question had not engaged his attention; at least not in any serious way. He had not thought of woman as having any active part in living. In the thoughtless way of the average man, he had ignored or idealized women according as they appealed to his eye. He had not risen to the point of pitying or condemning, or in any way consciously placing them in the social economy.

The speaker had appealed to his imagination before, and now again he sat absolutely motionless while great new thoughts and impersonal emotions sprang up in his brain. He saw women in a new light, and the aloofness of the speaker grew upon him again. He felt that she was holding her place as his teacher. Around him he heard the rustle of approval upon the gown she wore, upon her voice, and some few favorable comments upon her ideas. He saw some of the people crowd forward to shake her hand, while others went out talking excitedly.

He lingered as long as he dared, longing to go forward to greet her, but he went slowly out at last, home to his boarding place and sat down in his habitual attitude when in deep thought, his elbow on his knee, his chin in his palm. He wanted to see her, he must see her and tell her how much she had done for him.

How to do it was the question which absorbed him now. He got away from the noisy merriment of the house, out into the street again. The stars were more congenial company to him now; under their passionless serenity he could think better. He felt that he must come to an understanding with himself soon, but he put it off and turned his attention to his future, and more immediately to the plans which must be carried out, of seeing her.

When he came in he was desperately resolved. He would go to see her on the next day in her hotel. He justified himself by saying that she was a lecturer, a person before the public, and that she would not think it strange; anyhow, he was going to do it.

In the broad daylight, however, it was not so easy as it seemed under the magic of the moon. The conventions of the world always count for less in the company of the moon and the stars. He heard during the morning that she was going away in the afternoon, and he was made desperate. He started out to go straight to the hotel, and he did, but he walked by it, once, twice, a half dozen times, each time feeling weaker and more desperate in his resolution.

At length he deliberately entered and astonished himself by walking up to the clerk and asking for Miss Wilbur.

The clerk turned briskly and looked at the pigeon-holes for the keys. "I think she is. Send up a card?"

True, he hadn't thought of that. He had no cards. He received one from the clerk that looked as if it had done duty before, and scrawled his name upon it, and gave it to the insolent little darky who served as "Front."

"Tell her I'd like to see her just a few minutes."

On the stairs he tried to prepare what he

should say to her. His mouth already felt dry, and his brain was a mere swirl of gray and white matter. Almost without knowing how, he found himself seated in the ladies' parlor, to which the boy had conducted him. It was a barren little place, in spite of its excessively florid gilt and crimson paper, and its ostentatious harsh red-plush furniture.

His heart sent the blood into his throat till it ached with the tension. His lips quivered and turned pale as he heard the slow sweep of a woman's dress, and there she stood before him, with smiling face and extended hand. "Are you Mr. Talcott? Did you want to see me?"

She had the frank gesture and ready smile a kindly man would have used. Instantly his brain cleared, his heart ceased to pound, and the numbness left his limbs. He forgot himself utterly. He only saw and heard her. He found himself saying:

"I wanted to come in and tell you how much I liked your speech last night, and how much I liked a speech you made up at Rock River, at the grange picinic."

"Oh, did you hear me up there? That was one of my old speeches. I've quite outgrown that now. You'll be shocked to know I don't believe in a whole lot of things that I used to believe in." As she talked, she looked at him precisely as one man looks at another, without the slightest false modesty or coquettishness. She evidently considered him a fellow-student on social affairs. "I'm glad you liked my talk on the woman question. It was dreadfully radical to the most of my audience."

"It was right," Bradley said, and their minds seemed to come together at that point as if by an electrical shock. "I never thought of it before. Women have been kept down. We do claim to know better what she ought to do than she knows herself. The trouble is we men don't think about it at all. We need to have you tell us these things."

"Yes, that's true. As soon as I made that discovery I began talking the woman question. One radicalism opened the way to the other. Being a radical is like opening the door to the witches. Are you one?" she asked, with a sudden smile, "I mean a radical, not a witch."

"I don't know," he replied simply, "I'm a student. I know I can't agree with some people on these things."

"*Some* people! Sometimes I feel it would be good to meet with a single person —a single

one — I could agree with! But tell me of yourself — are you in the grange movement?"

"Well, not exactly, but I've helped all I
could."

"What is the condition of the grange in your
county?"

"It seems to be going down."

She was silent for some time. Her face saddened with deep thought. "Yes, I'm afraid it
is. The farmers can't seem to hold together.
Strange, aint it? Other trades and occupations
have their organizations and stand by each other,
but the farmer can't seem to feel his kinship.
Well, I suppose he must suffer greater hardships
before he learns his lesson. But God help the
poor wives while he learns! But he *must* learn,"
she ended firmly. "He must come some day to
see that to stand by his fellow-man is to stand by
himself. That's what civilization means, to stand
by each other."

Bradley did not reply. He was looking upon
her, with eyes filled with adoration. He had
never heard such words from the lips of anyone.
He had never seen a woman sit lost in philoso-
phic thought like this. Her bent head seemed
incredibly beautiful to him, and her simple flowing dress, royal purple. Her presence destroyed

his power of thought.   He simply waited for her to go on.

"The farmer lacks comparative ideas," she went on.   "He don't know how poor he is.   If he once finds it out, let the politicians and their masters, the money-changers, beware!   But while he's finding it out, his children will grow up in ignorance, and his wife die of overwork.   Oh, sometimes I lose heart."   Her voice betrayed how strongly she perceived the almost hopeless immensity of the task.   "The farmer must learn that to help himself, he must help others.   That is the great lesson of modern society.   Don't you think so?"

"I don't know.   I'm losing my hold on things that I used to believe in.   I've come to believe the system of protection is wrong."   He said this in a tone absurdly solemn as if he had somehow questioned the law of gravity.

"Of course it is wrong," she said.   "The moment I got East, I found free-trade in the air, and my uncle, who is a manufacturer, admitted it was all right in theory, but it wouldn't do as a practical measure.   That finished me.   I'm a woman, you know, and when a thing appears right in theory, I believe it'll be right in practice. Expediency don't count with me, you see.   But tell me, do you still live in Rock River?"

" Yes, I'm only studying law down here."

"Oh, I see.   I suppose you know many of the people at Rock River."   She asked about Milton, whom she remembered, and about Mr. Deering. Then she returned again to the subject of the grange.   "Yes, it has been already a great force, but I begin to suspect that the time is coming when it must include more or fail.   I don't know just what — I aint quite clear upon it — but as it stands now, it seems inadequate."

She ended very slowly, her chin in her palm, her eyes on the floor.   She made a grand picture of thought, something more active than meditation.   Her dress trailed in long, sweeping lines, and against its rich dark purple folds her strong, white hands lay in vivid contrast.   The most wonderful charm of her personality was her complete absorption in thought, or the speech of her visitor.   She was interested in this keen-eyed, strong-limbed young fellow as a possible convert and reformer.   She wanted to state herself clearly and fully to him.   He was a fine listener.

"I'm afraid I see a tendency that is directly away from my ideal of a farming community. There is a force operating to destroy the grange and all other such movements."

"You mean politics?"

"No, I mean land monopoly. I believe in thickly settled farming communities, communities where every man has a small, highly cultivated farm. That's what I've been advocating and prophesying, but I now begin to see that our system of ownership in land is directly against this security, and directly against thickly-settled farming communities. The big land owners are swallowing up the small farmers, and turning them into renters or laborers. Don't you think so?"

"I hadn't though of it before, but I guess that's so — up in our county, at least."

"It's so everywhere I've been. I don't understand it yet, but I'm going to. In the meantime I am preaching union and education. I don't see the end of it, but I know" — Here she threw off her doubt — "I know that the human mind cannot be chained. I know the love of truth and justice cannot be destroyed, and marches on from age to age, and that's why I am full of confidence. The farmer is beginning to compare his mortgaged farm with the banker's mansion and his safe, and no one can see the end of his thinking. The great thing is his thinking."

She arose and gave him her hand. "I'm glad you came in. Give my regards to Mr. Deering and other friends, won't you? Tell them not to think I'm not working because I'm no longer their lecturer. You ought to be in the field. Will you read something which I'll send?" she asked, the zeal of the reformer getting the upper hand again.

"Certainly. I should be very glad to."

"I'll send you some pamphlets I've been reading." Her voice seemed to say the interview was ended, but Bradley did not go. He was struggling to speak. After a significant pause, he said in a low voice:

"I'd — I'd like to write to you — if you don't — mind."

Her eyes widened just a line, but they did not waver. "I should like to hear from you," she said cordially. "I'd like to know what you think of those pamphlets, which I'll surely send."

He had the courage to look once more into her brown eyes, with their red-gold deeps, as he shook hands. The clasp of her hand was firm and frank.

"Good-by! I hope I shall see you again. My address is always Des Moines, though I'm on the road a great deal."

Out into the open air again he passed like a man sanctified. It seemed impossible that he had not only seen her, but had retained his self-possession, and had actually dared to ask permission to write to her!

The red-gold sunlight was flaming across the snow, and the shadows stood out upon the shining expanse vivid as stains in ink. The sky, aflame with orange and gold clouds, was thrown into loftier relief by the serrate blue rim of trees that formed the western horizon. As he walked, he had a reckoning with himself. It could not longer be delayed.

He had been a boy to this day, but that hour made him a man, and he knew he was a lover. Not that he used that word, for like the farm-born man that he was, he did not say, "I love her," but he lifted his face to the sky in an unuttered resolution to be worthy her.

He had come under the spell of her womanly presence. He had seen her in her house-dress, and his admiration for her intellect and beauty had added to itself a subtle quality, which rose from the potential husbandship and fatherhood within him.

Now that he was out of her immediate presence, thoughts came thick and fast. Every word she had spoken seemed to have a magical power of arousing long trains of speculation. He walked far out into the quiet evening, walked until he grew calmer, and the emotion of the hour faded to a luminous golden dusk in his mind as the day changed into the beautiful winter night.

As he sat down at his desk, an hour later, he saw a letter lying there. It was one of Nettie's poor little school-girl love letters. A feeling of disgust and shame seized him. He crumpled the letter in his hands, and was on the point of throwihg it away, when his mood changed, and he softened. By the side of Miss Wilbur poor little Nettie was a willful child. He couldn't retain his anger very long.

A few days after there came to him a pamphlet directed in a woman's hand. Its title page struck him as something utterly new, but it was only the first of a flood of similar publications.

"The Coming Conflict. A Series of Lectures prophetic of the Coming Revolution of the Poor, when they will rise against the National Banks and against all Indirect Taxation."

Its dedication was marked with a pencil and he read it over and over: "To the Toiling Millions who produce all the wealth, yet because they have never controlled legislation, have been impoverished by unjust laws made in the interests of the Land-holder and the Money-changer, who seize upon and hold the surplus wealth of the nation by the same right that the slave-master held his slave, *legal* right and that alone, this tract is inscribed by the author."

It was Bradley's first intimation of the mighty forces beginning to stir in the deeps of American society. He found the pamphlet filled with great confusing thoughts. He confessed frankly in his letter to Miss Wilbur that he got nothing satisfactory out of it, though it made him think.

It was astonishing to himself to find his thoughts flowing out to her upon paper with the greatest ease. He was stricken with fear after he had mailed his letter, it was so bulky. He was appalled at the length of time which must pass before he might reasonably expect to hear from her. He counted the days, the hours that intervened. Her note came at last, and it made his blood leap as the clerk flung it out with a grin. "She's blessed yeh this time!" It was a red-headed clerk, and his grin, by reason of a quid of tobacco in his thin cheek, was particularly offensive. Bradley felt an impulse to call him out of his box and whip him.

When he opened the letter in his own room he felt a sort of fear. How would she reply? The letter gave out a faint perfume like that he remembered floated with her dress. It was a

rather brief note, but very kind. She called his
attention to two or three passages in the pamphlet, and especially asked him to read the chap-
ters touching on the land and money questions.
But the part over which he spent the most time
was the paragraph at the close:

"I liked your letter very much. It shows a sincere desire for
the truth. You will never stop short of the truth, I'm sure, but
yon will have sacrifices to make — you must expect that. I shall
take great interest in your work.

"Very sincerely,
"IDA WILBUR."

XIV

BRADLEY CHANGES HIS POLITICAL VIEWS.

THE West had always been Republican. Its States had come into the Union as Republican States. It met the solid South with a solid North-west year after year, and it firmly believed that the salvation of the nation's life depended on its fidelity to the war traditions and on the principle of protection to American industries.

Its orators waved the bloody shirt to keep the party together, though each election placed the war and its issues farther into the background of history, and an increasing number of people deprecated the action of fanning smouldering embers into flame again. Iowa and Kansas and Nebraska were Stalwarts of the Stalwart. Kansas was the battle-ground of the old Abolition and

Free Soil forces, and their traditions kept alive a love and reverence for the Republican party long after its real leaders had passed away, and long after it had ceased to be the party of the people.

Iowa was hopelessly Republican, also. A strong force in the Rebellion, dominated by New England thought, its industries predominantly agricultural, it held rigidly to its Republicanism, and trained its young men to believe that, while "all Democrats were not thieves, all thieves were Democrats," and, when pressed to the wall, admitted, reluctantly, that there were "*some* good men among the Democrats."

In the fall of Bradley's last year at Iowa City, another presidential campaign was coming on, but few men considered that there was any change impending. Local fights really supplied the incitement to action among the Republican leaders. There was no statement of a general principle, no discussion of economic issues by their political leaders. They carefully avoided anything like a discussion of the real condition of the people.

Rock County had been the banner Republican county. For years the Democrats of Rock County had met in annual convention to nominate a ticket which they had not the slightest

expectation of electing.   There was something
pathetic in the habit.   It was not faith — it was a
sort of desperation ; and yet the Republicans as
regularly had their joke about it, regardless of
the pathos presented in the action of a body of
men thus fighting a forlorn and hopeless battle.
Each year some old-fashioned Democrat dropped
away into the grave, and yet the remnant met and
nominated a complete ticket, and voted for it
solemnly, even religiously.

The young Republicans of the county called
this remnant " Free traders " and "Copperheads,"
exactly as if the terms were synonymous.   The
Republican boys of the country felt that there
was something mysteriously uncanny in the term
"Free Trader," and always associated "Copperhead" with the yellowed-backed rattlesnakes that
were abundant in the limestone cliffs, and in
their snowballing took sides with these mysterious
words as shibboleths.

In truth, many of these Democrats were very
thoughtful men — old-line Jeffersonians, who held
to a principle of liberty.   Others had been born
Democrats a half-century ago, and had never been
able to make any change.   They continued the
habit of being Democrats, just as they continued
the habit of wearing fuzzy old plug hats, of old-

fashioned shapes, and long, polished frock coats. Then there were a few of that perpetually cross-grained class who will never agree with anybody else if they can help it. They belonged to the Democracy because the Democrats were in the minority, and considered it wrong to belong to a majority, anyhow. Of this sort were men like Colonel Peavy and old Judd Colwell.

The Colonel had been nominated for treasurer and Colwell for sheriff on the Democratic ticket year after year, and each year the leaders of the party had prophesied decided gains, but they did not come. The State remained apparently hopelessly Republican. The forces which were really preparing for change were too far below the surface for these old-line politicians to understand and measure.

As a matter of fact, the schools and debating clubs and newspapers were preparing the whole country for a political revolution. Radicals were everywhere being educated. Men like Radbourn, who still remained nominally a Republican, and a host of other young men and progressive men were becoming disabused of the protective idea, and were ready for a revolt. There needed but a change of leadership to make a change of the relation of parties and of party names.

The Grange, which was still non-partisan, seemed not destined to play a very strong part in politics, though it was still at work wresting some advanced forms of legislation from one or the other of the old parties.

But the deeper change was one which Judge Brown and a few of the progressive men had only just dimly perceived. The war and the issues of the war were slowly drawing off. The militant was being lost in the problems of the industrial. Each year a larger mass of people practically said, "The issues of to-day are not the issues of twenty-five years ago. The bloody shirt is an anachronism."

Here and there a young man coming to maturity caught the spirit of the new era, and turned away from the talk of the solid South, and addressed himself to a consideration of the questions of taxation and finance. These men formed a growing power in the State, and chafed under the restraint of their leaders.

And above all, death, the great pacificator, unlooser of bonds, and aider of progress, was doing his work. The old men were dying and carrying their prejudices with them, while each year thousands of young voters, to whom the war was an echo of passion, sprang to the polls and faced the future policy of the parties, not their past. Not only all over the State of Iowa, but all over the West, they were silent factors, in many cases kept so by the all-compelling power of party ties; but they represented a growing power, and they were to become leaders in their turn.

This spreading radicalism reached Bradley in the quiet of his life in Iowa City. The young fellows in the school were debating it with fierce enthusiasm, and several of them capitulated. They all recognized that the liquor question once out of the way, the tariff was the next great State issue. At the Judge's suggestion, Bradley did not return to Rock River during vacation, but spent the time reading with a prominent lawyer of the town who had a very fine law library.

He did not care to return particularly, for the quiet studious life he led, almost lonely, had grown to be very pleasant to him. He read a great deal outside his law, and enjoyed his days as he had never done before. Uuconsciously he had fallen into a mode of life and a habit of thought which were unfitting him for a politician's career. He gave very little thought to that, however; his ambition for the time had taken a new form. He wished to be well read; to be a scholar such as he imagined Miss Wilbur to be.

He began reading for that purpose, and kept at it because he really had the literary perception. He wrote to her of his reading; and when in her reply she mentioned some book which he had not read, he searched for it, and read it as soon as possible. In this quiet way he spent his days, the happiest he had ever known.

He had just two disturbing factors: one was Nettie's relation to him, and the other was his desire to see Miss Wilbur. Nettie wrote quite often at first, letters all very much alike, and very short, sending love and kisses. She was not a good letter writer, and even under the inspiration of love could not write above two pages of repetitious matter. "It's dreadfully hard work to write," she kept saying. "I wish you was to home. When are you coming back?"

It was very curious to see the different way in which he came to the writing of letters to these two persons.

"Dear Nettie," he would begin, with a scowling brow, "I *can't* write any oftener, because in the first place I'm too busy, and in the second place nothing happened here that you would care to hear about. I don't know when I'll be home. I ought to finish my course here. No, I don't expect you to mope. I expect you to have a good time, go to parties and dances all you want to."

But when Miss Wilbur's letters arrived, he devoured them with tremulous eagerness, and sat up half the night writing an elaborate answer, while Nettie's letters lay unanswered for days.

"Miss Ida Wilbur, Dear Miss." (That was the way he addressed her. He was afraid to call her Dear Miss Wilbur, it seemed a little too familiar.) In the body of his letters there was no expressed word of his regard for her. It was only put indirectly into the length of his letters, and was shown in the eager promptness of his reply. She wrote kindly, scholarly replies, giving him a great deal to think about. Her letters were very far apart, however, as she was moving about so much. She advised him to read the modern books.

"I'm always on the wrong side of everything," she wrote once, "so I'm on the side of the modern novel. I champion Mr. Howells. Are you reading his story in the *Century?* I like it because it isn't like anybody else; and Mr. Cable, too, you should read, and Henry James and Miss Jewett; they're all of this modern school, that most Western people know nothing about. The West is so afraid of its own judgments. My friends go about praising the classics because they know it's safe to do so, I suppose, while I am an image breaker to them. Mr. Howells says the idea of progress in art does not admit of the conception that any art is finished. Just like the question of social advance, there is always new work to be done and new victories to be won."

But more often she wrote upon economic subjects, as being more impersonal; and then her wish to make Bradley a reformer was greater than her desire to make him a lover of modern art.

"The spirit of reform is beginning to move over the face of the great deep," she wrote at another time. "No one who travels about as I do, can fail to see it. The labor question in the cities, and the farmer question in the country, will soon be the great disturbing factors in politics. The protective theory will go down: it is based on a privilege; and the new war, like the old war, is going to be against all kinds of special privileges."

It was with a peculiar feeling of pain and relief that he read Miss Wilbur's renunciation of her home-market idea. It seemed as if something sweet and fine had gone with it; and yet it strengthened him, for he had come to believe that a home-market built up by legislation was unnatural and a mistake. Judge Brown's constant hammerings had left a mark.

He wrote to her something of his hesitation, and she replied substantially that there was no abandonment of the home-market idea; only the method of bringing it about had changed. She had come to believe in what was free and natural, not what was artificial and forced.

"If you will study the past," she went on, "you will find that advance in legislation has always been in the direction of less law, less granting of special privileges. Take the time of the Stuarts, for example, when the king granted monopolies in the sale of all kinds of goods. It is abhorrent to us, and yet I suppose those protected merchants believed their monopolies to be rights. Slowly these rights have come to be considered wrongs, and the people have abolished them. So all other monopolies will be abolished, when people come to see that it is an infringement of liberty to have a class of men enjoying any special privilege whatever. The way to build up a home-market is to make our own people able to buy what they want.

"There never was a time when our own people were not too poor to buy what they wanted. Goods lie rotting in our Eastern factories, and we export many products which the farmer would be very glad to consume, if he were able. The farmer is poor; but it isn't because he needs protection, it isn't because he doesn't produce enough — it's because what he does produce is taken from him by bankers and corporations."

Bradley read her letters over and over again. Every word which she uttered had more significance than words from any one else. She seemed a marvellous being to him. He looked eagerly in every letter for some personal expression, but she seemed carefully to avoid that; and though his own letters were filled with personalities, she remained studiously impersonal. She replied cordially and kindly, but with a reserve that should have been a warning to him; but he would not accept warnings now — he was too deeply moved. Under the influence of her letters he developed a tremendous capacity for work. The greatest stimulus in the world had come to him, and remained with him. If it should be withdrawn at any time, it would weaken him. He did not speculate on that.

XV.

HOME AGAIN WITH THE JUDGE.

THE day that came to close his work at Iowa City had something of an awakening effect in it. The mere motion of the train brought back again in intensified form the feelings he had experienced on the day he left Rock River. Life was really before him at last. His studies were ended, and he was prepared for his entrance into law. He looked forward to a political career indefinitely. He left that in the hands of the Judge.

It was in June, and the country was very beautiful. Groves heavy with foliage, rivers curving away into the glooms of bending elm and basswood trees, fields of wheat and corn alternating with smooth pastures where the cattle fed — a long panorama of glorified landscape which his escape from manual labor now enabled him to see the beauty of, its associations of toil and dirt no longer acutely painful.

He thought of the June day in which he had first met Miss Wilbur — just such a day! Then he thought of Nettie with a sudden twinge. She had not written for several weeks; he really didn't remember just when she had written last. He wondered what it meant; was she forgetting him? He hardly dared hope for it; it was such an easy way out of his difficulty.

The Judge met him at the depot with a carriage. There were a number of people he knew at the station, but they did not recognize him: his brown beard had changed him so, and his silk hat made him so tall.

"Right this way, colonel," said the Judge, in a calm nasal. He was filled with delight at Bradley's appearance. He shook hands with dignified reserve, all for the benefit of the crowd standing about. "You paralyzed 'em," he chuckled, as they got in and drove off. "That beard and hat will fix 'em sure. I was afraid you wouldn't carry out my orders on the hat."

"The hat was an extravagance for your benefit alone. It goes into a band-box to-morrow," replied Bradley. "How's Mrs. Brown."

"Quite well, thank you; little older, of course. She caught a bad cold somewhere last winter, and she hasn't been quite so well since. We keep a girl now; I forced the issue. Mrs. Brown had done her own work so long she considered it a sort of high treason to let any one else in."

Mrs. Brown met him at the door; and she looked so good and motherly, and there was such a peculiar wistful look in her eyes, that he put his arm around her in a sudden impulse and kissed her. It made her lips tremble, and she was obliged to wipe her glasses before she could see him clearly. Supper was on the table for him, and she made him sit right down.

"How that beard changes you, Bradley! I would hardly have known you. What will Nettie think?"

"How is Nettie?"

"Haven't you heard from her lately?"

"Not for some weeks."

"Then I suppose the neighborhood gossip is true." He looked at her inquiringly, and she went on, studying his face carefully, "They say she's soured on you, and is sweet on her father's new book-keeper."

Bradley took refuge in silence, as usual. His face became thoughtful, and his eyes fell.

"I've hoped it was true, Bradley, because she was no wife for you. You'd outgrown her, and she'd be a drag about your neck. I see her out riding a good deal with this young fellow; he's just her sort, so I guess she isn't heart-broken over your absence."

There was a certain shock in all this. He recurred to his last evening with her, when in her paroxysm of agony she had thrown herself at his feet. Much as he had desired such an outcome, it puzzled him to find her in love with some one else. It was not at all like books.

"Well, Mrs. Brown, what do you think of my junior partner?" said the Judge, coming in and looking down on Bradley with a fatherly pride.

"I suppose, Mr. Brown, you refer to our adopted son."

Bradley dressed for church the next day with a new sort of embarrassment. He felt very conscious of his beard and of his tailor-made clothes, for he knew everybody would observe any change in him. He knew he would be the object of greater attention than the service; but he determined to go, and have the whole matter over at once.

The windows were open, and the sound of the bell came in mingled with the scent of the sunlit flowers, the soft rustle of the maple leaves, and the sound of the insects in the grass. His heart turned toward Miss Wilbur now whenever any keen enjoyment came to him ; instinctively turned to her, with the wish that she might share his pleasure with him. He sat by the open window, dreaming, until the last bell sounded through the heavy leaf-scented air.

"Won't you go to church with me, Judge?" he said, going out.

The Judge turned a slow look upon him. He was seated on the shady porch, his feet on the railing, a Chicago daily paper in his lap. He said very gravely: "Mrs. Brown, our boy is going to church."

"Can't you let him, Mr. Brown? It'll do him good, maybe," said Mrs. Brown, who was at work near the window.

"Goes to see the girls. Know all about it my-self. Go ahead, young man, and remember the text now, or we'll put a stop to this " — Bradley went off down the walk. He passed by a tiny little box of a house where a man in his shirt sleeves was romping with some children.

"Hello, Milton," called Bradley cheerily.

The young man looked up. His face flashed into a broad smile. "Hello! Brad Talcott, by thunder! Well, well. When'd you get back?"

"Last night. Yours?" he inquired, nodding toward the children.

"Yep. Well, how are you, old man? You look well. Couldn't fool me with that beard. Come in and sit down, won't yeh?"

"No, I'm on my way to church. Can't you come?"

"Great Cæsar, no! not with these young hyenas to attend to." He had grown fat, and his chin beard made him look like a Methodist minister; but his sunny blue eyes laughed up into Bradley's face just as in the past. "Say!" he exclaimed, "you struck it with the old Judge, didn't you? He's goin' to run you for governor one of these days. County treasurer ain't good enough for you. But say," he said, as a final word, "I guess you'd better not wear that suit much; it's too soft altogether. Stop in when you come back. Eileen'll be glad to see you," he called after him.

The audience had risen to sing as he entered, and he took his place without attracting much attention. As he stood there listening to the familiar Moody and Sankey hymn, there came again the touch of awe which the church used to put upon him. He was not a "religious" man. He had no more thought of his soul or his future state than a powerful young Greek. His feeling of awe arose from the association of beauty, music, and love with a church. It was feminine, some way, and shared his reverence for a beautiful woman.

The churches of the town were the only things of a public nature which had any touch of beauty or grace. They were poor little wooden boxes at best; and yet they had colored windows, which seemed to hush the dazzling summer sun into a dim glory, transfiguring the shabby interior, and making the bent heads of the girls more beautiful than words can tell. It was the one place which was set apart for purposes not utilitarian, and a large part of what these people called religious reverence was in fact a pathetic homage to beauty and poetry, and *rest*.

When they all took their seats, and while the preacher was praying, Bradley was absorbing the churchy smell of fresh linen, buoyant perfumes, (camphor, cinnamon, violets, rose) and the hot, sweet odor of newly-mown grass lying under the sun just outside of the windows. The wind pulsed in through the half-swung window, a bee came buzzing wildly along, a butterfly rested an instant on the window sill, and the preacher prayed on in an oratorical way for the various departments of government.

Bradley felt a sharp eye fixed upon him, and, turning cautiously, caught Nettie looking at him.

She nodded and smiled in her audacious way. Two or three of the young fellows saw him and nodded at him, but mainly the people sat with bowed heads, feeling some presence that was full of grace and power to banish, for a short time at least the stress of the struggle to live.

The young fellows were mainly in the back seats; and while they were decorously quiet, it was evident that they had very little interest in the prayer. Death and hell and the grave! Why should one trouble himself about such things when the red blood leaped in the heart, and the June wind was flinging a flickering flight of leaf shadows across the window pane? There sat the girls with roguish eyes, the rounded outline of their cheeks (as tempting as peaches), displayed with miraculous skill at just their most taking angle. Their Sunday gowns and gloves and hats transfigured them into something too dainty and fine to be touched, and yet every glance and motion was an invitation and a lure.

Here was the proper function of the church; to enable these young people to see each other at their best, and to bring into their sordid lives some hint, at least, of music and beauty.

Bradley did not hear the sermon. He was wondering just what Nettie's smile meant, and what he was going to say to her. He was not subtle enough to take a half-way or an ambiguous stand. He must either treat her tenderness as a forgotten thing or hold himself to his promise as something which he was under orders from his conscience to fulfill.

When the service was over he went out into the anteroom with the young fellows, who were anxious to meet him. Quite a number of farmers were in from the country, and they all crowded about, shaking his hand with great heartiness. He moved on with them to the sidewalk, where many of the congregation stood talking subduedly in groups. The women came by in their starched neatness, leading rebellious boys in torturing suits of winter thickness topped with collars, stiff as sauce pans; while the little girls walked as upright as dolls, looking disdainfully at their sulking brothers. Some of the merchants passing by discussed the sermon, some talked about crops with the farmers, and those around Bradley dipped into the political situation guardedly.

While he was talking to some of the town people, he saw Nettie come up and join a young man at the door whom he had recognized as the tenor in the choir; and they sauntered off together under the full-leafed maples — she in dainty white and pink, he in a miraculously modish suit of gray, a rose in his lapel. Bradley looked after them without special wonder. It was only as he went back to his room that he began to see how fully Nettie had outgrown her passion for him.

He met her the next day as he was going home from the office.

"Hello, Bradley," she said, without blushing, though her eyes wavered before his.

He held out his hand with a frank smile. "Hello, Nettie, which way are you going?"

"Going home now, been up to the grocery. Want to go 'long?"

"I don't mind. How are you, anyway?"

"Oh, I'm all right. Say! that beard of yours makes you look as funny as old fun."

"Does it?" he said.

"You bet! It makes you look old enough to go to Congress. Say! heard from Radbourn lately?" Bradley shook his head. "Well, I haven't, but Lily has. He's writing — writing for the newspapers, she said."

"Is that so? I haven't heard it."

"E-huh! Say, do you know Lily's all bent on him yet! Funny, ain't it? I ain't that way, am I?" she ended, with her customary audacity.

"No, it's out o' sight, out o' mind with you," he replied, with equal frankness.

"Oh, not quite so bad as that. Ain't yeh comin' in?" They were at the gate.

"Guess not. You remember your father's command; I must never darken his door."

She laughed heartily. "I guess that don't count now."

"Don't it? Well, some other time then."

"All right, but gimme that basket. Goin' to lug that off with you?"

XVI.

NOMINATION.

On the Monday evening following Bradley's return, there was quite a gathering at Robie's along about sundown. Colonel Peavy and Judge Brown came down together, and Ridings and Deering were there also, seated comfortably under the awning, in mild discussion with Robie, who had taken the side of free trade, to be contrary, as Deering said.

"No, sir; I take that side for it's right." There was something sincere in his reply, and Ridings stared.

"How long since ?"

"About a week."

"What's got into yeh, anyhow ?"

"A little horse sense," said Robie. "I've been a readin' the other side ; an' if a few more of yeh'd do the same, you'd lose some of your damn pig-headed nonsense." The Democrats cheered, but the Republicans stared at Robie, as if he had suddenly become insane.

"Well, I'll be damned!" said Smith, his brother-in-law. "I'd like to know what you'd been a readin' to make a blazin' old copperhead of you."

Robie held up two or three tracts. The Judge took them, looked them over, and read the titles out loud to the wondering crowd.

"'The Power of Money to Oppress.' 'Free Trade Philosophy.' 'The Money Question.' 'The Right to the Use of the Earth,' by Herbert Spencer. 'Land and Labor Library.' 'Progress and Poverty,' by Henry George."

"Oh, so you've got hold of Spencer and George, have you?" said the Judge.

"No; they've got hold 'f me."

"*Spencer!*" said Smith, in vast disgust. "What the hell has he to do with it?" The rest sat in silence. The occasion was too momentous for jokes.

"Where'd you get hold o' these?" said the Judge, fingering the leaves.

"Radbourn sent 'em out."

"I'll bet yeh! If there was a rank, rotten book anywhere on God's green footstool, that feller'd have it," said Smith.

The Judge ruminated: "Well, if that's the

effect, guess I'll circulate a few copies 'mong the young Republicans of the county. Gentlemen, this is our year."

"You've been a sayin' that for ten years, Judge," said Ridings.

"And it's been a comin' all the time, gentlemen. I tell you, I've had my ear to the ground, and there's something moving. The river is shifting its bed. Look out for a flood. I'm going to make an entirely new move this fall; I'm going to put up a man for legislature that'll sweep the county; and you'll all vote for 'im, too. He's young, he's got brains, he's an orator, and he can't be bought."

Robie brought his fist down on the counter in an excitement such as he had never before manifested. "Brad Talcott! We'll elect him sure as hell!"

Amos hastened to put in a word. "Brad's a Republican."

"He's a Free Trade Republican," said the Judge, quietly.

"How do yeh know?"

"Oh, I know. Haven't I been a workin' 'im for these last two years? Did you expect a man to live with me and not become inoculated with the Simon-pure Jeffersonian Democracy?"

"I don't believe it," Amos replied; "and I won't till I hear him say so himself. I want to see him go to Des Moines, but I want to see him go as a Republican."

"Well, you attend the Independent convention next week, and you'll hear something that'll set you thinking. Your Grange is losing force. You failed to elect your candidate last year. Now, if we put up a man who is a farmer and a clean man — a man that can sweep the county and carry Rock River — why not join in and elect him?"

The railroad interest was the great opposing factor; and the Judge, who was a great politician, had calculated upon a fusion of the farmer Republicans and the Democrats. He was really the ablest man in that part of the State, and could wield the Democratic party like a pistol. He succeeded in getting Amos, Councill, Jennings, and a few other leading grangers to sign his call for a people's convention to nominate county officers and the member of the legislature. It really amounted to a union of the independent Republicans and the young Democrats.

The old liners, however, were there, and set out from the first to control the convention, as was shown in the opening words of the chairman, old man Colwell, whom the Judge had kindly allowed in the chair, in order that he might have a chance to speak on the floor.

"This is a great day for us," said the chairman. "We've waited a long time for the people to see that Republican rings were sapping the foundations of political honesty, but they see it now. This crowded convention, fellow-citizens, shows that the deathless principles of Jacksonian Democracy still slumber under the ashes of defeat."

He went on in this strain, calmly taking to himself and the other old moss-backs (as young Mason contemptuously called them) all the credit of the meeting, and bespeaking, at the same time, all the offices.

Following this intimation, Colonel Peavy presented a slate, wherein all the leading places on the ticket had been given "to the men who stood so long for the principles of Jackson and Jefferson. It was fitting that these men should be honored for their heroic waiting outside the gates of emolument."

Young Mason was on his feet in an instant. "Mr. Chairman," he said, penetratingly.

"Mr. Mason."

"While I appreciate, sir, the fortitude, the patience, of the men who have been waiting outside the gates of emolument so long, I want to say distinctly, that if that slate is not broken, we'll all wait outside the gates of emolument twenty years longer. But I want to say further, Mr. Chairman, that the strength of this new movement is in its freedom from spoils-seeking; is in its independence from the old party lines. Its strength is in its appeal to the farmer, in its support of his war against unjust tariff and against railway domination. Its strength also is in its appeal to the young men of this county, sir."

Applause showed that the young orator had his audience with him. He was a small man, but his voice was magnificent, and his oratory powerful, self-contained, full of telling points.

"If we win, gentlemen of this convention," he said, turning, "we must put at the head of this movement a man who is absolutely incorruptible — a man who can command the granger vote, the temperance vote, the young man's vote, and the Independent vote. That man"—

"Mr. Chairman," snarled Colonel Peavy, rising with impressive dignity and drawing his coat around him with ominous deliberation.

"Colonel Peavy," acknowledged the chairman.

"Mr. Chairman," shouted young Mason, "I

have the floor. I deny the right of your recognition of another member while I'm speaking."

"Mr. Chairman, I rise to a point of information," said the Colonel.

"State your point, Colonel."

"I would like to ask this young gentleman who holds the floor how many votes he has cast in his whole life."

Young Mason colored with anger, but his voice was cool and decisive. "For the gentleman's information, Mr. Chairman, I will say that I have voted once, but that vote entitles me to stand here as a delegate, and I have the floor."

The delegates were mainly with young Mason, and the Colonel sat down grimly in the midst of the Old Guard. Milton and Bradley, sitting together, rejoiced in the glorious attitude of the young champion, who went on —

"I say, Mr. Chairman and gentlemen, that we cannot win this election on old party lines. I'm a Democrat." (Applause.) "But we are not strong enough as a party in this district to elect, and I'm willing to work with the Independents. There is just one man who can be elected from this convention. He is a young man; he is sound on the tariff; he is an orator; he can sweep the county. I present, as nominee for our next representative, Bradley Talcott, of Rock River."

Bradley sat still, stunned by the applause which burst forth at the mention of his name. Brown had prepared him for the presentation of his name, but he had not dared to hope that any considerable number of delegates would support him.

Judge Brown rose to his feet. "I second the nomination, Mr. Chairman. I am a Democrat — an old Democrat, but I'm damned if I'm a moss-back. I don' allow any young man to get ahead of me on radicalism. I stand for progress; and because I know Bradley Talcott stands for progress, I second his nomination. His canvass will be an honor to himself, and a historical event in this county."

Amos Ridings arose. "Mr. Chairman, I second that nomination as a Granger-Republican. I second it because I know Brad Talcott can't be bought, and because I know he's honest in his convictions. I'll stand by him as long as he stands by principle."

This practically brought to Bradley's support the winning force, for Amos was a power in the county. Somebody called for Milton Jennings, and after some hesitation he got upon his feet.

"Mr. Chairman, I'm not a delegate to this convention, and so it isn't my place to speak here; but I want to say that if I was, I should second this nomination. It's a complete surprise to me to have him nominated. If I had known of it before, I would have been working for him all along. I'm pledged in another direction; but if I could honorably withdraw my support from the regular nominee, I would do everything I could to elect my old classmate and esteemed colleague."

With this boom, the vote was wildly enthusiastic. The chairman pronounced it unanimous.

"Give us a speech!" shouted the crowd.

Young Mason leaped up, a sardonic gleam in his eye. "Mr. Chairman, I move that Colonel Peavy and Amos Ridings escort the nominee to the platform."

The motion was put and carried amid laughter. As they dragged Bradley out of his chair and pushed him up the aisle, everybody laughed and cheered. William Councill kicked the Colonel as he went past and Robie hit him a sounding slap between the shoulders. The Colonel bore it all with astonishing good nature. As they reached the platform, young Mason stepped into the aisle and shouted:

"Three cheers for the Honorable Bradley Talcott!"

With the roar of these cheers in his ears, Bradley turned and faced his fellow-citizens. His knees shook, and his voice was so weak he could hardly be heard.

"Fellow-citizens, do you know what you're doing?" he said, in a curiously colloquial tone.

"You bet we do!" roared the crowd. "What d'ye think we've done?"

"You've nominated a man for your legislature who hasn't got a dollar in the world."

"So much the better! The campaign 'll be honest!" shouted young Mason.

Bradley's throat was too full to speak, and his head whirled. "I can't make a speech now, gentlemen; I aint got any breath. All I can say is, I'm very thankful to have such friends, and I'll try to do my duty in the campaign, and in the legislature, if I'm elected."

The delegates swarmed about him to shake his hand and promise him their support. Bradley, dazed by the suddenness of it, could only smile and grip each man's hand. The Judge was jubilant. Had Bradley been his son, he couldn't have felt more sincerely pleased.

"We'll see such a campaign this fall as this

county never had," he said to everybody; "a campaign with a principle; a campaign that will be educational."

Bradley had now a greater work before him than he had ever undertaken before. He had now to go to his old friends and neighbors in a new light, practically as a Democrat. He had to face audiences mainly hostile to his ideas, and defend opinions which he knew not only cut athwart the judgment of the farmers of the county, but squarely across their prejudices.

But he had something irresistible on his side; he was debating a principle. He was widening the discussion, and he made men feel that. He rose above local factions and local questions to the discussion of the principles of justice and freedom. He voiced this in his speech of acceptance in the Opera House the next day. The house was packed to its anteroom with people from every part of the county. A curious feeling of expectancy was abroad. Men seemed to feel instinctively that this was the beginning of a change in the thought of Rock River. Everybody remarked on the change in Bradley, and his beard made him look so much older.

Judge Brown and Dr. Carver sat on the stage with the speakers, young Mason and Bradley.

The Judge was very dignified, but there was an exultant strut in his walk and a special deliberation in his voice which proclaimed his pride in his junior partner. He alluded, in his dry, nasal way, to the pleasure it gave him to inaugurate the new era in politics in Rock River. "The liquor question I regard as settled in this State," he said. "And now the discussion of the tariff has free sailing. But you don't want to hear us old fellows, with our prejudices; you want to hear our young leaders, with their principles."

He introduced young Mason, who made one of his audacious speeches. "Death is a great friend of youth and progress," he said. "The old men die, off, thank God! and give young men and new principles a chance. I tell you, friends and neighbors, the Democratic party is being born again — it must be born again, in order to be worth saving."

When Bradley stepped forward, he was very pale.

"Friends and fellow-citizens," he began, after the applause had ended, "I can't find words to express my feeling for the great honor you have done me. I thank the citizens of Rock River for their aid, but I want to say — I'm going to run this campaign in the farmers' interest, because the interests of this county and of this State are agricultural, and whatever hurts the farmer hurts every other man in the State. There is no war between the town and the country. The war is between the people and the monopolist wherever he is, whether he is in the country or in the town. It is not true that the interests of the town dweller and of the farmer are necessarily antagonistic; the cause of the people is the same everywhere. It's like the condition of affairs between England and Ireland. People say that Ireland is fighting England — fighting the English people, but that is not the fact. The antagonism is between the Irish people and the English landlord. So the fight in America is the people against the special privileges enjoyed by a few. It's because these few generally live in towns that we *seem* to be fighting the towns.

"As the Judge said, we've settled the liquor question in this State; it won't come up again unless office seekers drag it up. It has been our State issue — that and the railroads; and now that is settled, we can turn our attention to the finishing up of the railway problem and to the discussion of the tariff."

"And the money!" shouted some one; "abolish the national banks!"

Bradley hesitated a little. " No, we can't do that, but we can destroy any special privilege they hold. But the first thing that stares us in the face is the war tariff that is eating us up. I'm going to state just what I think in this campaign, and you can vote for me or not. It is sheer robbery to continue a tariff that was laid at a time when we needed enormous revenue. See the surplus piling up in the public vault. You say it's better to have a surplus than a deficit. Yes, but I'd rather have the surplus in the pockets of the people. This taxing the people to death, in order to have a surplus to expend in senseless appropriations, is poor policy."

In this strain his whole speech ran, and it had an electrical effect. They cheered him tremen-dously, and the meeting broke up, and discussion burst out all over the hall with appalling fury, and continued each day thereafter. The railroad question and the tariff question began right there to divide the county into two camps. The young leader carried the same disturbing influence into every township in which he spoke, and the whole county became a debating school. It took a position far ahead of the other counties of the State in the questions.

Men stopped each other, and talked from plow

to plow across the line fence.   They met in the
road upon dusty loads of wheat, and sat hours at
a time under the burning August sun to discuss
the matter of railroad commissions, and the fixing
of rates, and the question or reducing the surplus
in the treasury.

The old greenbackers came out of their tempo-
rary retirement, and helped Bradley's cause simply
because he was young and a dissenter.   They
were a power, for most of them were deeply read
on the tariff and on the railroad problem ; in fact,
were all round radicals and fluent speakers.

Judge Brown kept out of it.   "I don't want to
seem too prominent in this campaign," he said to
Colonel Peavey.   "We old Mohawks are a dam-
age to any man's campaign just now.   The time
is coming, Colonel, when we'll help, but not now.
We've set the mischief afoot; now let the young
fellows and the farmers do the rest of it.   Besides, my young man here is quite able to look
out for himself.   All that scares me is he'll get
too radical, even for the Democracy, one of these
days.   If he does, all is we ll have to build a
party up to his principle, for he'll be right, Colonel; there's no two ways about that."

XVII.

ELECTION.

THE interest of the election was very great; and as the vote of Rock River practically settled the contest, the centre of interest was the Court House, which was crowded to suffocation on election night. There was a continual jam and a continual change. Crowds stood around the doorway, or moved up and down the sidewalk. Crowds were constantly running up and down the stairway, and crowding in and out the dingy, dimly lighted court-room, which was roaring with voices, blue with smoke, and foul as a dungeon — with tobacco and vitiated breaths.

All the men of the town seemed to be present, from old man Dickey, the chicken thief and fisherman, to cold, aristocratic R. F. Russell, the banker. Rowdyish boys pushed and banged and howled, playing at hide-and-seek among the legs of the men, who filled every foot of standing space, or were perched on the railings or tables near the Judge's bench, from which the returns were being called. The kerosene lamp shed a dim light, through the smoke. There was no fire, and the excited partisans kept their hats and coats on, and warmed themselves by wild gestures and stamping.

Occasionally a boy's shrill yell or whistle, or some excited Democrat's calling, "It's a whack! I'll take yeh!" rose above the clamor. Upon the benches piled up along the wall, to leave the middle space free, groups of the less demonstrative citizens of both parties sat discussing the chances of the different candidates. Bradley was not there, but young Mason and Milton were considered his representatives, and were surrounded by a constant crowd of sympathizers. It was about nine o'clock at night before the decisive returns began to come in.

Occasionally the sound of furious pounding was heard, and a momentary lull was enforced while the clerk read some telegraphic message or report of a neighboring town. While he stood upon the Judge's bench, at about nine o'clock, the crowd, aware in some mysterious way of the arrival of decisive news, made a wild surge toward the clerk, and shouted for silence, while he announced in a high nasal key: "Rock River gives a hundred and ninety-one for Kimball, two hundred and twenty-five for Talcott." At this a wild cheer broke forth, led by Milton and young Mason.

"That means victory!" said Milton.

"Don't be too sure of it! Wait for Cedarville."

The reading went on, with occasional yells from either the Democrats or Republicans, according to the special quality of the report, but it was plain that the most interest was centered in the contest for representative.

As the evening wore on, messengers clattered up on horseback from other towns of the county, and amid yells and cheers were hustled up the stairway, through the crowd to the clerk, carrying in their hands envelopes filled with election returns. These returns from the townships were almost entirely in Bradley's favor, but Cedarville was the decisive vote. Messengers from the little telegraph station dashed to and fro, and the excitement was fanned into greater fury by the accounts of Democratic gains from other counties and other States. "It is a political landslide," exclaimed Mason. "The Democrats are in it this time."

At length there rose the cry of "Cedarville! Cedarville!" and a messenger bearing a telegraph blank was rushed through to the reading-desk, where his message was snatched by the clerk. Again there was a wild surge toward the desk, and a silence, broken only by derisive cheers from the boys, while the clerk glanced over it.

"Cedarville gives seventy votes for Kimball, and a hundred and ten for Talcott."

The Independents shouted themselves hoarse, and flung their caps in the air. Talcott had carried both of the towns of the county; he was sure of the farmers. The boys howled like savages, and tripped each other over the railings and seats, boxed hats, punched the men in the back, and hid around their legs; while the clerk went on with his reading, at more and more frequent intervals, of reports from other States and districts of the congressional field. The old-line Democrats were delirious with joy. The promised land was in sight.

It was about half past twelve o'clock when Colonel Russell conceded Bradley's election, and two stout men toiled up the stairs, bringing his forfeit of two barrels of apples. Amid wilds yells from the crowd, they threw the barrels to the floor, where they burst, and sent Northern Spys rolling in every direction.

Then came a wilder roar and scramble, that

outdid everything that had gone before, and a surging mass of struggling men and boys covered the apples. They threw themselves upon each other's backs. They clawed like wild-cats, barked like wolves. They kicked each other out of the way, and scratched and mauled each other, crushing hats, tearing coats, bruising shins. As fast as one man filled his hands or arms or pockets, the others set upon him, struck them from his arm, snatched them from his hands, tore them from his pockets, or tripped him headlong to the floor, where he rolled in the filthy sawdust, under the feet of the crazy mob.

The wrestle of starving wild hogs for corn or potatoes could not have been more tumultuous or ear-splitting than this ferocious, jovial scramble. It ceased only when the last apple was secured, so that none could snatch it away. Then began the fusilade of cores and parings. Shining stove-pipe hats were choice game, and to throw a core clean through a silk hat was a distinction which everybody seemed to covet. In five minutes not a tall hat was to be seen. Colonel Peavy wrapped his handkerchief around his, thus drawing upon himself the attack of the entire crowd, and he was forced to retreat.

Then they threw at faces and bald heads. The

uproar redoubled. No one was drunk, no one was mad; but the scene was furious with mirth. It was contagious. Word spread outside, and the whole male population of the town jammed into the stairway, and struggled furiously to reach the court-room, where the fun was going on. A stranger would have imagined it the loosing of the hordes of hell.

In the streets of the town, the boys, without the slightest care about who was elected, were stealing kerosene barrels and dry-goods boxes, in order to keep the bonfire going. When they heard of the free apples which they had missed by their zeal in bonfiring, a bitterness came upon them, and they came together and tried to organize a committee to go down and see Judge Brown and state their grievance.

At last one desperate young fellow took the lead, and the rest marched after. He moved off down the street, shouting through his closed lips *"Bum, bum, bum, bum, bum!"* The rest took up the drum-like cry, and marched after him two and two. They made straight toward Judge Brown's office, where they knew Bradley was. They halted and raised a great shout.

"Three cheers for the Honorable Brad," and gave them wildly.

This brought the Judge out; and when they saw him, they yelled in lugubrious tones, as if they were starving, "Apples! apples!"

The Judge shouted down, "All right, boys, I'll send Robie up. He'll roll out all the apples you want." The boys gave another cheer, and left.

Bradley sat there in the Judge's office in a sort of daze. He could not say a word. His thought was not clear. He was not at all anxious. Somehow he could not feel that it was his fate that was being decided. On the contrary, it seemed to be some other person. He was not excited; he was only puzzled and wondering.

At last the crowd was heard coming from the Court House. Wild cheers sounded faintly far up the street. The sound of a band was heard, and the marching of feet, rhythmic on the sidewalks. There came the sound of rapid footsteps, and so familiar was Bradley with the sidewalk that he knew exactly where the runners were by the different note given out by each section of planking. They were crossing the street. Now they came across the warped and clattering length before the butcher shop. Then over the crisp, solid planking before Robie's. Then came a rush up the stairway, and Milton and young Mason burst into the room.

"Hurrah, we've carried you through! You're elected, sure as guns!"

"Three cheers for Democracy and progress," shouted the Judge, in high excitement, from the open windows. They were given with tremendous vigor by the crowd from below and the band struck up "Hail Columbia."

*   *   *   *   *   *

It was two o'clock when Bradley and the Judge got away from the crowd and went home to bed. They found Mrs. Brown sitting up. With the customary thoughtlessness of men, neither of them had taken her anxiety into account.

"Well, Mrs. Brown, are you up?"

"Yes, Mr. Brown; I wanted to hear the news. You didn't suppose I could go to bed without it," she replied calmly, though she was trembling with eagerness.

"Well, we're elected, Mrs. Brown," said the Judge proudly.

She came up to Bradley timidly, a longing mixed with pride expressed in her face. Bradley took her in his arms, and laid her cheek on his shoulder. She stood before him like a mother now. He felt her pride in him, and she had grown very dear to him.

XVIII.

"DON'T BLOW OUT THE GAS."

DES MOINES appeared to Bradley to be **very** great and very noisy. It was the largest city he had ever seen. He was born in Eastern Wisconsin on a farm, and his early life had been spent far from any populous centre; very largely, indeed, in the timber-lands. He had been in Lacrosse, that is to say, he changed cars there, and Rock River and Iowa City were the only towns he had ever lived in.

He had the preconception that Des Moines was a fine city, but its streets seemed endless to him that cold, clear night that he got off the train and walked up the sidewalk. He had been told to go right to the Windom House, because there was the legislative headquarters. He walked, carrying his valise in his hand, and looking furtively about him. He knew he ought not to do so, but the life about him and the endless rows of vast buildings fascinated him — drew his attention constantly.

The portico of the hotel awed him with its red sandstone magnificence, and he moved timidly on toward the centre of the rotunda with hesitating and uncertain steps. It seemed to be the realization of his imaginings of Chicago. It subdued him into absolute clownishness; and the porter who rushed toward him and took his valise from his hands, classified him off-hand as another one of those country fellows who must be watched and prevented from blowing out the gas. Bradley signed his name on the book without any flourishes, and without writing the "Honorable" before his name, as most of the other members had done.

"Front!" yelled the clerk, in an imperative voice. Bradley started, and then grew hot over his foolishness. "Show this gentleman to No. 30. Like dinner?" the clerk asked, in a kindly interest. Bradley nodded, suddenly remembering that in fashionable life dinner came at six o'clock. "All ready in about ten minutes," the clerk said, looking at the clock.

Bradley followed the boy to the elevator. He noticed that the darkey did not enter with him, but ran up the stairs. He could see him rushing around the curves, his hands sliding on the railings. He met him at the door of the elevator and motioned to him — "This way, suh." There was something in his tone that puzzled Bradley; and as he walked along the hall, he thought of the soft carpet under his feet (it must have been two inches thick) and of that tone in the boy's voice.

A dull fire of soft coal was burning on the grate, and the boy punched it up, and said, "'Nother gent jes' left. I git some mo' coal."

The room, like all hotel rooms, was a desolate place, notwithstanding its one or two elaborate pieces of furniture, its fine carpet, and its easy chair. It had a distinctly homeless quality. Bradley sat down in the big chair before the fire, and took time to think it all over. He was really here as a legislator for a great State. The responsibility and honor of the position came upon him strongly as he sat there alone in this great hotel looking at the fire. That he, of all the men in his county, should have been selected for this office, was magnificent. He drew a long sigh, and said inwardly:

"I'll be true to my trust." And he meant, in addition, to be so dignified and serious that he would not seem young to the other legislators.

He was reading, from a little frame on the wall, the rules of the house when the boy knocked on the door, and started away toward the fire so that the boy should not suspect what he had been doing. He returned to the reading, however, after the boy had gone out. He read "Don't Blow out the Gas," without feeling it an impertinence, and went over to read the code of signals posted above the bell punch.

RING ONCE FOR BELL BOY.
RING TWICE FOR ICE WATER.
RING THREE FOR FIRE.
RING FOUR FOR CHAMBERMAID.

His mind went off in a pursuit of trivial matters concerning this code. What would happen if he rang three times — which he thought stood for alarm of fire. In imagination he heard the outcries throughout the various floors and rooms of the house. Then his mind went back to the fact that the boy was not allowed to ride in the elevator. He wondered if this touch of southern feeling would ever get any farther north. For the first time in his life he had met the question of caste.

He went down to supper, as he called it himself, in the dining-room, which he found to be a very large and splendid apartment. A waiter in a dress coat (he had never seen a live figure in a dress coat before) met him at the door, and with elaborate authority called another darkey, in a similar dress coat, to show him to a chair.

The second darkey led his way down the polished floor (which Bradley walked with difficulty), his coat tails wagging in a curious fashion, by reason of the action of his bow legs. He was obliged to take the uncomprehending Bradley by the arm, while he shoved the chair under him; but he did it so courteously that no one noticed it. He was accustomed to give this silent instruction in ceremonials. Bradley noticed that, notwithstanding the splendor of his shirt-front, collar and dress-coat, his shoes were badly broken, though highly polished.

A man sat at the opposite side of the table reading a paper over his coffee. He attracted Bradley's attention because he had a scowl on his face, and his hair was tumbled picturesquely about his forehead. Even his brown moustache contrived to have an oddly dishevelled look.

They ate in silence for some time, or rather Bradley did; the other man read and sipped his coffee, and continued to frown and swear under his breath. At length he burst forth in a suppressed exclamation: "Well, I'll be damned." When he looked at Bradley, his eyes were friendly, and he seemed to require some one to talk to.

"These devilish railroads will own the country, body and breeches yet."

"What are they up to now?" said Bradley.

"They've secured Joe Manley as their attorney, one of the best lawyers in the State. It's too cussed bad." He looked sad. "I can't account for it. I suppose he got hard up, and couldn't stand the pressure. I wonder if you know how these infernal corporations capture a State!"

"No, but I'd like to know. I'm down here to fight 'em."

"That so? From where?"

"From Rock County. I'm the representative; Talcott is my name," Bradley said, seizing an excuse to announce himself.

"*Is* that so! Well, now, I'm an old cock in the pit, and I want to warn you. I've known many a fine, honest fellow to get involved. Now I'll tell you how it's done. Before you have been here a week, some of these railroads will send for you, and tell you they've heard of you as a prominent young lawyer of the State. Oh, they've heard of you, we've all heard of your canvass; and as they are in need of an attorney in your county, they'd like very much to have you take charge, etc., of any legislation that may arise there, and so on. There may not be a week's work during the year, and there may be a great deal, etc., but they will be glad to pay you six hundred dollars or eight hundred dollars, if you will take the position.

"Well, we'll suppose you take it. You go back to Rock, there is very little business for the railroad, but your salary comes in regularly. You say to yourself that, in case any work comes in which is dishonorable, you'll refuse to take hold of it. But that money comes in nicely. You marry on the expectations of its continuance. You get to depending upon it. You live up to it. You don't find anything which they demand of you really dishonest, and you keep on; but really cases of the railroad against the people do come up, and your sense of justice isn't so acute as it used to be. You manage to argue yourself into doing it. If you don't do it, somebody else will, etc., and so you keep on."

After an impressive pause, during which the speaker gazed in his face, he finished: "Suddenly the war of the corporation against the people is on us, and you find you are the paid tool of the corporation, and that the people are distrustful of you, and that you are practically helpless."

The man spoke in a low voice, but somehow his words had the quality of exciting the imagination. Bradley thrilled at the picture of moral disintegration hinted at. The imaginative tragedy was brought very close to him.

"Do they really do that?" he asked.

"That's a part of their plan. The proof of it will be in the offer which they'll make to you in less than ten days. They're always on the lookout for such men, especially men who have the confidence of the farmers. The next war in this State and in the nation is to be a railway war."

"You think so. I think the tariff"—

"What is the tariff, compared to the robbery that makes Gould and Sage and Vanderbilt? I tell you, young man, the corporations in this country are eating the life out of it. This power of three men to get together, steal the privilege from the people, and by their joint action to produce a fourth body (*corpus*), behind which they hide and push their schemes — an intangible something which outlives them all — that is the power that is undermining this government. It's against the Constitution. Old Chief Justice Marshall in

his verdict (which ushered in the reign of corporations, in this country) distinctly said that it
was based on usurpation, dating back to the
Stuarts or the Georges; and the hint in that was,
that it was un-American and un-Constitutional."

Bradley perceived that he was in the presence
of another reformer like himself. He wondered
if he seemed so cranky to other men. He was
interested by the man's evident thought and honesty of purpose and by the sympathy of a city
man with a farmer's fight.

"You're with us in our fight against the
railroads?"

The man threw one arm back over the top of
his chair and looked at Bradley out of his half-
closed eyes. "Of course. Only you're so damned
narrow. Excuse me. You don't see that you've
got to kill *every* corporation. *Every* corporation
is an infringement of individual rights. When
three men go into business as a firm, they should
every one be liable for every contract which they
make. The creation of an intangible corporate
personality is a trick to evade liability. Make
war against the whole system," he said, rising.
"Don't go fooling about with regulating fares and
forming commissions. Declare corporations ille-
gal, and let the people know their practices."

They went down to the rotunda floor together. The electric lights flooded the brilliant marbles with a dazzling light.   Groups of men were gathered around spittoons, talking earnestly, gesticulating with fists and elaborate broad-hand, free-arm movements — political gestures, as Bradley recognized.

"These are your colleagues and their parasites," said Bradley's companion, whose name was Cargill.   "Know any of 'em?"

"No; I don't know any of the legislators."

Cargill led Bradley up to a group which surrounded a gigantic old man who leaned on a cane and gesticulated with his powerful left hand.

"Senator Wood, let me introduce Hon. Bradley Talcott, of Rock."

"Ah, glad to see you, sir.   Glad to see you. Gentlemen, this is the young man who made that gallant fight up in Rock.   This is the Hon. Jones of Boone, Mr. Talcott, and this is Sam Wells of Cerro Gordo, one of the most remorseless jokers in the House.   Look out for him!"

After shaking hands all about, Bradley hastened to say, "Don't let me interrupt.   Go on, senator. I want to listen."   This made a fine impression on the senator, who loved dearly to hear the sound of his own voice.   He proceeded to enlarge upon his plan for gerrymandering the state — to the advantage of the Democratic party, of course.

In the talk which followed, Bradley was brought face to face with the fact that these men were more earnest in maintaining the hold of their parties upon the offices than principles of legislation. They were not legislators in any instances; they were gamesters.

"Now, let me tell you something more," said Cargill, as he led his way back to a settee near the wall. He drew up a chair for his feet, lighted his cigar, pulled his little soft hat down to the bridge of his nose, put one thumb behind his vest, and began in a peculiarly sardonic tone: "Now, here is where the legislation really takes place — here and at the Iowa House. See those fellows?" He waved his hand in a circle around the rotunda, now filled with stalwart men laughing loudly or talking in confidential, deeply interested groups, with their heads close together. "There are the supposed law-makers of the State. What do you think of them, anyway?"

Bradley was silent. He was so filled with new sensations and ideas that he could not talk.

Cargill mused a little. "I suppose it all appears to you as something very fine and very important. Now, don't make a mistake. The most of these fellows are not even average men. I have a theory that, take it one ten years with another, the legislatures of our country must be necessarily beneath the average, because the man who is a thinker or a moralist necessarily represents a minority. Anyhow, these men support my theory, don't they?"

There was a distinct bitterness in his tone that made his words sink deep. There was a touch of literary grace also in his phrases, quite unlike anything Bradley had ever heard. "You imagine these men honest. You say 'they differ from me' honestly. But I know there is no question of principle in their action. They simply say No. 1 first, party next, and principle last of all. I remember how awe-struck I was during my first term. Now, don't waste any nervous energy on admiring these men or standing in awe of them. Jump right in and take care of yourself. Vote for party, but make arrangements before you vote —no; I forgot. You stand for a real principle, and success may lie for you in standing by it. Yes, on the whole, I believe I would stand by principle; it will bring you out in greater relief from the rest of them, and then the people may begin to think. I doubt it, however."

"You are a pessimist, then," said Bradley, feeling that there was an undercurrent of dark philosophy in Cargill's voice.

"I am. The whole damned thing is a botch, in my opinion. You may find it different," he said, with a mocking gleam in his eyes as he rose and walked away. Bradley did not believe the man meant half he said, and yet his bitterness had thrown a sombre shadow over his heart. The vista ahead was not quite so bright as it had been except where Miss Wilbur seemed to walk. He longed to go out and find her, and tried to content himself with walking up and down the street, which seemed incredibly brilliant with its lighted windows and streams of gay young people coming and going.

At last he came to a corner where he saw the name of her street upon the lamp post, and the hunger to see her was irresistible. He rushed up the street with desperate haste. He wished he had started sooner. It was eight o'clock and there was danger that she might be gone out. The electric cars hardly diverted him as they came floating weirdly down the line — the trolley invisible, the wheels emitting green sheets of light at the crossings.

The street grew more quiet as it climbed the hill, and at last became quite like Rock River, with its rows of small wooden houses on each side of the maple-lined streets, through which the keen wind went hissing. The stars glittered through the clear cold air like crystals of green and gold and white fire. As he walked along, his newly acquired honors fell away from him, together with his war for the grange, and his ambitious plans displayed their warmer side. He began to feel that all he was and was to do must be shared with a woman in order that he could enjoy it himself, and he had known for a long time that Ida was that woman.

His face lifted to the stars as he implored their aid in a vast and dangerous enterprise. It meant all or nothing to him. He was in the mood to risk all his life and plans that night if she had been with him. The strangeness of the city had exalted him to the mood where his timidity was gone.

When he came to the house, he found it all dark save a dim light in the rear, and it made him shiver with a premonition of failure. A servant girl answered his ring. He had the hope that this was the wrong house after all.

"Can you tell me if Miss Wilbur lives here?"

"Yassir, but she nat haar," answered the girl, with the Norwegian accent.

"Where is she?"

"Ay nat know. Ay tank she ees good ways off; her moder she ees gawn to churtz."

Bradley no longer looked at the stars as he walked along the street. All his doubts and fears and his timidity and his reticence came back upon him, and something warm and sweet seemed to go out of the far vista of his life. He felt that he had lost her.

XIX.

CARGILL TAKES BRADLEY IN HAND.

CARGILL was not at the table the next morning, but he came in later, and greeted Bradley brusquely, as he flung his rag of a hat on the floor.

"Well, legislator, what is on the tapis this morning? Anything I can do for you?"

"No, I guess not. I am going to look up a new boarding-house."

"What's the matter with this?"

"Too rich for my blood."

"Just repeat that, please."

"Can't stand the expense."

Cargill poured the cream on his oatmeal before he replied: "But, dear sir, nothing is too good for a representative. Young man, you don't seem to know how to farm yourself out."

All day Saturday the Richwood rotunda was

crowded with men. The speakerships, the house offices, were being contested for here; the real battle was being fought here, and under Cargill's cynical comment the scene assumed great significance to Bradley's uninitiated eyes. They took seats on the balcony which ran around the "bear pit," as he called it. Around them, flitting to and fro, were dozens of bright, rather self-sufficient young women.

"This is one of the most dangerous and demoralizing features of each legislature," he said to Bradley. "These girls come down here from every part of the State to cajole and flatter their way into a State House office. You see them down there buttonholing every man they can get an introduction to, and some of them don't even wait for an introduction. They'd be after you if you were a Republican."

Bradley looked out upon it all with a growing shadow in his eyes. He suddenly saw terrible results of this unwomanly struggle for office. He saw back of it also the need for employment which really forced these girls into such a contest.

"They soon learn," Cargill was saying, "where their strength lies. The pretty ones and the bold ones succeed where the plain and timid ones fail. It has its abuses. Good God, how could it be otherwise! It's a part of our legislative rottenness. Legal labor pays so little, and vice and corruption pay so well. Now see those two girls button-holing that leprous old goat Bergheim! If it don't mean ruin to them both, it will be because they're as knowing as he is. Every year this thing goes on. What the friends and parents of these girls are thinking of, I'll be damned if I know."

Bradley was dumb with the horror of it all. He had such an instinctive reverence for women that this scene produced in him a profound, almost despairing sorrow. He sat there after Cargill left him, and gazed upon it all with stern eyes. There was no more tragical thing to him than the woman who could willingly allure men for pay. It made him shudder to see those bright, pretty girls go down among those men, whose hard, peculiar, savage stare he knew almost as well as a woman.

They did not know that he was a legislator, and he escaped their importunities; but he overheard several of them, as they came up with some member — sometimes a married man — and took seats on the balcony near him.

"But you had no business to promise Miss Jones! How could you when I was living?"

"But I didn't know you then!"

"Well, then, now you've seen me, you can tell Miss Jones your contract don't go," laughed the girl.

"Oh, that wouldn't do, she'd kick."

"Let'er kick. She aint got any people who are constituents. My people are your constituents."

Bradley walked away sick at heart. As he passed a settee near the stairway, he saw another girl with a childish face looking up at a hard-featured young man, and saying with eager, wistful voice, her hands clasped, "Oh, I *hope* you can help me. I need it so much."

Her sweet face haunted him because of its suggested helplessness and its danger. His heart swelled with an indefinable and bitter rebellion. Everywhere was a scramble for office — everywhere a pouring into the city from the farms and villages. Why was it? Was he not a part of the movement as well as these girls? Did it not all spring from the barrenness and vacuity of rural life?

Bradley went to church, for the reason that he had nothing better to do, and, in order to get as much out of it as possible, went to the largest sanctuary in the city. The hotels were thronged by men who took little thought of the day. The rotunda echoed with roaring laughter and the tramp of feet. Every new member was being introduced and manipulated, but Bradley shrank from declaring himself. His name, B. Talcott, conveyed no information to those who saw it on the register, and so he sat aside from the crowd all day, untouched by the male lobbyist or the girl office seekers.

He went next day, according to promise, to call at Cargill's office, which was on the fifth floor of a large six-story building on the main street. There were two ornamental ground-glass doors opening from the end of a narrow hall. One was marked, " Bergen & Cargill, Commission Merchants, Private," and Bradley entered. A man seated at a low table was operating a telegraphic machine. He was in his shirt sleeves, and wore blue checked over-sleeves, and carried a handkerchief under his chin to keep his collar from getting soiled. He sat near two desks which separated the private room from the larger room, in which were seated several men looking at one side of the wall, which was a blackboard checked off in small squares by red lines. Columns of figures in chalk were there displayed.

Cargill did not seem to be about, and the busy operator did not see the visitor. A brisk young man of Scandinavian type was walking about in the larger office with a piece of chalk in his hand. He came to the desk and looked inquiringly at Bradley, who started to speak, but the sonorous voice of the operator interrupted him.

"Three eighths bid on wheat," he called, and handed a little slip of paper to the brisk young man with the flaxen mustache.

"Wheat, three eighths," he repeated in a resonant tone, and proceeded to put the figures in a small square under the section marked "Wheat" on the blackboard. When he came back, Bradley asked for Cargill.

"He'll be in soon; take a seat."

"Three eighths bid. They still hammer the market, as they sold short," shouted the operator.

Bergen repeated the telegram to the crowd. "Of course they'll do that," said one of the smokers, a young man with an assumption of great wisdom on all matters relating to wheat. He looked prematurely knowing, and spit with a manly air.

As Bradley took a seat at the desk, Bergen was calling into the telephone in a high, sonorous, monotonous voice, "Wheat opened at ninety-three, three quarters; sold as high as ninety-four; is now ninety-three and three eighths. Corn opened at forty-two; is now forty-one and seven eighths. Bradstreet's decrease on both coasts the past week, two and a quarter millions. Cables very strong."

Cargill came in a little later, and greeted Bradley with a nod while crossing the room to look at the blackboard.

"Draw up a chair," he said, and they took a seat at the table, while the business of the office went on. "You'll be interested in knowing something about this business," he said to Bradley. "It's as legitimate as buying or selling real estate on a commission; but so far as the popular impression goes, there is no difference between this and a bucket-shop."

"It's all very new to me," said Bradley. "I don't know the difference between this and the bucket-shop."

"Ninety-three and seven eighths bid on wheat," called Bergen from a slip, as he walked back and chalked the latest intelligence upon the board.

"Well, there is a difference. In this case, we simply buy and sell on commission. These are real purchases and sales. The order for wheat is transmitted to Chicago and registered, and has its effect upon the market; whereas in a bucket-shop the sale does not go out of the office, and, if there

is a loss to the customer, the proprietor gains it.
In other words, we buy and sell for others, with
no personal interest in the sale ; the bucket-shop
is a pure gambling establishment, where men bet
on what other men are going to do. But that
ain't what I had you call to talk over. I want
you to meet Bergen. Chris, come over here,"
he called. "I want to introduce the Honorable
Talcott of Rock River. He's started in, like
yourself, to reform politics.

"The reason why I wanted you to meet Bergen," Cargill went on, "is because he is a sincerer
lover of literature than myself, and like yourself, I
imagine, believes thoroughly in the classics. He's
translating Ibsen for the Square Table Club.
His idea of amusement ain't mine, I needn't say."

" New York still hammers away on the market.
Partridge quietly buying to cover on the decline."

"Excuse me a moment," said Bergen, returning
to business.

Cargill took an easy position. "I don't know
why I have sized you up as literary in general
effect, but I have. That's one reason why I took
to you. It's so damned unusual to find a politician that has a single idea above votes. And
then I'm literary myself," he said, his face a mask
of impenetrable gravity. " I wrote up the sheep

industry of Iowa for the Agricultural Encyclopæ dia. That puts me in the front rank of Des Moines literary aspirants.

"Towns like this," he said, going off on a speculative side track, "have a two-per-cent. population who are inordinately literary. They recognize my genius. The other ninety-eight per cent. don't care a continental damn for Shakespeare or anybody else, barring Mary Jane Holmes, of course, and the five-cent story papers. But literary Des Moines *is* literary. They stand by Shakespeare and Homer, I can tell you, and they recognize genius when they see it. By the way, Bergen," he said, calling his brother-in-law to him again, "we must make this young man acquainted with our one literary girl."

"Wheat is ninety-four bid. New York strong." It was impossible to hold Bergen's attention, however, with a sharp bulge on the market, and Cargill was forced to turn to Bradley again.

"There is a girl in this town who has the literary quality. True, she has recognized my ability, which prejudices me in her favor, of course. In turn I presented her with my report on the sheep industry."

Bradley laughed, but Cargill proceeded as if there were nothing funny in the situation —

"And she read it, actually, and quoted it in one of her great speeches. It made the reporter bug out his eyes. He said he had observed of late quite a vein of poetry running through Miss Wilbur's speeches, which lifted them out of the common rut."

Bradley lost sight of the humor in this speech at the sound of Ida's name, and his face flushed. He had not heard her name spoken by a third person in months, and had never dared to say it out loud himself.

Cargill went on: "She's an infernal heretic and suffragist and all that, but she's a power. Her name is Wilbur — Ida Wilbur. Used to lecture for the Grange or something of that kind. Is still lecturing, I believe, but the Grange has snuffed out."

Six or eight men came into the larger room talking loudly and excitedly about the market, and Cargill's attention was drawn off by the resonant reports of the Chicago market.

"The market shows great elasticity. Western advices contribute to the Bull feeling."

"Do you know Miss Wilbur?" Bradley asked when Cargill came back, being afraid Cargill might forget the topic of conversation.

"Yes, I meet her occasionally. I meet her at

the Square Table Club, where we fight on literature. They call it the Square Table Club, because they disagree with the opinions of the most of us real literary people of the town."

Bradley managed to say, in a comparatively firm tone of voice, that he had heard of Miss Wilbur as a Grange lecturer, and that he would like to know more about her.

"Well, I'll introduce you. She aint very easy to understand. She is one of these infernal advanced women. Now, I like thinkers, but what right has a woman to think? To think is our manly prerogative. I'm free to admit that we don't exercise it to much better advantage than we do our prerogative to vote; but then, damn it, how could we stand wives that think?"

Bradley had given up trying to understand when Cargill was joking and when he was in earnest. He knew this was either merciless sarcasm or the most pig-headed bigotry. Anyhow he did not care to say anything for fear of drawing him off into a discussion of an impersonal subject, just when he seemed likely to tell something about Ida's early life.

It was a singular place to receive this information. He sat there with his elbow on the desk, leaning his head on his palm, studying Cargill's face as he talked. Over at the other end of the room, the operator was feeding himself on a pickle with his left hand, and receiving the telegrams from the far-off, roaring, tumultuous wheat exchange, every repeated message being a sort of distant echo of the ocean of cries and the tumult of feet in the city. They were as much alone and talking in private as if they were in Cargill's own room at the hotel. Cargill talked on, unmindful of the telephone, the telegraphic ticking, and the brisk, business-like action of his partner.

"Yes, I have known her ever since she was a girl. Her father was a queer old seed of a farmer, just out of town here, cranky on religion — a Universalist, I believe. Had the largest library of his town; I don't know but the largest private library outside of a city in the State. His house was literally walled with books. How he got 'em I don't know. It was currently believed that he was full of information, but I never heard of any one who was able to get very much out of him. His wife had been a beauty; that was her dowry to her daughter.

"The girl went to school here at sixteen. I was a student then, six or seven years older than she, and I remember there were about six of us who used to stand around the schoolhouse door to carry her books for her; but she just walked past us all without a turn of the head. She didn't seem to know what ailed us. She was one of these girls born all brains, some way. I never saw her face flushed in my life, and her big eyes always made me shiver when she turned them on me."

"Wheat falls to ninety-three and a fourth. There is a break in the market. New York is still hammering," called the operator, his mouth full of pie.

Cargill was distinctly talking to himself, almost as much as to Bradley. The hardness had gone out of his eyes, and his voice had a touch of unconscious sadness in it.

"Does Miss Wilbur live here?" Bradley asked, to start him off again.

"Yes, she went into the Grange when she was eighteen, just after she graduated from our university here. Had a good deal of your enthusiasm, I should judge. Expected to revolutionize things some way. I don't take very much interest in her public work, but I thoroughly appreciate her literary perception." He had got back to his usual humor.

"Chris, when does the club meet next?"

"Friday night, I believe."

"All right. I'll take you up, and introduce you into the charmed circle. They pride themselves on being modern up there, though I don't see much glory in being modern."

Bradley stood for a moment at the door, looking at this strange scene. It appealed to him with its strangeness, and its suggestion of the great battles on the street which he had read of in the papers. The telegraph machine clicked out every important movement in Chicago and New York. The manager called up his customers, and bawled into the telephone the condition of the market and the significant gossip of the far-off exchange halls. It was so strange, and yet so familiar, that he went away with his head full of those cabalistic sentences —

"New York still hammering away. Partridge quietly buying to cover on the decline."

XX.

AT THE STATE HOUSE.

THAT the invitation to attend the Square Table Club over-shadowed the importance and significance of Bradley's entrance into public life, was an excellent commentary upon his real character. The State House, however, appealed to his imagination very strongly as he walked up its unfinished lawn, amid the heaps of huge limestone blocks, his eyes upon the looming façade of the west front. He walked the echoing rotunda with a timid air; and the beautiful soaring vault was so majestic in his eyes, he wondered if Washington could be finer. There were a few other greenhorns, like himself, looking the building over with the same minute scrutiny. He entered all of the rooms into which it was possible to penetrate, and at last into the library, a cheerful, rectangular room, into which the sun streamed plenteously.

There was hardly any one in either the Senate or the Representative Halls except farmer-like groups of people, sometimes a family group of four or five, including the grandmother or grandfather. They were mainly in rough best suits of gray, or ostentatiously striped cassimere. The young men wore wide hats, pushed back, in some cases, to display a smooth, curling wave of hair, carefully combed down over their foreheads. He was able to catalogue them by reference to his old companions, Ed Blackler, Shep Watson, Sever Anderson, and others.

Soon the crowds thickened, and groups of men entered, talking and laughing loudly. They were wholly at their ease, being plainly old and experienced members. They greeted each other with boisterous cries and powerful handshaking.

"Hello, Stineberg, I hoped you'd git snowed under. Back again, eh?"

"Well, I'll be damned! Aint your county got any more sense than to send such a specimen as you back? Why weren't you around to the caucus?"

Bradley stood around awkwardly alone, not knowing just what to do. Perhaps some of these men would be glad to see him if they knew him, but he could not think of going to introduce him-

self.   Being new in politics, there was not a man
there whose face he recognized.   The few that he
had met at the hotel were not in sight.   He felt
as if he had been thrust into this jovial company,
and was unwelcome.

The House was called to order by one of the
members of the capital county, and prayer was
offered.   He sat quietly in his seat as things went
on.   The session adjourned after electing tem-
porary speaker, clerk, etc.   Bradley felt so alien
to it all that he scarcely took the trouble to
vote ; and when the committee on credentials was
appointed, he felt nervously in his pocket to see
that his papers were safe.   He felt very much as
he used to when, as a boy, he went to have his
hair cut, and sat in torture during the whole operation, in the fear that his quarter (all he had with
him) might be lost, and trembling to think what
would happen in such a case.

That night he moved to a new boarding-place.
He secured a room near the Capitol, and went to
supper in a small private house near by, which
had a most astonishing amplitude of dining-room.
He felt quite at home there, for the food was put
on the table in the good old way, and passed
around from hand to hand.   The mashed potato
tasted better, piled high, with a lump of butter in

the top of it; and the slices of roast beef, outspread on the platter, enabled him to get the crisp outside, if it happened to start from his end of the table. There were judges and generals and senators and legislators of various ranks all about him. Crude, rough, wholesome fellows, most of them, with big, brawny hands like his own, and loud, hearty voices. It was impossible to stand in awe of a judge who handled his knife more deftly than his fork, and spooned the potato out of the big, earthen-ware dish with a resounding slap. He began to see that these men were exactly like the people he had been with all his life. He argued, however, that they were perhaps the poorer and the more honorable part of the legislature.

He wrote a note to Judge Brown, telling him that he was settled, but was taking very little part in the organizing of the House. He did not say that he was disappointed in his reception, but he was; his vanity had been hurt. His canvass had attracted considerable attention from the Democratic press of the country, and he expected to be received with great favor by them. He had come out of Republicanism for their sake, and they ought to recognize him. He did not consider that no one knew him by sight, and that recognition was impossible.

He was at the Capitol again early the next morning, and found the same scene being re-enacted. Straggling groups of roughly-dressed farmers loitered timidly along the corridors; brisk clerks dashed to and fro, and streams of men poured in and out the doors of the legislative halls. Bradley entered unobserved, and took a seat at the rear of the hall on a sofa. He did not feel safe in taking a seat.

It was a solemn moment to the new legislator as he stood before the clerk, and, with lifted hand, listened to the oath of office read in the clerk's sounding voice. He swore solemnly, with the help of God, to support the Constitution, and serve his people to the best of his ability ; and he meant it. It did not occur to him that this oath was a shuffling and indefinite obligation. The room seemed to grow a little dimmer as he stood there; the lofty ceiling, rich in its colors, grand and spacious to him, seemed to gather new majesty, just as his office as lawmaker gathered a vast and sacred significance.

But as he came back to his seat, he heard a couple of old members laugh. "Comin' down to save their country. They'll learn to save their bacon before their term is up. That young feller looks like one of those retrenchment and reform cusses, one of the fellers who never want to adjourn — down here for business, ye know."

Their laughter made Bradley turn hot with indignation.

The selection of seats was the next great feature. The names of all the members were written upon slips of paper and shaken together in a box, while the members stood laughing and talking in the back part of the house. A blind-folded messenger boy selected the slips; and as the clerk read, in a sounding voice, the name on each slip, the representative so called went forward and selected his seat.

Bradley's name was called about the tenth, and he went forward timidly, and took a seat directly in the centre of the House. He did not care to seem anxious for a front seat. The Democratic members looked at him closely, and he stepped out of his obscurity as he went forward.

A young man of about his own age, a stalwart fellow, reached about and shook hands. "My name is Nelson Floyd. I wanted to see you."

Floyd took the first opportunity to introduce him to two or three of the Democratic members, but he sat quietly in his seat during the whole session, and took very little interest in the speakership contest, which seemed to go off very smoothly. He believed the speaker implicitly, when he stated the usual lie about having no pledges to redeem, and that he was free to choose his committee with regard only to superior fitness, etc., and was shocked when Floyd told him that a written contract had been drawn up and signed, before the legislature met, wherein the principal clerkships had been disposed of to party advantage. It was his second introduction to the hypocrisy of officialism.

If he had been neglected before, he was not now; all sorts of people came about him with axes to grind.

"Is this Mr. Talcott? Ah, yes! I have heard of your splendid canvass — splendid canvass! Now — ahem! — I'd like you to speak a good word for my girl, for the assistant clerkship of the Ways and Means"; while another wanted his son, Mr. John Smith, for page.

He told them that he had nothing to say about those things. "I am counted with the Democrats, anyhow; I haven't any influence."

They patted him on the shoulder, and winked slyly. "Oh, we know all about that! But every word helps, you know."

Going out at the close of the session, he met Cargill.

"Well, legislator, how goes it?"

"Oh, I don't know; smoothly, I guess. I've kept pretty quiet."

"That's right. The Republicans have everything in their hands this session."

"Hello, Cargill!" called a smooth, jovial voice.

"Ah, Barney! Talcott, this is an excellent opportunity. This is Barney, the great railway lobbyist. Barney, here is a new victim for you — Talcott, of Rock."

"Glad to see you, Mr. Talcott."

Bradley shook hands with moderate enthusiasm, looking into Barney's face with great interest. The lobbyist was large and portly and smiling. His moustache drooped over his mouth, and his chin had a jolly-looking hollow in it. His hazel eyes, once frank and honest, were a little clouded with drink.

"Cargill is an infernal old cynic," he exclaimed, "and he is corporation mad. Don't size us up according to his estimate."

It did not seem possible that this man could be the great tool of the railway interest, and yet that was his reputation.

Cargill moralized on the members, as they walked on: "Barney's on his rounds getting hold of the new members. He scents a corruptible man as the buzzard does carrion. Every session young fellows like you come down here with high and beautiful ideas of office, and start in to reform everything, and end by becoming meat for Barney and his like. There is something destructive in the atmosphere of politics."

Bradley listened to Cargill incredulously. These things could not be true. These groups of jovial, candid-looking men could not be the moral wrecks they were represented. He had expected to see men who looked villainous in some way, with bloated faces — disreputable, beery fellows. He had not risen to the understanding that the successful villain is always plausible.

When he left the Capitol and went down the steps with Cargill, he felt that he had fairly entered upon the work of his term.

"Now, young man," said Cargill, as they parted, "let me advise you. The fight of this session is going to be the people against the corporations. There are two positions and only two. You take your choice. If you side with the corporation, your success will be instantaneous. You can rig out, and board at the Richwood, and be dined out, and taken to see the town Saturday nights, and retire with a nice little boost and a record to apologize for when you go back to Rock

River; that is, you can go in for all that there is in it, or you can take your chances with the people."

"I will take the chances with the people."

"Well, now, hold on! Don't deceive yourself. The people are a mob yet. They are fickle as the flames o' hell. They don't know what they do want, but in the end the man that leads them and stands by them is sure of success."

The daily walk down from the Capitol was very beautiful. As the sun sank low it struck through the smoke of the city, and flooded the rotunda of the building with a warm, red light, which lay along the floor in great streams of gold, and warmed each pillar till it glowed like burnished copper. At such moments the muddy streets, the poor hovels, the ugly bricks, lost to sight beneath the majesty and mystery of the sun-transfigured smoke and the purple deeps of the lower levels (out of which the searching, pitiless light had gone), became a sombre and engulfing flood of luminous darkness.

"Here, here!" Cargill said one day, when Bradley called his attention to the view, "a man can swear and get drunk and be a politician; but when he likes flowers or speaks of a sunset, his goose is cooked. It is political death."

XXI.

BRADLEY had come to like Cargill very much. He was very thoughtful in his haphazard way, but not at all like Radbourn. Bradley compared every man he met with Radbourn and Judge Brown, and every woman suffered comparison with Ida Wilbur.

He went down to meet Cargill on the night of the promised call. He found him seated on the small of his back, his hands in his pockets. His absurd little hat (that seemed to partake of his every mood) was rolled into a point in front, and pulled down aggressively over his eyes. He was particularly violent, and paid no attention whatever to Bradley.

"No, sir; I am not a prohibitionist. My position is just this: If we vote prohibition in Iowa, the government has no business to license men to sell contrary to our regulations."

"That's state's rights!" burst in the other man who was trembling with rage and excitement.

Cargill slowly rose, transfixing him with a glare. "Go way, now; I won't waste any more time on you," he said, walking off with Bradley. "Let me see, we were going to the club to-night." He looked down at his boots. "Yes, they are shined; that puts a dress suit on me." As he walked along, he referred to Miss Wilbur. "She is a great woman, but she is abnormal from my point of view."

"Why so?" inquired Bradley.

"Well, look at the life she leads. On the road constantly, living at hotels. A woman can't hold herself up against such things."

"It depends upon the woman," was Bradley's succinct protest against sweeping generalizations.

It was crisp and clear, and the sound of their feet rang out in the still air as if they trod on glass at every step. They talked very little. Bradley wanted to tell Cargill that he had already met Miss Wilbur, but he could not see his way clear to make the explanation. Cargill was unwontedly silent.

The Norwegian girl ushered them into a pretty little parlor, where a beautiful fire of coal was burning in an open grate. While they stood warming their stiffened hands at the cheerful blaze, Ida entered.

"Mr. Cargill, this is an unexpected pleasure."

"I wonder how sincere you are in that. This is my friend Mr. Talcott."

Ida moved toward Bradley with her hand cordially extended. "I think we have met before," she said.

"I call him my friend," said Cargill, "because he has not known me long enough to become my enemy."

"That is very good, Mr. Cargill. Sit down, won't you? Please give me your coats." She moved about in that pleasant bustle of reception so natural to women.

Cargill slid down into a chair in his disjointed fashion. "We came to attend the intellectual sit-down."

"Why, that doesn't meet to-night! It meets every other Friday, and this is the other Friday."

"Oh, is it? So much the better; we will see you alone."

Ida turned gravely to Bradley. "Mr. Cargill is not often in this mood. I generally draw him off into a fight on Mr. Howell's, Thackeray or Scott."

"She prefers me in armor," Cargill explained, "and on horseback. My intellectual bowleggedness, so to say, and my moral squint are less obtrusive at an altitude."

Ida laughed appreciatively. "Your extraordinary choice of figures would distinguish you among the symbolists of Paris," she replied."

This all seemed very brilliant and droll to Bradley, and he sat with unwavering eyes fixed upon Ida, who appeared to him in a new light, more softly alluring than ever — that of the hostess. She was dressed in some loose, rich-colored robe, which had the effect of drapery.

"When did you get back?" Cargill inquired, a little more humanly.

"Yesterday, and I am just in the midst of the luxury of feeling at home, with no journeys to make to-morrow. I have a friend I would like to introduce to you," she said, rising and going out. She returned in a few moments with a tall young lady in street dress, whom she introduced as Miss Cassiday.

In a short time Cargill had involved Miss Cassiday in a discussion of the decline of literature, which left Ida free to talk with Bradley. It was the most beautiful evening in his life. He talked as never before. He told her of his reading, and of his plans. He told her of his election to the legislature.

"Ah, that is good!" she said; "then we have one more champion of women in our State House."

"Yes, I will do what I can," he said.

"I will be here to hear you. I am one of the committee in charge of the bill."

The firelight fell upon her face, flushing its pallor into a beauty that exalted the young farmer out of his fear and reticence. They talked upon high things. He told her how he had studied the social question, since hearing her speak in Iowa City. He called to her mind great passages in the books she had sent him, and quoted paragraphs which touched upon the fundamental questions at issue. He spoke of his hopes of advancement.

"I want to succeed," he said, "in order that I may teach the new doctrine of rights. I want to carry into the party I have joined the real democracy. I believe a new era has come in our party."

"I am afraid not," she said, looking at the fire. "I begin to believe that we must wait till a new party rises out of the needs of people, just as the old Free-soil Party rose to free the slaves. Don't deceive yourself about your party in this State. It is after the offices, just the same as the party you have left. They juggle with the tariffs and the license question, because it helps them. They will drop any question and any man when they think they are going to lose by retaining him. They will drop you if you get too radical. I warn you!" she said, looking up at him and smiling with a touch of bitterness in her smile; "I am dangerous. My counsel does not keep men in office. I belong to the minority. I am very dangerous."

"I'm not afraid," he said, thrilling with the intensity of his own voice. "I will trust human reason. I'm not afraid of you — I mean you can't harm me by giving me new thoughts, and that's what you've done ever since that day I heard you first at the picnic. You've helped me to get where I am."

"I have?" she asked, in surprise. His eyes fell before hers. "It will be strange if I have helped any one to political success."

Bradley was silent. How could he tell her what she had become to him? How could he tell her that she was woven into the innermost mesh of his intellectual fibre.

"You've taught me to think," he said, at last. "You gave me my first ambition to do something."

"I am very glad," she replied, simply. "Some-times I get discouraged. I speak and people applaud, and I go away, and that seems to be all there is to it. I never hear a word after-wards; but once in a while, some one comes to me or writes to me, as you have done, and that gives me courage to go on; otherwise I'd think people came to hear me simply to be amused."

She was looking straight into the fire; and the light, streaming up along her dress, transfigured her into something alien and unapproachable. The easy flex of her untrammelled waist was magnificent. She had the effect of a statue, draped and flooded with color.

Cargill's penetrating voice cut through that sacred pause like the rasp of a saw file. He had been listening to his companion till he was full of rebellion. He was a bad listener.

"But what is success? Why, my dear young woman " —

"Don't patronize us, please," Ida interposed. "I speak for poor Miss Cassiday, because she's too timid to rebel. Nothing angers me more than that tone. Call us comrades or friends, but don't say 'My dear young woman!'" She was smiling, but she was more than half in sober earnest.

Cargill bowed low, and proceeded with scowling brow and eyes half-closed and fixed obliquely upon Ida. "Dear comrades in life-battle, what is success? You remember the two lords in Lilliput who could leap the pack thread half its width higher?"

"Don't drag Swift into our discussion," Ida cried. "Mr. Cargill's a sort of American Swift," turning to Bradley. "Don't let him spoil your splendid optimism. There is a kind of pessimism which is really optimism; that is to say, people who believe the imperfect and unjust can be improved upon. They are called pessimists because they dare to tell the truth about the present; but the pessimism of Mr. Cargill, I'm afraid, is the pessimism of personal failure."

There was a terrible truth in this, and it drove straight into Cargill's heart. Bradley was pleased to see Ida dominate a man who was accustomed to master every one who came into his presence. There was a look on her face which meant battle. She did not change her attitude of graceful repose, but her face grew stern and accusing. Cargill looked at her, wearing the same inscrutable expression of scowling attention; but a slow flush, rising to his face, showed that he had been struck hard.

There was a moment's pause full of intense interest to Bradley. The combatants were dealing with each other oblivious of every one else.

"I admire you, friend Cargill," Ida went on, "but your attitude is not right. Your influence upon young people is not good. You are always crying out against things, but you never try to help. What are you doing to help things?"

"Crying out against them," he replied, curtly.

Ida dropped her glance. "Yes, that's so; I'll admit that it has that effect, or it would if you didn't talk of the hopelessness of trying to do anything. Don't feel alarmed," she said, turning to the others, "Mr. Cargill and I understand each other very well. We've known each other so long that we can afford to talk plain."

"This is the first time she ever let into me so directly," Cargill explained. "Understand we generally fight on literature, or music, or the woman question. This really is the first encounter on my personal influence. I'm going home to stanch my wounds." He rose, with a return to his usual manner.

Ida made no effort to detain them. "Come and see me again, Mr. Talcott, and don't let Mr. Cargill spoil you."

After leaving the house, the two men walked

on a block in silence, facing the wind, their over-coats drawn up about their ears.

"There's a woman I like," Cargill said, when they turned a corner and were shielded from the bitter wind. "She can forget her sex occasion-ally and become an intellect. Most women are morbid on their sex. They can't seem to escape it, as a man does part of the time. They can't rise, as this woman does, into the sexless region of affairs and of thought."

Bradley lacked the courage to ask him to speak lower, and he went on. "She's had suitors enough and flattery enough to turn her into a simpering fashion-plate; but you can not spoil brains. What the women want is not votes; it's brains, and less morbid emotions."

"She's a free woman?" said Bradley.

"Free! Yes, they'd all be free if they had her brains."

"I don't know about that; conditions might still" —

"They'd make their own conditions."

"That's true. It all comes back to a question of human thinking, doesn't it?"

This seemed a good point to leave off the dis-cussion, and they walked on mainly in silence, though two or three times during the walk Cargill broke out in admiration. "I never saw a woman grow as that woman has. That's the kind of a woman a man would never get tired of. I've never married," he went on, with a sort of confession, "because I knew perfectly well I'd get sick of my choice, but" —

He did not finish — it was hardly necessary; perhaps he felt he had gone too far. They said good-night at the door of the Richwood, and Bradley went on up the avenue, his brain whirling with his new ideas and emotions.

Ida had rushed away again into the far distance. It was utter foolishness to think she could care for him. She was surrounded with brilliant and wealthy men, while he was a poor young lawyer in a little country town. He looked back upon the picture of himself sitting by her side, there in the light of the fire, with deepening bewilderment. He remembered the strange look upon her face as she rebuked Cargill. He wondered if she did not care for him.

XXII.

THE JUDGE PLANS A NEW CAMPAIGN.

THE first three or four weeks of legislative life
sickened and depressed Bradley. He learned in
that time, not only to despise, but to loath some
of the legislators. The stench of corruption got
into his nostrils, and jovial vice passed before his
eyes. The duplicity, the monumental hypocrisy,
of some of the leaders of legislation made him
despair of humankind and to doubt the stability
of the republic.

He was naturally a pure-minded, simple-hearted
man, and when one of the leaders of the moral
party of his State was dragged out of a low resort,
drunk and disorderly, in company with a leader of
the Senate, his heart failed him. He was ready
to resign and go home.

Trades among the committees came obscurely
to his ears ; hints of jobs, getting each day more
definite, reached him. Railway lobbyists swarmed

about and began to lay their cajoling, persuasive hands upon members; and he could not laugh when the newspaper said, for a joke, that the absent-minded speaker called the House to order one morning by saying: "Agents of the K. C. & Q. will *please* be in order." It seemed too near the simple fact to be funny. The School Book Lobby, the University Lobby, the Armour Lobby, each had its turn with him, through its smooth, convincing agent.

He reached his lowest deep one night after a conversation with Floyd Smith, an ex-clerk, and a couple of young fellows who called upon him at his room. Floyd noticed his gloomy face, and asked what the trouble was. He told them frankly that he was disgusted.

"Oh, you'll get used to it!" the ex-clerk said. "When I first went into the House, I believed in honesty and sincerity, like yourself; but I came out of my term of office knowing the whole gang to be thieves. My experience taught me that legislators in America think it's a Christian virtue to break into the government treasury."

The others broke out laughing, believing him to be joking; but there was a ferocious look on his face, and Bradley felt that he might be mistaken, but he was not joking.

"They stole stationery, spittoons, waste baskets, by God! They stole everything that was loose, and at the end of the term, they seemed to be looking around unsatisfied, and I told 'em there was just one thing left — the gold leaf on the dome."

The others roared with laughter, and Bradley was forced to join in. But the face of the ex-clerk did not lose its dark intensity.

"Take salary grabbing. Why! they wanted me to certify to their demands for Sunday pay for themselves and their clerks, and I refused, and they were wild. I'm not an angel nor a Christian man, but I won't sign my name to a lie, and blamed if they didn't pass the order without my signature! Yes, sir; it's there on the record.

"Take nepotism. The members bring their wives and daughters down here, put them in as pages and clerks, or divide the proceeds when they have no relatives. Every device, every imaginable chicanery, every possible scheme to break into the State money box, is legitimate in their eyes, and worthy of being patented. Public money is fair game; and yet," he said, with a change of manner, "we have the fairest, purest and most honorable legislators, take it as a whole,

that there is in the United States, because our
State is rural, and we're comparatively free from
liquor. Our legislature is a Sunday School, compared to the leprous rascals that swarm about the
Capitol at Albany or Springfield."

"What is the cure?" asked Bradley, whose
mind had been busy with the problem.

"God Almighty! there is no cure, except the
abolition of government. Government means that
kind of thing. Look at it! Here we enthrone
the hungry, vicious, uneducated mob of incapa-
bles, and then wonder why they steal, and gorge
and riot like satyrs. The wonder is they don't
scrape the paint off the walls."

"Oh, you go too far; a legislator wouldn't
steal a spittoon."

"No, but the fellow he recommends for clerkship does."

"My idea is that there are very few men who
take money."

"I admit that, but they'll all trade their job
for another job. Honesty is impossible. The
Angel Gabriel would become a boodler under
our system of government. The cure is to abolish government."

This conclusion, impotent to Bradley, was practically all the savage critic had to offer. Either

go back to despotism or go ahead to no government at all.

After they went out, Bradley sat down and wrote a letter to Judge Brown, embodying the main part of this conversation: "It's enough to make a man curse his country and his God to see how things run," he said, at the end of writing out the ex-clerk's terrible indictment. "I feel that he is right. I'm ready to resign, and go home, and never go into politics again. The whole thing is rotten to the bottom."

But as the weeks wore on, he found that the indictment was only true of a certain minority, but it was terribly true of them; but down under the half-dozen corruptible agents, under the roar of their voices, there were many others speaking for truth and purity. The obscure mass meant to be just and honest. They were good fathers and brothers, and yet they were forced to bear the odium that fell on the whole legislature whenever the miscreant minority rolled in the mire and walked the public streets.

There was one count, however, that remained good against nearly all of the legislators: they seemed to lack conscience as regards public money. Bradley remembered that this dishonesty extended down to the matter of working on the roads in the country. He remembered that every man esteemed it a virtue to be lazy, and to do as little for a day's pay as possible, because it "came out of the town." He was forced to admit that this was the most characteristic American crime. To rob the commonwealth was a joke.

He ended by philosophizing upon it with the Judge, who came down in late February to attend the session during the great railway fight.

The Judge put his heels on the window sill, and folded his arms over the problem.

"Well, now, this thing must be looked at from another standpoint. The power of redress is with the voter. If the voter is a boodler, he will countenance boodling. Here is the mission of our party," he said, with the zeal of an old-fashioned Democrat, "to come in here and educate the common man to be an honest man. We have got a duty to perform. Now, we mustn't talk of resigning or going out of politics. We've got to stay right in the lump, and help leaven it. It will only make things worse if we leave it." The Judge had grown into the habit of speaking of Bradley as if he were a partner.

Bradley, going about with him on the street, suddenly discovered that the Judge's hat was just a shade too wide in the brim, and his coat a little bit frayed around the button-holes. He had never noticed before that the Judge was a little old-fashioned in his manners. No thought of being ashamed of him came into his mind, but it gave him a curious sensation when they entered a car together for the first time, and he discovered that the Judge was a type.

When Bradley made his great speech on the railroad question, arraigning monopoly, the Judge had a special arrangement with a stenographer. He was going to have that speech in pamphlet form to distribute, if it took a leg. He was already planning a congressional campaign.

Ida sat in the balcony on the day he spoke for woman's suffrage, and he could not resist the temptation of looking up there as he spoke. Everything combined to give great effect to his speech. It was late in the afternoon and the western sun thrust bars of light across the dim chamber which the fresh young voice of the speaker had hushed into silence. Ida had sent a bunch of flowers to his desk and upon that bouquet the intrusive sun-ray fell, like something wild that loved the rose, but as the speaker went on it clambered up his stalwart side and rested at last upon his head as though to crown him with victory.

But defeat came as usual. The legislators saw nothing in the sun-ray except a result of negligence on the part of the door-keeper. They all cheered the speech, but a majority tabled the matter as usual. The galleries cheered and the women swarmed about the young champion, Ida among them. Her hand-shake and smile was his greatest reward.

"Come and see me," she said. "I want to thank you."

The Judge was immensely proud of him. "A great speech, Brad; if I wasn't so old-fashioned and set — you'd have contented me. In private I admit all you say, but it aint policy for me to advocate it just now."

"Policy! I'm sick of policy!" cried Bradley. "Let's try being right awhile."

The Judge changed the subject. He told the members at the boarding-house that it wouldn't hurt Bradley's chances. "People won't down a man on that point any more."

"Perhaps not in your county, but I don't want to experiment down in my county," said Major Root, of MacIntosh.

"I don't believe the people of Iowa will down any man for stating what he believes is right."

"Don't bet too high on that," said the Major in final reply.

The Judge dined with Bradley at the dining-room in the little cottage, and it gave Bradley great satisfaction to see that he used his fork more gracefully than the Supreme judge, who sat beside him, and better than the senator, who sat opposite. They had a most delightful time in talking over old legal friends, and the Judge was beaming as he came to pudding. He assured them all that the Honorable Talcott would be heard on the floor of Congress.

"We're the winning party now," he said. "We're the party of the future."

The others laughed good naturedly. "Don't be too certain of that." They all rose. "You surprised us sleeping on our arms," the general said, "but we're awake now, and we've got pickets out."

The Judge enjoyed his visit very much, and only once did he present himself to Bradley with a suspicious heaviness in his speech. He had reformed entirely since he had adopted a son, he explained to his old cronies.

On the day when the Judge was to return, as they walked down to the train together, he said, "Well, Brad, we'll go right into the congressional campaign."

"I don't believe we'd better do that, Judge."

"Why not?"

"Well, I could not be elected — that's one thing."

The Judge allowed an impressive silence to intervene.

"Why not? I tell you, young man, they're on the run. We can put you through. You've made a strong impression down here."

"I don't believe I want to be put through. I'm sick of it. I don't believe I'm a politician. I'm sick all through with the whole cussed business. I never'd be here only for you, pulling wires. I can't pull wires."

"You needn't pull wires. I'll do that. You talk, and that's what put you here, and it'll put you in Congress."

Bradley was in a bad mood.

"What's the good of my going there? I can't do anything. I've done nothing here."

"Yes, y' have. You've been right on the railroad question, on the oleo question, and the bank question. It's going to count. That speech of yours, yesterday, I'm going to send broadcast in Rock County. The district convention will meet in June early. Foster will pave the way for your nomination, by saying Rock County should have a congressman. We'll go into the convention with a clear two-thirds majority, and then declare your nomination unanimous. You see, your youth will be in your favor. Your election will follow, sure. The only fight will be in the convention."

"Looks like spring, to-day," Bradley said. It was his way of closing an argument.

"Well, good-by. You'll find the whole pot boiling when you come home," the Judge said, as the train started.

As Bradley looked on these suggestive scenes, the earth-longing got hold upon him again. It was almost seed time, with its warm, mellow soil, .. sweeping flights of prairie pigeons, its innumerable swarms of tiny clamorous sparrows, its whistling plovers, and its passing wild fowl. The thought came to him there, for the first time, that nature was not malignant nor hard; that life on a farm might be the most beautiful and joyous life in the world. The meaning of Ida's words at last took definite and individual shape in his mind. He had assimilated them now.

Bradley gave himself up to the Judge's plans. He went home in April with eagerness and with reluctance. He was eager to escape the smoke of the city and reluctant to leave behind him all chance to see Ida. This feeling of hungry disappointment dominated him during his day's ride. He had seen her but twice during his stay in Des Moines, and now — when would he see her again?

This terrible depression and sharp pain wore away a little by the time he reached home, and the active campaign which followed helped him to bear it. He still wrote to her, and she replied without either encouragement and without explicit displeasure. The campaign was really the Judge's fight. Bradley was his field officer. Victory in the convention only foreshadowed the sweeping victory in October. He resigned as legislator, to become a congressman.

XXIII.

ON TO WASHINGTON.

IN the west (as in rural America anywhere), the three types of great men in the peoples' eyes are the soldier, the politician and the minister. The whole people appear to revere the great soldier, the men admire the successful politician, and the women bow down before the noted preacher.

These classes of hero-worshipers melt into each other, of course, but broadly they may be said to separately exist. In colonial days the minister came first, the soldier second, the politician last. Since the revolution the soldier has been the first figure in the triumvirate, and in these later times the politician and his organ of voice the newspaper have placed the preacher last.

And there is something wholesome in such an atmosphere, the atmosphere of the West, at least by contrast. The worship of political success, low as it may seem, is less deplorable than the worship of wealth, which is already weakening the hold of the middle-class Eastern man upon the American idea. In the West mere wealth does not carry assurance of respect, much less can it demand subservience.

Bradley never dreamed of getting rich, but under Radbourn and the Judge he had developed a growing love for the orator's dominion. He hungered to lead men. Notwithstanding his fits of disgust and bitterness he loved to be a part of the political life of his time. It had a powerful fascination for him. The deference which his old friends and neighbors paid him as things due a rising young man, pleased him.

He looked now to Washington, and it fired his imagination to think of sitting in the hall where the mighty legislators of generations now dead had voiced their epoch-marking thoughts. It amazed the Judge to see how the wings of his young eagle expanded. The transformation from a farmer's hired man to a national representative appealed to him as characteristically American, and he urged Bradley to do his best.

The election which the young orator expected to be another moment of great interest really came as a matter-of-fact ending to a long and triumphant canvass. He had held victory in his hand until she was tamed. The election simply confirmed the universal prophecy. He was elected, and while the Democrats went wild with joy, Bradley slept quietly in his bed at home — while the brass band played itself quiescent under his window.

Now he fixed his eyes on Washington as an actuality. It was a long time before his term began, and at the advice of Judge Brown and others he packed his trunk in January to go on and look around a little in the usual way of new members. He went alone, the Judge couldn't spare the time.

That ride from Chicago to Washington was an epic to him. It was his next great departure, his entrance into another widening circle of thinking. He had never seen a mountain before; and the wild, plunging ride among the Alleghany Mountains was magnificent. He sat for hours at a time looking out of the window, while the train, drawn by its two tremendous engines, crawled toward the summit. He saw the river drop deeper and deeper, and get whiter and wilder; and then came the wooded level of the summit, and then began the descent.

While the reeling train alternately flung him to the window and against the seat, he gazed out at the wheeling peaks, the snow-laden pines, and the mighty gorges, through which the icy river ran, green as grass in its quiet eddies. On every side were wild hillsides meshed with fallen trees, and each new vista contained its distant peak. It was the realization of his imagination of the Alleghanies.

As the train swooped round its curves, dropping lower and lower, the valley broadened out, and the great mountains moved away into ampler distances. The river ran in a wide and sinuous band to the east and the south. He realized it to be the Potomac, whose very name is history. He began to look ahead to seeing Harper's Ferry, and in the nearing distance was Washington!

He had the Western man's intensity of feeling for Washington. To him it was the centre of American life, because he supposed the laws were made there. The Western man knows Boston as the centre of art, which he affects to despise, and New York appeals to him as the home of the millionaire, of the money-lender; but in Washington he recognizes the great nerve centre of national life. It is the political ganglion of the body politic. It appeals to the romantic in him as well. It is historical; it is the city that makes history.

Slowly the night fell. After leaving Harper's Ferry the outside world vanished, and when the brakeman called "Washington," it was nearly eight o'clock of a damp, chilly night. He was so eager to see the Capitol, which the kindly fat man behind him had assured him was but a few steps away from the station, that he took his valise in his hand, and started directly for the dome, which a darkey with a push-cart, pointed out to him with oppressive courtesy.

There was an all-pervasive, impalpable, blue-gray mist in the air, cold and translucent; and when he came to the foot of the grounds, and faced the western front of the Capitol building, he drew a deep breath of delight. It thrilled him. There it loomed in the misty, winter night, the mightiest building on the continent, blue-white, sharply outlined, massive as a mountain, yet seemingly as light as a winter cloud. Weighing myriads of tons, it seemed quite as insubstantial as the mist which transfigured it. Against the cold-white of its marble, and out of the gray-white enveloping mist, bloomed the warm light of lamps, like vast lilies with hearts of fire and halos of faint light.

He stood for a long time looking upon it, mus-
ing upon its historic associations.   Around him
he heard the grinding wheels, the click of the
horses' hoofs upon the asphalt pavement, and
heard the shouts of drivers.   Somewhere near
him water was falling with a musical sound in a
subterranean sluiceway.   At last he came to himself with a start, and found his arm aching with
the fatigue of his heavy valise.   He struck off
down the avenue.   It seemed to swarm with colored people.   They were selling papers, calling
with musical, bell-like voices —

"Evenin' Sty-ah!"   "Evenin' Sty-ah!"

Horse cars tinkled along, and a peculiar form
of elongated 'bus, with the word "Carette" painted
upon it, rolled along noiselessly over the asphalt
pavement.   An old man in business dress, with
rather aristocratic side-whiskers, came toward
him, walking briskly through the crowd, an open
hand-bag swung around his neck; and as he
walked he chanted a peculiar cry —

"Doc-tor Ferguson's, selly-brated, double X,
Philadelphia cough-drops, for coughs *and* colds,
sore throat or hoarseness; five *cents* a package."

Innumerable signs invited him to "meals at 15
and 25 cts."   "Rolls and French drip coffee, 10
cts."   "Oysters in every style," etc.

The oyster saloons were, in general, very attractive to him, as a Western man, but specifically he did not like the looks of the places in which they were served. He came at last to a place which seemed clean and free from a bar, and ventured to call for a twenty-five cent stew.

After eating this, he again took his way to the street, and walked along, looking for a moderate-priced hotel. He did not think of going to a hotel that charged more than seventy-five cents for a room. He came at length to quite a decent-looking place, which advertised rooms for fifty cents and upwards. He registered under the clerk's calm misprision, and the brown and wonderfully freckled colored boy showed him to his room.

It was all quite familiar to him — this hotel to which a man of moderate means is forced to go in the city. The dingy walls and threadbare carpet got geometrically shabbier at each succeeding flight of stairs, until at length the boy ushered him into a little room at the head of the stairway. It was unwarmed and had no lock on the door; but the bed was clean, and, as he soon found, very comfortable.

XXIV.

RADBOURN SHOWS BRADLEY ABOUT THE CAPITAL.

He woke in the morning from his dreamless sleep with that peculiar familiar sensation of not knowing where he had lain down the night before. There was something boyish in the soundness of his sleep. He heard the newsboys calling outside, although it was apparently the early dawn. Their voices made him think of Des Moines, for the reason that Des Moines was the only city in which he had ever heard the newsboys cry. He sprang from his bed at the thought of Radbourn. He would hunt him up at once! He was surprised to find that it had snowed during the night, and everywhere the darkies were cleaning the walks.

Walking thus a perfect stranger in what seemed to him a great city he did not feel at all like a rising young man. In fact the farther he got from Rock River the smaller his importance grew, for he had the imagination that comprehends relative values.

On the street he passed a window where a big negro was cooking griddle-cakes, dressed in a snowy apron and a paper cap. He looked so clean and wholesome that Bradley decided upon getting his breakfast there, and going in, took his seat at one of the little tables. A colored boy came up briskly.

"I'd like some of those cakes," said Bradley, to whom all this was very new.

"Brown the wheats!" yelled the boy, and added in a low voice, "Buckwheat or batter?"

"Buckwheat, I guess."

"Make it bucks!" the boy yelled, by the way of correction, and asked again in a low voice, "Coffee?"

"If you please."

"One up light."

While Bradley was eating his cakes, which were excellent, others came in, and the waiters dashed to and fro, shouting their weird orders.

"Ham *and*, two up coff, a pair, boot-leg, white wings."

Bradley had a curiosity to see what this order would bring forth, and, watching carefully, found that it secured ham and eggs, two cups of coffee, a beefsteak, and an omelet. He was deeply interested in the discovery.

He recognized the most of the men around him as Western or Southern types. Many of them had chin whiskers and wore soft crush hats. The negroes interested and fascinated him : they were so grimly ugly of face, and yet apparently so good natured and light hearted.

On the street again he saw the same types of men. He wondered if they were not his colleagues. As for them, they probably took him for a Boston or New York man, with his full brown beard and clear-skinned face.

The negroes attracted his eyes constantly. They drifted along the street apparently aimlessly, many of them. Their faces were *mainly* laughing, but in a meaningless way, as if it were a habit. He soon found that they were swift to struggle for a chance to work. They asked to carry his valise, to black his boots; the newsboys ran by his side, in their eagerness to sell.

As he went along, he noticed the very large number of " Rooms to Let," and the equally large number of signs of " Meals, Fifteen and Twenty-five Cents." Evidently there would be no trouble in finding a place to board.

As he entered Radbourn's office, he saw a young lady seated at a desk, manipulating a typewriter. She had the ends of a forked rubber tube hung in her ears, and did not see Bradley. He observed that the tube connected with a sewing-machine-like table and a swiftly revolving little cylinder, which he recognized as a phonograph. At the window sat Radbourn, talking in a measured, monotonous voice into the mouthpiece of a large flexible tube, which connected with another phonograph. His back was toward Bradley, and he stood for some time looking at the curious scene and listening to Radbourn's talk.

"Congress brings to Washington a fulness of life which no one can understand who has not spent the summer here," Radbourn went on, in a slow, measured voice, his lips close to the bell-like opening of the tube. It had a ludicrous effect upon Bradley—like a person talking to himself.

"The city may be said to die, when Congress adjourns. Its life is political, and when its political motor ceases to move the city lies sprawled out like a dead thing. Its streets are painfully quiet. Its street cars shuttle to and fro under the burning sun, and its teamsters loaf about the corners drowsily. The store-keepers keep shop, of course, but they open lazily of a morning and close early at night. The whole city yawns and rests and longs for the coming of the autumn and Congress.

"It is amusing and amazing to see it begin to wake up at the beginning of the session. Then begins the scramble of the hotels and boarding-houses to secure members of Congress. Then begins " —

The girl suddenly saw Bradley standing there, and called out, "Some one to see you, Mr. Radbourn!"

Radbourn stopped the cylinder, and turned.

"Ah, how do you do," he said, as if greeting a stranger.

Bradley smiled in reply, knowing that Radbourn did not recognize him. "I'm very well. I don't suppose you remember me, but I'm Brad Talcott."

Radbourn rose with great cordiality. "Well, well, I'm glad to see you," he said, his sombre face relaxing in a smile, as he seized Bradley by the hand. "Sit down, sit down. I'm glad to see an old class-mate."

"Don't let me interrupt your work. I was interested in hearing you talk into that thing there."

"Oh, yes, I was just getting off my syndicate letter for this week. Sit down and talk; you don't interrupt me at all. Now tell me all about yourself. Of course I have heard of your success, State Legislature and Congress and all that, but I would like to have you tell me all about it."

"There aint very much to tell. I had very little to do with it," said Bradley.

They took seats near the window, looking out upon the square, and upon the vast, squat, Egyptian, tomb-like structure, that rose out of the centre of the smooth, snow-covered plat, across which the sun streamed with vivid white radiance.

There was a little pause after they sat down. Radbourn leaned his head on his arm, and studied Bradley earnestly. He seemed older and more bitter than Bradley expected to see him. He asked of the old friends in a slow way, as if one name called up another in a slowly moving chain of association. They talked on for an hour thus, sitting in the same position. At last Radbourn said —

"How far I've got from all those scenes and people! and yet the memory of that little old town and its people has a powerful fascination. I never'll go back, of course. To tell the truth, I am afraid to go back; it would drive me crazy.

I am a city man naturally. I am gregarious. I like to be in the centre of things. It'll get hold of you, too. This city is full of ruined young men and women, who came here from the slow-moving life of inland towns and villages, and, after two or three years of a richer life, find it impossible to go back; and here they are, struggling along on forty-five cents a day at hash-houses, living in hall bedrooms, preferring to pick up such a living, at all kinds of jobs, than to go back home. I'd do it myself, if I were" —

He broke off suddenly, and looked at Bradley in a keen, steady way. "And so your're a congressman, Talcott? Well, I'm glad of your success, because it shows a man *can* succeed on the right lines — in a measure, at least."

"Well, I've tried to live up to most of your principles," smiled Bradley. "I've read all the things you've sent me."

"Well, you're the wildest and most dangerous lunatic that ever got into Congress," Radbourn said, gravely. "Do you expect to talk any of that stuff on the floor?"

"Well, I — I hoped to be able to say something before the session closes."

"If you do, it will be a miracle. The House is under the rule of a Republican Czar, and men with your ideas or any ideas are to be shut out remorselessly. Let me tell you something right here; it will save time and worry: You want to know the Speaker, cultivate him. He's the real power. That's the reason the speakership becomes such a terrible struggle. It decides the most tremendous question. In his hand is the appointing of committees, which should be chosen by the legislators themselves. The power of these committees is unlimited, you'll find. They can smother bills of the utmost importance. Theoretically they are the servants of the House. Actually they are its autocrats."

"I didn't realize that."

"I don't suppose it is realized by the people. This appointing of the committee is supposed to save time, and yet the speakership contest consumes weeks, sometimes months. It will grow in ferocity."

"Can't something be done?"

"Try and see," he said rising. "Well, suppose we got out and walk about a little. I infer you're on to see the town. Where are you stopping?"

Bradley named the hotel with a little reluctance. He knew how cheap it was; and since he had discovered that congressmen were at a premium in boarding-houses, he saw that he must get more sumptuous quarters than he had hitherto occupied. They went out into the open air together. The sun was very brilliant and warm. The eaves were running briskly. The sky was gentle, beautiful, and spring-like. The fact that he was in Washington came upon Bradley again, as he saw the soaring dome of the capitol at the head of the avenue.

"What you want to do is to get on good social terms with the so-called leaders," Radbourn was saying. "Recognition goes by favor on the floor of the House. We might go up to the capitol and look about," Radbourn suggested.

They walked up the steps leading to the west front of the building. Everywhere the untrodden snow lay white and level.

"This is the finest part of the whole thing," Radbourn remarked, as they reached the level of esplanade. "It has more beauty and simple majesty than the main building itself, or any structure in the city."

It was magnificent. Bradley turned and looked at it right and left with admiring eyes. It gleamed with snow, and all about was the sound of dripping water, and in the distance the roll of wheels and click of hoofs. The esplanade was a broad walk extending the entire width of the building, and conforming to it. It was bottomed with marble squares, and bordered with a splendid wall, breast-high on one side, and by the final terrace running to the basement wall on the other. Here and there along the wall gigantic brazen pots sat, filled with evergreens, whose color seemed to have gradually dropped down and entered into the marble beneath them. The bronze had stained with rich, dull green each pedestal and irregular sections of the marble wall itself.

Below them the city was outspread. Radbourn pointed out the Pension Office, the White House, the Treasury, and other principal buildings with a searching word upon their architecture. The monument, he evidently considered, required no comment.

As they entered the dome, they passed a group of men whose brisk, bluff talk and peculiar swagger indicated their character — legislators from small country towns.

"Some of your colleagues," Radbourn said, indicating them with his thumb. As they paused a moment in the centre of the dome, one of the group, a handsome fellow with a waxed mustache and hard, black eyes, gave a stretching gesture, and said, " I'm in the world now."

His words thrilled Bradley to the heart. He was in the world now. Des Moines and its capitol were dwarfed and overshadowed by this great national city, to which all roads ran like veins to a mighty heart. He lifted his shoulders in a deep breath. It was glorious to be a congressman, but still more glorious to be a citizen of the world.

They passed through the corridors in upon the house floor, which swarmed with legislators, lobbyists, pages, newspaper men and visitors. Radbourn led the way down to the open space before the speaker's desk, and together they turned and swept the semi-circular rows of seats.

"Everywhere the visitor abounds," said Radbourn. "Western and Southern men predominate. It's surprising what deep interest the negro takes in legislation," he went on, lifting his eyes to the gallery, which was black with their intent and solemn faces. "See this old fellow with his hat off as if he were in the midst of a temple," he said, nodding at a group before the speaker's desk.

Bradley looked at the poor, bent, meek, old man with a thrill of pity. He observed that many of the negroes were splashed with orange-colored clay.

Members began to take their seats and to call pages by clapping their hands. The cloak-rooms and barber-shop resounded with laughter. News-paper men sauntered by, addressing Radbourn and asking for news. And here and there others, like Radbourn, were acting as guides to groups of visitors.

In the midst of the growing tumult a one-armed man entered the speaker's desk and called out in snappy tenor —

"Gentlemen, I am requested by the door-keeper to ask all persons not entitled to the floor to please retire."

Bradley started, but Radbourn said, "No hurry, you have fifteen minutes yet. As a member-elect you have the courtesy of the floor anyway. Do you want to meet anybody?"

"No, I guess not. I just want to look on for to-day."

"Well, we'll go up in the gallery."

Looking down upon the floor and its increas-ing swarm of individuals, Bradley got a complete sense of its vastness and its complexity and noise.

"It makes the Iowa legislature seem like a school-room," he said to Radbourn.

At precisely noon the gavel fell with a single sharp stroke, and the speaker called persuasively,

"The house will *please* be in order." The members rose and stood reluctantly, some of them sharpening their pencils, others reading while the chaplin prayed sonorously with many oratorical cadences, taking in all the departments of government in the swing of his generous benediction.

Instantly at the word "Amen," like the popping of a cork, the tumult burst out again. Hands clapped, laughter flared out, desks were slammed, papers were rattled, feet pounded, and the brazen monotonous clanging voice of the clerk sounded above it all like some new steam calliope whose sounds were words.

"You see how much prayer means here," said Radbourn.

A good deal of the business which followed was similar in character to the proceedings at Des Moines. Resolutions were passed with two or three aye votes and no noes at all, while the rest of the members looked over the Record, read the morning papers, or wrote on busily. The speaker declared each motion carried with glib voice.

At last a special order brought up an unfinished debate upon some matter, and the five minute rule was enforced.

"You're in luck," said Radbourn. "The whole procession is going to pass before you."

As the debate went on he pointed out the great men whose names suggested history to Bradley and whose actual presence amazed him. There was Amos B. Tripp, whom Radbourn said resembled "a Chinese god"—immense, featureless, bald, with a pout on his face like an enormous baby. The "watch dog of the house," Major Hendricks, was tall, thin, with the voice and manner of an old woman. His eyes were invisible, and his chin-beard wagged up and down as he shouted in high tenor his inevitable objection.

An old man with abundant hair, blue-white under the perpendicular light, arose at the back part of the room, making a fine picture outlined against the deep red screen. His manner was courtly, his ruddy face pleasing, his voice musical and impassioned.

"He's the dress parade orator of the house," observed Radbourn.

"I like him," said Bradley, leaning forward to absorb the speaker's torrent of impassioned utterance. When he sat down the members applauded.

Most of the orators conformed to types familiar to Bradley. There was the legal type, monotonously emphatic, with extended forefinger, which pointed, threatened and delineated. His speaking wore on the ear like a saw-filing. Then there was the political speaker, the stump orator, who was full of well-worn phrases, who could not mention the price of wool or the number of cotton bales without using the ferocious throaty-snarl of a beast of prey.

He was followed by the clerical type, a speaker who used the most mournful cadences in correcting the gentleman on his left as to the number of cotton bales. His voice and manner formed a distinct reflection of the mournful preacher, and the tune of his high voice had the power of calling up the exact phraseology of sermons — "Repent, my lost brother, ere it be too late," "Prepare for the last great day, my brother," while he actually asserted the number of cotton bales had been grossly over-stated by the gentleman from Alabama.

On going down the stairs, Radbourn called his attention to the paintings, hanging here and there, which he called "hideous daubs" with the reckless presumption of a born realist to whom allegory was a personal affront. Radbourn showed him about the city as much as he could spare time to do, and when he released him, Bradley went back to the capitol, which exercised the profoundest fascination upon him.

He had not the courage to go back to the private gallery into which Radbourn had penetrated, but went into the common gallery, which was full of negroes, unweariedly listening to the dry and almost unintelligible speeches below.

He sat there the whole afternoon and went back to his hotel meek and very tired.

Radbourn introduced him to a few of the members the next day. It was evident that nobody cared very much whether he had been elected or not. Each man had his own affairs to look after, and greeted him with a flabby hand-shake and looked at him with cold and wandering eyes. It was all very depressing.

He grew nervous over the expenses which he was incurring, although he constantly referred himself back to the fact that he was a Congressman, at a salary of six thousand dollars. His economy was too deeply ingrained to be easily wiped out. He seldom got into a street-car that he did not hold a mental debate with himself to justify the extravagance.

He went about a good deal during the next two or three days, but he continued at the cheap hotel, where he was obliged to keep his overcoat on in order to write a letter or read a newspaper. He went twice to the theatre. He bought a dollar seat the first time, which worried him all through

the play, and he did penance the following evening by walking the twenty blocks (both ways),
and by taking a fifty-cent seat. He figured it a
clear saving of sixty cents. He really enjoyed
the play more than he would have done in a dollar
seat and consoled himself with the reflection that
no one knew he was a Congressman, anyway.

He told Radbourn at the station that he had
enjoyed every moment of his stay. As the train
drew out he looked back upon the city, and the
great dome its centre, with a deep feeling of
admiration, almost love. It had seized upon him
mightily. He had only to shut his eyes to see
again that majestic pile with its vast rotundas, its
bewildering corridors and its tumultuous representative hall. Life there would be worth while.
He began to calculate how long it would be
before he should return. It seemed a long while
to wait.

XXV.

AFTER his return home he accepted every invitation to speak, because that relieved the tedium of his life in Rock River. He took an active part in the fall campaign in county politics, and he delivered the Fourth of July address at the celebration at Rock River amid the usual blare of bands and bray of fakirs and ice-cream vendors, while the small boys fired off crackers in perfect oblivion of anybody but themselves.

It was magnificent to occupy a covered carriage in the parade and to sit on the platform as the centre of interest, and to rise amid cheers to address the citizens of the United States, to point to cloud-capped towering peaks, to plant the stars and stripes upon battlements of ancient wrong, and other equally patriotic things.

No occasion was complete now without him.

The strawberry festival that secured his presence felicitated itself upon the fact and always insisted on "just a few words, Mr. Congressman."

The summer passed rather better than he had anticipated. About a month before his return to Washington he received a letter from Ida asking him to be present at a suffrage meeting in Des Moines, and he accepted the invitation with great pleasure. He had been wondering how he could see her again without making the journey for that purpose, which he could not bring himself to do.

It was a soft, hazy October day and the ride to Des Moines was very beautiful. The landscape seemed to be in drowse, half-sleeping and half-waking. The jays flew from amber and orange-colored coverts of maples and oaks across the blue haze of the open, and quails piped from the hazel-thickets. Crows flapped lazily across the fields where the ploughmen were at work. The threshing machines hummed and clattered with a lower, quieter note, and as Bradley looked upon it all, the wonder of his release from the toil of reaping and threshing and ploughing came upon him again.

Ida was glad to see him. She gave him her hand in a frank, strong clasp.

"You'll stay to tea with us, of course," she said. "There is no one here but mother and I, and we can talk things all over. This is my mother," she said, presenting an elderly lady with a broad, placid face. She said nothing whatever during his stay, but listened to all that was said with unchanging gravity. It was plain she worshipped her daughter, and never questioned what she said.

They sat down at the table.

"Mr. Talcott, this is Christine," said Ida, introducing a comely Norwegian girl who came in with the tea. "Christine takes care of mother while I'm away."

"Ay tank sometime she take care of me," smiled Christine.

Avoiding family matters, Ida talked on general subjects while the rest listened. She over-estimated Bradley's education, his reading, but he was profoundly thankful for it. He had never heard such talk. It was literature to him. She spoke with such fine deliberation and such choice of words. He felt its grace and power without understanding it. It seemed to him wonderful.

"I should like to be a novelist," she said. "I'd like to treat of this woman's movement."

"Why can't you do it?" he asked.

"I lack the time, the freedom from other interests. But if I could be a novelist, it would be a novelist of life."

He never remembered all that she said, but she made an impression that was almost despair upon him by her incidental mention of books that he had never read, and of authors of whom he had never even heard.

They walked to the church together along the side-walks littered with fallen leaves, and when they entered the side door she began to introduce him to the ladies who swarmed about her the moment they caught sight of her. Bradley felt embarrassed by their multiple presence, but was proud to be introduced by Ida. They moved to the platform. He had never spoken at such a meeting before and he was nervous. He spoke first and spoke well, but he would have done better with Ida's face before him. When she spoke he sat looking up at the beautiful head and feeling rather than seeing the splendid lines of her broad, powerful and unconfined waist. The perfume of her dress and its soft rustle as she moved to and fro before him made him forget her words.

Cargill came up to the platform after the speaking and said jocosely, "Well, Legislator, you're getting ahead. You're laying a foundation for post-mortem fame, anyway. I hear you've been on to Congress."

"Yes, I went on and stayed a few days."

"How'd you like it?"

"How do you do, Mr. Cargill," said Ida at his elbow. "Aren't you out of place here?"

"Not more than usual," replied Cargill. "I'm always out of place."

"Do you know Mr. Birdsell?" she asked, presenting a powerful young man with a singularly handsome face. He had clear brown eyes and a big, graceful mustache. For just a moment as he stood beside Ida, Bradley shivered with a sudden suspicion that they were lovers.

"Mr. Birdsell happens to be on from Muscatene," Ida explained, "and happened in to see a suffrage meeting. He's trying to reconcile himself to the idea of woman's emancipation."

"He'll find a sympathizer in me," put in Cargill.

Bradley studied Birdsell with round-eyed steady stare. He was a superb type of man. It gave Bradley a feeling of awkwardness to stand beside him and a consciousness of stupidity to listen to their banter, but Ida dismissed Cargill and Birdsell summarily and walked home with Bradley. He was not keenly perceptive enough to see that

Ida put Birdsell off with a brusqueness that argued a perfect understanding.

They walked home by the risen moon side by side. He had not the courage to take her arm and she did not offer it. He referred again to Washington and she asked him to remember the women in his legislation.

"I don't know what I'm going to do next, but I must reach the farmer's wives again as I did in the days of the grange. I feel for them. They are to-day the most terrible proofs of man's inhumanity. My heart aches for them. There is a new farmer's movement struggling forward, the Alliance. I'm thinking of going into that as a lecturer. Do you know anything about it?"

"No, not much."

They had reached the gate, and they stood there like lovers in the cold, clear moonlight just an instant, but in that lingering action of the woman there was something tender which Bradley seized upon. He asked again—

"You'll let me write to you again, won't you?"

"Certainly. I shall follow your career with the deepest interest. I wish you'd think of this alliance movement and advise me what to do. Goodby." She extended her hand.

"Good-by," he said, and his voice choked. When he turned and walked away Washington was very far away indeed and political honors cheap as dust.

XXVI.

CONGRESSIONAL LIFE.

HE found Washington less lonely for him on his return. There were many new members, and they sought each other socially and soon managed to have a good deal of talk among themselves, notwithstanding the studied slights of the old members. One member, Clancy, who grew profane at times said, "These old seeds think they're hell's captains, but I guess we can live if they don't shake hands."

Most of the members were married and lived with their families in rented houses, but others, who were too poor to bring their families or who were bachelors like Bradley, lived in boarding houses. Bradley secured a room and board in a house near the capitol, because he seemed to be nearer the centre of things when he could look out upon the dome.

It surprised him to learn how humbly most of the congressmen lived. They were quite ordinary humans in all ways. Of course some of the senators of great wealth lived in fine houses, but they were the exception, and the poorer members did not conceal their suspicion of these great men.

"It aint a question of how much a man's got," Clancy of Iowa said, "but how he got it. I've simmered the thing down to this: Living in a hash-house aint a guarantee of honesty any more than living in a four-story brown-stone is a sure sign of robbery, but it's a tolerably safe inference."

These rich senators and representatives, owners of vast coal tracts, or iron mines, or factories, rode up to the capitol with glittering turn-outs, their horses' clanking bits and jingling chains, warning pedestrians like Clancy and Talcott, to get out of the way. For the first time in his life Bradley met great wealth with all of its power. It shocked him and made him bitter.

He took little interest in the organizing of the house. His experience in Des Moines taught him to sit quietly outside the governing circle. He accepted a place on one of the minor committees and waited to see what would develop.

His life was very quiet. Nothing was done before the holidays but organize, and he found a great deal of time to study. Radbourn came back during the early weeks of the session and resumed his work.

Clancy went to the theatre very often and attended all manner of shows, especially all that were free or that came to him as a courtesy.

" I've lived where I couldn't get these things," he said, "and I propose to improve each shining hour."

Attending Congress was quite like attending the legislature. Every morning the members went up to the great building, which they soon came to ignore, except as a place to do business in. They trooped there quite like boys going to school. It was the state legislature aggrandized —noisier, more tumultuous and confusing.

In a little while, Bradley ceased to notice the difference in gilding and jim-crackery between the senate and representative ends of the corridors. He no longer noticed the distances, the pictures, or the statues in the vaulted dome, but passed through the vast rotundas with no thought of them. The magnificence of it all grew common with familiarity.

The vast mass, and roar, and motion of the hall

itself soon ceased to confuse or abase him. In proportion to membership, he doubted whether there were more able men there than in the State legislature. They were more acute politicians; they were wilier, and talked in larger terms, manipulating states instead of counties — that was all. The routine of the day was of the same general character, and gave him no trouble.

Some of the more famous of the leaders he absolutely loathed — great, bloated, swaggering, unscrupulous, treacherous tricksters. "I'll lend you my *support*," they said, as if it were something that could be loaned like a horse. He often talked them over with Radbourn, whose experience in and about Congress as a newspaper correspondent had given him an intimate knowledge of men, and had rendered him contemptuous, if not rebellious.

"The men counted party leaders are manipulators, as a matter of fact. They subordinate everything to party success. We've got to have another great political revolution to — to de-centralize and de-machinize the whole of our political method. Our system will break of its own weight; it can't go on. It is supposed to be popular, when in fact, it is getting farther and farther away from the people every year. Just see the departments.   Do you know anything about them ?"

" No, I don't," Bradley admitted.

"You're like all the rest.   Every year the army of useless clerks increases; every year the numbers of useless buildings increases.   The whole thing is appalling, and yet the people are getting apparently more helpless to reform it. Laws pile upon laws, when the real reform is to abolish laws.   Wipe out grants and special privileges.   We ought to be legislating toward equality of opportunity in the world, and here we go with McKinley bills, and the devil knows what else.   By the way, to change the subject, what has become of Milton Jennings ?   He started out to be a great Republican politician."

" Well, he lives there yet ; he's still in politics, but doesn't seem to get higher than a county office."

" He was a brilliant fellow, but he started in on the wrong side ; there is no hope for him on that side in the West."

"He's married, lives just opposite the Seminary, seems to be reasonably contented."

Radbourn turned suddenly.   "You are not married ?"

Bradley colored. · " No, I'm not."

Radbourn mused a little.   "Seems to me, I remember some talk about your marrying that little — Russell girl?"

"Well, I didn't."   Bradley had just a moment's temptation to tell Radbourn his whole secret, but he gave it up as preposterous.

Legislation was incredibly slow.

"Beats the devil how little we fellows amount to here," Clancy said one night after they had been sitting all day in their seats, while Brown of Georgia, Dixon of Maine, and others of their like had wasted hour after hour in all sorts of tedious discussions upon mere technicalities. "We can't even vote, by thunder! I'm going to make a great break one of these days and make a motion to adjourn."

Bradley laughed dutifully, for this was the ancient joke.

"It's an outrage," Clancy fumed.   The speaker had refused to recognize him and he was furious. "The speaker's got everything in his hands. Say, do you know that it's all made up the day before who's goin' to be recognized?"

"Yes, I found that out some time ago," said Bradley quietly.

"Well, I feel like making a great big kick."

"It wouldn't do any good."

"Yes, it would, it would relieve my feelings. It's a pretty how de do, to send a man here to represent his constituents and then put the whole power of the house into the hands of the speaker and the committee on rules."

Bradley's seat came between two of the old members, Samuels of Mississippi and Col. Maxwell of South Carolina, and they were constantly talking across Bradley's back or before his face, ignoring him completely. It wore on him so that he fell into the habit of sitting over beside the profane Clancy in Bidwell's seat. Bidwell occupied the leather-covered lounge behind the screen so industriously that no one else felt privileged to throw himself down there.

The drinking disgusted Bradley, and the obscene talk which he heard in snatches as he went past sickened him. The same sort of attitude toward the female clerks was expressed by a certain class of the legislators. He began to wonder if he were not abnormal in some way by reason of his repugnance to all this desolating derision of really holy things. He found that while he had less religion than these men, they had infinitely less reverence for the things which he considered sacred.

Some of the better class of members invited him to their houses and he went occasionally, and if he found them uncongenial he never went again. He could not make calls out of duty. It seemed to him that they took very little interest in the higher side of politics and some of them he found were unaware of any higher side of life.

He could not help noticing that Washington was a city full of beautiful girls. His idolatry of Miss Wilbur could not prevent him from admiring them as they streamed along the walk to church. He sometimes looked wistfully at this flood of sunny laughing life that moved by him so near and yet so completely out of his reach. He knew at such times that he had missed something sweet out of his own lonely life.

But these moments were few. He realized that there was no place in the social life of the city for him, and the librarian knew him better than the butlers in the houses of rich senators. He attended one or two public receptions and was thoroughly disgusted with the crush, and felt the essential vulgarity of the whole thing.

His life at the capital was not entirely that of the politician. He had in him capabilities for appreciating art and literature, which most of his colleagues had not. He studied upon economic problems, rather than upon partisan politics, and tried to grasp the meaning of social change and social condition, and to comprehend economic causes and tendencies. He spent many hours upon problems which were unconsciously unfitting him for partisan success.

His life was very full and happy, save for the dull hunger at his heart whenever he thought of Ida. He wrote to her still, but her replies still kept their calm, impersonal tone. One night, when he returned from the capitol, he found a letter from her enclosing some clippings.

"I have joined the Farmers' Alliance," she wrote. "I begin to believe that another great wave of thought is about to sweep over the farmers. The *spirit* of the grange did not die. It has passed on into this new organization. The difference is going to be that this new alliance of the farmers will be deeper in thought and broader in sympathy. I never believed the grange a failure. It taught people by its failure. I'm going to Kansas to speak for them there. The alliance is very strong there. This order will become political. Its leaders are very enthusiastic."

She passed on to write of other things, but Bradley was deeply affected by this news. He had heard of the alliance obscurely, but had felt that it was only an attempt to revive the old grange movement, and that it could not succeed. But her letter set him thinking.

He wrote away on a speech till nine o'clock, and then went out for his usual walk about the capitol and its grounds, which had never lost their charm, as the city itself had. He had grown into the habit of going out whenever he wished to escape the paltry decoration, the hot colors, the vitiated air, of his boarding-place and the importunities of his fellow-boarders. He went out whenever he wanted to think great and refreshing thoughts, or whenever he felt the need of beauty or the presence of life.

XXVII.

BRADLEY'S LONG-CHERISHED HOPE VANISHES.

IT had been snowing all the afternoon, and the shrubbery hung heavy and silent with heaped, clinging, feathery snow, dazzling white by contrast with the dark sustaining branches, and the yellow lamps flamed warmly amid the all-surrounding steely blue and glistening white. The damp pavements, where the snow had melted, were banded with gold and crimson from the reflected light of the lamps and the warning glare of car and carriage lights.

As Bradley breathed the pure air and walked soundlessly along the narrow paths and looked across the unflecked, untrodden snow up to the vast and silent dome, he shuddered in wordless delight. He hungered to share it with Ida. It was like fairy-land — so far removed from daylight reality; and yet the sound of sleigh-bells, the occasional shouts of coasters, and the laughter of girls added a familiar human quality to it all, and added an ache to the mysterious shuddering delight of it all. It was so evanescent; it would decay so quickly. The wind, the morning sun, would destroy it.

He walked up to the lonely esplanade, and saw the city's lights shine below him like rubies and amethysts, and saw far beyond the snow-heaped highlands, above which Jupiter hung poised, serene and lone, the king of the western sky.

How far away all this seemed from the brazen declamation, the monotonous reiterations of the reading-clerk, and from the sharp clank of the speaker's gavel! His ear wearied, his heart sick of the whole life of the farcical legislature, with its flood of corrupt bills, got back serenity and youth and repose in the presence of the snows, the silences, and the stars.

Again the impulse seized him to write to Ida and show her his whole soul; to dare and end once for all his ache of suspense. He went back to his room, and seized pen and paper. Everything he wrote seemed too formal or too presumptuous. At last he finished a short letter —

Dear Miss Wilbur : —

I do not know how to begin to say what I want to say. I am afraid of losing you out of my life by not writing, and I'm afraid if I write, I will lose you It is impossible for me to say what you've done for me. I never would have been anything more than a poor farmer, only for you. I don't want to apologize to you for telling you how much you are to me. I want to appeal to you to give me a chance to work for you; that's all. I want you to give me some hope, if you can.

I know I am asking a great deal even in that. I realize how unreasonable it is. You've only seen me a few times; and yet I'm not going to apologize for it. I must have it over with; I can't go on in this way. Won't you write to me and tell me that I can look forward to the future with hope?

Yours sincerely,

Bradley Talcott.

For the next ten days he was of little service to his country except the day he made his speech on the tariff question. It was his first set speech, and he had twenty minutes yielded to him by the gentleman from Missouri, who had charge of the bill. He had the close attention of the House, not only for his thoughts, which were fresh and direct, but also for the natural manner in which he spoke. He had lost a good deal of his "oratory," but had gained a powerful, flexible and colloquial style which made most of the orators around him seem absurd. The fine shadings of emotion and of thought in his voice struck upon the ear wearied with rancous yells and monotonous brazen declamations, with a cool and restful effect. At the close, the menbers crowded about to congratulate him upon his efforts, and for the moment he felt quite satisfied with himself.

It gave him a shock to see Ida's fateful letter lying upon the hat-rack in his boarding-house, where it had been pawed over by the whole household. He hastened to his room, and dropped into a chair with that familiar terrible numbness in his limbs, and with his heart beating so hard it shortened his breathing. He was like a man breathless with running. When his eyes fell on the writing, his hands ceased to shake, and his quick breathing fell away into a long, shuddering inspiration. He read the first page twice without moving a muscle. Then he turned the page, and finished it. It was not long, and it was very direct.

Dear Mr. Talcott:—

Your letter has moved me deeply, very deeply. I would have prevented its being written if I could. It is the greatest tribute — save one — that has ever come to me; and yet I wish I had not read it. I'm not free to make you any promise. I'm not free to correspond with you any more — now. I've been trying to find a way to tell you so indirectly, but your letter makes it necessary for me to do so directly.

The rest of the letter was an attempt to soften the blow, but it fell upon him very hard.

The possibility which he had always feared had become a fact, the hope which he had kept in the obscure processes of his thought and which had filled a vital place in his action, dropped out and left him purposeless. This hope of somehow, someway having her near to him had been the mainspring of his action and it could not be withdrawn without leaving him disabled.

He returned to the letter again, and again studying each word, each mark. He saw in it her acceptance of some other — probably Birdsell.

Then he saw that she had withdrawn the privilege — the blessed privilege — of writing to her. She was determined to go out of his life completely. At times as he imagined this strongly, his throat swelled till he could hardly breathe. He would have cried if nature had not denied him that relief.

He saw how baseless his hope had been, and he exonerated her from all blame. She had been kind and helpful till he spoiled it all by a fool's presumption. He had always exaggerated her social position and her attainments, but in the depths of his self-abasement and despair every kindness she had done him and every letter she had written took on a new significance. On every one he saw her warnings. Every meeting he had ever had with her he now went over and over with the strange pleasure one takes in bruising an aching limb.

She had never been other than reserved, impersonal in his presence. She had shown him again and again that her intimate life was not for him to know. He remembered now the peculiar look of perfect understanding which flashed between Birdsell and Ida, which troubled him at the time, but which his cursed egotism had brushed away as of no significance.

His speech lay there on the table, it was waste paper now. He had no one left to address it to. His utter loneliness came back to him. His mind went back over the line of his life till it came again into the little opening in the Wisconsin woods where the pines wept or snarled ceaselessly — till his mother died in the moan and the snarl and shadow of them. His heart went out to her as never before since Ida came into his life.

The gloom and reticence of those dark-green forests had wrought him into the reticent, serious man he was. He was not gloomy naturally, he was strong and hopeful, but this was one of those moments which appall a man, even a young man — or more properly, especially a young man.

He did not go down to dinner, but sat in his room till late; then when hunger compelled, he went out to a vast cafe, where he could be more alone. It seemed that night as if all incentive to live were gone; but he went to the session next day in a mechanical sort of a way, and each day thereafter in the same way, though he took no interest in the proceedings.

Clancy had his suspicions and had to verify them.

"Talcott, your're off y'r feed. Girl gone back on ych?"

Bradley refused to reply and Clancy took delight in spreading the story among his gang. They respected Bradley's physique too much to push him unduly, however.

Nature slowly reasserted itself, and as the weeks went by he regained his interest in the work; but the sparkle, the allurement of life, was gone, and he went about with more of the purely mechanical in his actions.

He read now every available bit of news relating to the farmers' rising in the West, in the hope that Ida's work would be mentioned in it. The papers were getting savage in their attack upon the movement in Kansas. It was said to mean repudiation; that it was a movement of the shiftless and unscrupulous citizens which destroyed the credit of the State and disturbed social conditions wantonly. The West seemed on the point of upheaval, and Kansas seemed to be the centre of the feeling of unrest.

XXVIII.

SPRING CONVENTIONS.

THE session wore along monotonously — at least to those who like Bradley took no interest in the bitter partisan wrangling — and suddenly it came upon him that spring was near. There came a couple of sunny days after three days of warm rain and the grass grew suddenly green. A robin hunting worms on the lawn laughed out audaciously one morning as Bradley went across the path. There seemed to be a mysterious awakening thrill in every plant and animal. The distant hills grew soft in outline.

A few days and the Spirea Japonica flamed out in yellow, the quince in the hedges showed its rose-colored tips of bursting blooms and on the red buds grew wonderful garnet-colored fists soon to open into beautiful palms of flowers. The gardeners got out with rakes and wheel-barrows and lazily plodded to and fro upon the beautiful seamless green of the lawns, or spaded about the flowers beds in the countless little parks of the the city.

A few days later and the old white mule and darkey driver came out upon the springing grass with the purring mower, and it made Bradley's blood leap with recollections of the haying field. The air began to grow sweet with the odor of flowers. The sky took on a warm look. The building took on a deeper blue in its shadows and the north windows became violet at noon. Brad-ley longed for the country, but the orange-colored mud of the suburbs kept him confined to the sidewalks.

On Easter Sunday the girls came out in their delicious dresses, looking dainty and sweet as the lilies each church displayed. New hats, new grasses and springing plants announced that spring had come. The "leaves of absence" indi-cated spring in the House.

As spring came on, the question of re-election began to trouble some of the members. They began to get "leave of absence on important business," and to go home to fix up their political fences. There was no sign of adjournment. It was the policy of the Republicans to keep the Democrats out of the field.

The profane Clancy was one of the first to go. He came to Bradley one day, "Say, Talcott, I wish yóu'd ask for indefinite leave for me, my fences are in a hell of a fix and besides I want to see my wife.　I'm no earthly use here —though you needn't state that in your request."

"What'll I say?"

"Oh, important business — or sickness — the baby's cutting a tooth — just as you like. It all goes."

"I guess I'll try important business. The other is too much worn."

"All right. It does beat hell the amount of sickness there is on pension bill nights and on convention week."

Clancy was a type of legislator whose idea of legislation was to have a good time and look out for re-election. Bradley, however, did not worry particularly about his re-election until he received a letter from the Judge asking him to come home and attend the convention.

"It's just as well to be on the ground," the Judge wrote; "there is a good deal of opposition developing in the north-west part of the district. Larson wants the nomination for the Legislature, and he is trying to swing the Scandinavians for Fishbein. They are making a good deal of your attitude on the pension bill, and that interview on the oleo business where you go back on your legislative vote is being circulated to do you harm."

This letter alarmed Bradley, and suddenly showed him what a fight the Judge was making. Suddenly he woke to the fact that defeat would be unwelcome. Congress had come at last to have a subtle fascination, and he loved the city and its noble buildings, its theatres, and its libraries. Since that fatal letter from Ida he had been forced to go more often to the theatres and concerts. They seemed now like necessities of life, and the thought of going back to private life was not at all pleasant. He therefore got leave of absence, and took the train for Rock River.

He did not see so much of the outside world on this return trip. His trouble came back upon him mixed, too, with something sweet which lay in the fact of a return to the West. He caught a thrill of this as the train dipped and swung round a peak on the west slope of the Alleghanies, and for a single instant the sea of sun-illumined swells and peaks of foliage broke upon the eyes and then was lost, and the train dropped down into the rising darkness of the valley.

It came to him again the next afternoon as he rode away over the wide, low swells of the prairies between Chicago and the Mississippi. It was a beautiful showery June day. A day of alternate warm rain and brilliant sunshine, and the rushing engine plunged into trailing clouds of rain only to burst forth into sunshine again with exultant shrieks of untamed energy, and listening to it one might have fancied it a living thing with capability to snuff the glorious west wind, and eyes to reflect the cool green swells of pasture.

It was a magnificent thing to step off the Chicago sleeper into the broad morning at Rock River. Soaring streamers of red and flame-color arched the eastern sky like the dome of a mighty pagoda. Birds were singing in the cool, sweet hush; roosters were crowing; the air was full of the scent of fresh leaves and succulent, springing grain. Bradley abandoned himself to the spring, and his walk up the quiet street was a keen delight. The town seemed wofully small and shabby and lifeless; but it had trees and birds and earth-smell to compensate for other things.

There was no one at the station to receive him, not even a 'bus. The station agent said:

"Guess the Judge didn't know you was comin' or he'd been down here with a band-wagon."

Mrs. Brown was in the kitchen bent above a pan of sizzling meat. A Norwegian girl with vivid blue eyes and pink and white complexion was setting the table with great precision. She smiled broadly as Bradley put his finger to his lips and crept toward Mrs. Brown, who gave a great start as she felt the clasp of his arm.

"Gracious sakes alive! Bradley Talcott!"

"Did I scare yeh?" he inquired, smiling. "Where's the Judge?"

She looked at him fondly as he held her a moment in his arms.

"He's out by the well — I think he's at work at something, for I've heard him swearing and groaning out there."

Bradley found the Judge weeding a bed of onions. He had a couple of folded newspapers under his knees and was in his shirt-sleeves. He looked like a felon condemned for life to hard manual labor.

"Judge, how are you?" called Bradley.

The Judge looked up with a scowling brow. "Hello, Brad." He wiped his hand on his thigh and rose with a groan to shake hands. "I'm slavin' again. Mrs. Brown insists on my working on the garden. How's Congress?"

"Piratical as ever. Nothing doing that ought to be done. How's everything here?"

The Judge put on his coat; "I guess I'll quit

for this time," he said, referring to the onions "Let's wash up for breakfast."

They washed at the kitchen sink as usual. Mrs. Brown watched Bradley with maternal pleasure as he hung his coat on a nail and went about in his shirt-sleeves scrubbing his face and combing his hair.

"It's good to see you around again, Bradley."

"Well, it seems good to me. Seems like old times to sit down here to your cooking with the kitchen door open and the chickens singing."

"We're all right in this county," said the Judge, referring back to politics; "but as I wrote you, it aint all clear sailing. We've got work to do. I've called the Convention at Cedarville, in order to keep some useful people in the field. We'll take dinner with old Jake Schlimgen — he's a power with the Germans."

Bradley avoided political talk as much as possible, but when on the street there seemed nothing else to talk about. Councill and Ridings assured him he was all right in the eastern part of the county, and under their flattery he grew quite cheerful. Their simple, honest admiration did him good.

On the day named Bradley and the Judge drove off up the road in a one-horse buggy. The

Judge talked spasmodically; Bradley was silent, looking about him with half-shut eyes. The wheat had clothed the brown fields; crows were flying through the soft mist that dimmed the light of the sun, but did not intercept its heat. Each hill and tree glimmered across the waves of warm air, and seemed to pulse as if alive. Blackbirds and robins and sparrows everywhere gave voice to the ecstasy which the men felt, but could not express.

The Judge roused up, slapping the horse with the reins. "It's going to be a fight; but Fishbein will be left on the first ballot by twenty-five votes."

Cedarville was wide-awake — feverishly so. The street was lined with knots of gesticulating politicians. As he alighted Bradley's friends swarmed about him with "three cheers for the Hon. Brad Talcott." He shook hands all round with unfeigned pleasure.

"Hurrah, boys, let's all go over to the Palace Hotel and have some dinner," said the Judge at last.

The rest whooped with delight. "That's the cooky, Judge."

They swarmed in upon Jake like the locusts into Egypt. They washed (some of them) in the wash-room, out of tin basins, laughing and talking in hearty clamor over the water and the comb. Others flung their nondescript wind-worn hats upon the floor, brushed their hair with their fingers and went into the dining-room as if going into a farm-kitchen in threshing time.

The girls were in a flutter of haste, and giggled and bumped against each other trying to serve the dinner to order —

"Quick as the Lord 'll let yeh."

Bradley's constituents were mostly farmers, clean-eyed and hearty. They all felt sure of success and jeered the opposition good-naturedly.

When the Judge and Bradley rode home that night, they were silent for another cause. They had been defeated on the tenth ballot, and bitter things had been said by both sides.

It was again beautiful around them, but they did not notice it. The low sun flung its level red rays of light across the flaming green of the springing grain, and lighted every western window-pane into burning squares of crimson. The train carrying the successful Waterville crowd passed them, and they waved their hats in return to their opponents' salute.

The Judge was as badly defeated as Bradley. He took it very hard. It seemed to give the

lie to all his prophecies of Democratic progress.
It seemed to him a defeat of Jeffersonian principle. He consoled himself by saying —

"Those fellows don't represent the people.
The thing to do is to bolt the convention";
and then he went on planning an independent
campaign.

Bradley maintained gloomy silence. The comment of his friends hurt him more than his defeat.
Their tone of pity cut him, and left him raw to
the gibes of his opponents. The fact that an
honorable, honest man could have enemies in his
own party was borne in upon him with merciless
force. What had he done that men should yell
in hell-like ferocity of glee over his defeat?

This defeat cut closer into the Judge's life than
anything that had come to him since the death of
his son. If Bradley had not been so blind in his
selfish suffering he would have seen how the
Judge had aged and saddened since the morning.

But the old man's vital nature would not rest
under defeat. He almost forced Bradley to issue
a card to the public announcing his independent
candidacy for Congress. Bradley had no heart
in it, however. The energy of youth seemed gone
out of him.

The Judge gathered his forces together for battle, but Bradley fled away from Rock River to escape the comments of his friends as well as his enemies. He was too raw to invite strokes of the lash. He dreaded the meeting with his colleagues at Washington, but there was a little more reserve in their comment and there were fewer who took a vital interest in his affairs.

He met Radbourn a few days after his return.

"Well," Radbourn said, "I see by the papers that your defeat in the convention was due to your advocacy of 'cranky notions.' I told you the advocacy of heresies was dangerous; I have no comfort for you. You had your choice before you. You can be a hypocrite and knuckle down to every monopoly or special act, or you can be an individual and — go out of office."

"I'll go out of office, I guess, whether I want to or not," was his bitter reply. He suffered severely for a few days with the commiseration of friends and the thinly-veiled ridicule of his political enemies, but each man was too much occupied to hold Bradley's defeat long in mind. He soon sank back into quiet, if not into repose.

As the hot weather came on, the city became almost as quiet as Rock River itself. Save taking care of the few tourists who drifted through, there was very little doing. The cars ground along ever more thinly until they might be called occasional. The trees put forth their abundance of leaf, and under them the city seemed to sleep. Congress had settled down into a dull and drowsy succession of daily adjournments and filibustering. The speaker ruled remorselessly, "counting the hats in the cloak-room to make up his quorum," his critics said.

Nothing was doing, but vast accumulations of appropriations were piling up, waiting the hurried action of the last few days of the session. The senators dawdled in and out dressed in the thinnest clothing; the House looked sparse and ineffectual.

Bradley grew depressed, and at last he became positively ill. He was depressed by the incessant relentless attacks made upon him through the *Waterville Patriot*, and by his apparently hopeless outlook. The *Patriot* published some of his radical utterances much garbled, of course, and called him "an anarchist and a socialist, a fit leader for the repudiating gang of *alleged* farmers in Kansas."

Radbourn became alarmed for him, and advised him to get indefinite leave of absence, and go home. "Go back into the haying-field; that's what you need; they won't miss you here. Go home and go out of politics, and stay out till the revolution comes; then go out and chalk death on your enemies' door."

The advice to go home was so obviously sound that Bradley took it at once. It seemed as if the atmosphere of the city would destroy him. As a matter of fact it was inactivity that was killing him. He found it so hard to exercise — except by walking, and that did not rest his over-active mind.

XXIX.

BRADLEY DISCOURAGED.

THE Judge and Mrs. Brown were alarmed at the change in him. He was gloomy and pale, but he protested he was all right.

"I'm going out on the farm. I believe it'll do me good to go out and help Councill put up his hay. It seems to me if I could get physically tired and wolfishly hungry again it would do me good."

The Judge drove him out to Councill's one afternoon. Everybody they met seemed delighted to see him. Mrs. Councill came out to the horse-block, her bare arm held up to shield her eyes.

"Well, Brad Talcott, how are yeh — anyway? you're jest in time to help me pick berries."

Bradley sprang out and shook hands with hearty force. "Give us your dish."

"H'yare!" yelled Councill from the load of hay he was driving in, "I can use you out here."

"Oh, you go long," replied Mrs. Councill. "He's got better company and a better job."

Out in the berry patch he talked over the neighborhood affairs and picked berries and killed mosquitoes, while the wind wandered by with rustling steps on the lombardy poplar leaves. The locusts sang and the grasshoppers snapped their shining wings. It was a blessed relief to his troubled older self, for he slipped back into the more tranquil life of his boyhood.

At supper he sat at the table with the men, whose wet shirts showed how fierce the work of pitching the hay had been.

"Be yeh out f'r play or work, Brad?" asked Councill.

"Work, need a hand."

"They's plenty to do — but I'm afraid you can't take a hand's place for a while."

"Try me and see."

They were all curious to hear of Washington, but he was more inclined to talk of the crops and the cattle.

He went to sleep that night in the bare garrett with the men and woke the next morning at sunrise at sound of Councill's voice calling him, just as he used to do when he was a hired man.

"*Hello !* Brad.   Roll out ! ' "

He went down to breakfast, sloshed his face at the cistern pump and was ready to eat when the men came in.

"We live jest the same as ever, Brad," said Mrs. Councill, "you'll haf to put up with it jest as if y' wa'n't a Congressman."

"I guess he can stand a few days what we stand all the while," laughed Councill.

There was a good deal of banter during the meal about "downing" the Congressman.

Bradley's physical pride was roused and he took his place in the field determined to show them their mistake.   Night came bringing weariness that was exhaustion, and next morning he was too lame to lift a fork.   It emphasized the unnatural inactivity into which he had fallen.

He improved physically and by the end of the week was able to pitch hay with the rest.   The Judge drove up for him on Saturday afternoon, and found him pitching hay upon the stack behind the wind-break, wet with sweat and covered with timothy bloom.   Councill was stacking.

"Hello, Congressman," called the Judge.

"Get off 'n take right hold, Judge," said Councill.   "A Judge aint no better'n a Congressman, not a darn bit."

"I'll take a hand at the table," the Judge replied.

"I've had about enough of it," Bradley said to him privately while Councill was putting his team up. "I'm better, but it begins to seem like a waste of time."

They drove home that night through the still, warm, star-lit air, like father and son in slow talk of the future.

The Judge told of the plan for the fall campaign, to which Bradley listened silently.

"We'll win yet if you only keep your grit."

He planned also a broadening out of their law business. A new block had just been built and they were to take two adjoining rooms.

"You need a library of your own and a chance to work where you wont be disturbed. I'll do the consulting business and leave you the business in court." For a time Bradley was interested and occupied in moving into the new office and in getting in some new books and arranging the shelves.

But the narrowness, the quiet, the mental stagnation of the life of Rock River settled down on him at last. There were days when he walked the floor of the office, wild with dismay over his prospect. How could he settle down again to this life of the country lawyer? The honors and ease that accompanied his office, the larger horizon of Washington, had ruined him for life in Rock River. Love might have enabled him to bear it, but he had given up the thought of marriage and he longed for the larger life he had left.

There was a sorrowful scene when the Judge read for the first time Bradley's letter of withdrawal from the canvass in the cause. The Judge was deeply hurt because he had not been consulted, and was depressed by Bradley's despair. He tried to reason with him, but Bradley was in no mood to reason.

"I'm out of it, Judge; it aint any use to go on; I'm beaten; that's all there is about it; we'd only get a minority vote, and show how weak we are; I'm a failure as a politician, and every other way. I give it up."

The Judge sat staring at him without words to express his terrible disappointment and alarm, for the condition into which his lieutenant had sunk scared him and he communicated his fear to Mrs. Brown.

They discussed the matter that night just before going to sleep. Bradley heard their voices still mumbling on when he sank to sleep.

"You don't suppose, Mrs. Brown," the Judge

said a little timidly, "it can't be possible it's a woman " —

"If it had been, Mr. Brown, he would have told me," she said convincingly. "It's just the heat, and then his defeat has told on him more than you admit."

"If I felt sure of that, Mrs. Brown," the Judge said in answer, "but I don't. All ambition seems to have gone out of him. I hate to acknowledge myself mistaken in the man. I've believed in Brad. I am alarmed about him. He aint right; I've a good mind to send him down to St. Louis and Kansas City on some collection cases."

"I think he'd better do that, Mr. Brown, if he will go."

"Oh, he'll go; he wants to get away from the campaign; it seems to wear upon him some way; he avoids everybody, and won't speak of it at all if he can help it."

As a matter of fact, Bradley was very glad to accept the offer, and made himself ready to go with more of his old-time interest than he had shown since his sickness. The Judge brightened up also, and said to him, as he was about to step into the train: "Now, Brad, don't hurry back; take your time, and enjoy yourself. Go around by Chicago, if you feel like it."

After the train pulled out, and they were riding home, the Judge said to his wife: "Mrs. Brown, you must take good care of me now. I want to live to see a party grow up to the level of that young man's ideas. This firm is crippled, but it aint in the hands of a receiver, Mrs. Brown."

"I'll be the receiver," Mrs. Brown said.

The Judge shifted the lines into his left hand.

The horse fell into a walk. "Mrs. Brown, if this weren't a public road, I'd be tempted to put my strong right arm around you and give you a squeeze."

"I don't see any one looking," she said, and her eyes took on a pathetic suggestion of the roguishness her face must have worn in girlhood.

He put his arm over her shoulder, and gave her a great hug. After that she laid her head against his shoulder, and cried a little; the Judge sighed.

"Well, we'll have to get reconciled to being alone, I suppose; we can't expect to keep him always."

XXX.

THE GREAT ROUND UP.

DURING his stay in St. Louis Bradley found the papers filled with the Alliance movement in Kansas, and looked for Ida's name each morning. She was in the western part of the State, but moving eastward ; and when a few days later he saw her announced in the Kansas City morning papers to speak at the great "round up" at Chiquita, he packed his valise on the sudden impulse, and started on the next train, determined to hear her speak once more at least.

It was just noon when he alighted from the train at Chiquita. The day was dry, hazy, resplendent October — a genuine Western day. The wind was strong but amiable, and was full of the smell of corn and of that warm, pungent, smoky odor which forms the Indian summer atmosphere of the West. The wind rushed up the broad street past him, carrying the dust and leaves in its powerful clutches, and laying strong hands upon his broad back. The sky was absolutely without speck, but a pale mist seemed to dim the radiance of the sun, and lent a milky white tone to the blue of the sky.

As he moved slowly off up the street, he studied the town and the people from the standpoint his life in the East had given him. Everywhere was an air of security. Men moved slower. Their faces were less anxious and more placid; they had leisure to talk as they met at the shop door. The *boss* seemed farther away. But all this security did not conceal the poverty which he now saw everywhere. The houses were mainly low, unpainted buildings, containing only three or four cramped rooms. They were a little smarter in appearance than the country type, but not much more commodious.

"I wonder if you are one of the speakers here to-day," said a voice behind him.

Bradley turned, and saw a small man with a stubby mustache, under whose derby hat-rim a pair of round black eyes shone with a keen glitter.

"No, sir, I'm not."

"Beg pardon, no harm done. Saw you get off with your valise; knew you wern't a native by the cut o' y'r jib. Excuse me, I hope?"

"Certainly; I'm just on to see some friends here."

"*Precisely*; I'm up from Kansas City to see the big 'round up,' as they call it. Here's my card. I represent what our Alliance friends call the 'plutocratic press.'" His card stated that his name was Mr. Davis, and that he represented the *Chronicle*. "I'm afraid the parade must be over by this time, but I missed my train. Perhaps we had better step along a little."

They had reached the main street, a broad avenue which ran north and south across a gentle swell in the prairie. There were a great many people on the sidewalks, and teams were moving in various directions slowly and in apparent confusion.

"Let's go over here to the Commercial House; that's the headquarters of all the brethren," said Davis.

They went across the street to the Commercial House, which they found full of men in groups, talking very earnestly, but quietly. Most of them were farmer-like looking figures, big and brown, and dressed in worn, faded clothing. Here and there was a young man, with a broad white hat, a gay handkerchief knotted loosely about his neck. On all sides could be heard the same soft, slightly drawling speech of the Kansan.

They went up to a little balcony which projected over the walk. There were four or five other young fellows seated there already. They all wore the wide, straight-brim hats, with the crowns uncrushed, which struck Bradley as being a characteristic Kansas hat. Some of them were magnificent-looking fellows, keen, wholesome, and picturesque in their dress.

"Excuse me now, gentlemen," said Davis. whipping out his note-book. "I'm the reporter. and here they come."

Up the broad street, under that soaring sky, from their homes upon a magnificently fertile soil, came the long procession of revolting farmers. There were no bands to lead them : no fluttering of gay flags ; no cheers from the bystanders. They rode in grim silence for the most part, as if at a funeral of their dead hopes — as if their mere presence were a protest.

Everywhere the same color predominated — a russet brown. Their faces were bronzed and thin.

Their beards were long and faded, and tangled like autumn corn silk. Their gaunt, gnarled, and knotted hands held the reins over their equally sad and sober teams. The women looked worn and thin, and sat bent forward over the children in their laps. The dust had settled upon their ill-fitting dresses. There were no smart carriages, no touch of gay paint, no glittering new harnesses; the whole procession was keyed down among the most desolate and sorrowful grays, browns, and drabs.

Slowly they moved past. In some of the wagons, banners, rudely painted on cotton cloth, uttered the farmers' protest in words.

"Good God!" said Davis, as he dashed away at his writing. "Did you ever see such a funeral in your life? See that banner!"

NO MORE FOURTEEN-CENT CORN.

"Go on voting for the monopolists in the Republican party, and you'll have ten-cent corn," Davis growled to the farmer who carried the banner.

LET US LEGISLATE FOR THE POOR, NOT FOR
THE BANKERS.

"That's the ticket. *Suppose* we do try that a while."

Down with Monopolies.

"All right, down with them; you're the doctor."

Free Trade, Free Land, Money at Cost,
Transportation at Cost.

"Now you *are* shouting, brother. See that old woman in the sunbonnet carrying that banner! Now, don't make no mistake; the old girl knows just what that means; that's *right!* They're all reading these days, even the babies. See that old father in Israel with a faded beard wagging up and down!"

If We Don't Own the Railways, the
Railways Will Own Us.

"Cert. That's right, daddy; stick to your text."

Abolish the National Banks.

"I guess you've got to wipe out *both* old parties to do that," said Davis, writing away furiously.

"That's *right!*" said one of the young fellows on the balcony, "and we'll do it in 1892."

"All right; I don't care a continental tee-cumpsy."

Equal Rights to All is as Dear to the
Heart of the Farmer as it was in
the Days of our Forefathers.

"Well, now, sure you mean that — that's all. Stop talking, and act. If you'll go ahead and carry out that motto, you'll do a work that has never been done in America or any other country on the face of the earth," said Davis. "That's the end of it; let's go down on the street."

Bradley had remained perfectly silent through it all. As these farmers passed before his eyes, there came into his mind vast conceptions that thrilled him till he shuddered — a realization that that here was an army of veterans, men grown old in the ferocious struggle against injustice and the apparent niggardliness of nature, — a grim and terrible battle-line. It was made up, throughout its entire length, of old or middle-aged men and women with stooping shoulders, and eyes dim with toil and suffering. There was nothing of lovely girlhood or elastic, smiling boyhood; not a touch of color or grace in the whole line of march. It was sombre, silent, ominous, and resolute.

It appeared to him the most pathetic, tragic, and desperate revolt against oppression and wrong ever made by the American farmer. It was the Grange movement broadened, deepened, and made more desperate and wide-reaching by changing conditions.

"Well! If they ain't a calamity crowd," sneered a flashily dressed man who stood in the doorway of a jeweler shop.

Bradley's indignation flared out against him. He stammered in trying to speak. "Calamity! What right have *you* got to sneer at men like that? A man that can sneer at such an exhibition of poverty and hard work and poor pay as that, is a damned scoundrel."

"That's right," cheered Davis, "all they needed in that procession was a few cannon or cans of dynamite. Then the parasites and boomers of this State wouldn't be so chipper in their remarks."

At Davis' suggestion they went off down the street, joining the crowd on the sidewalk, which was streaming away towards the fair grounds. A roasted ox was to be served there, and speeches were to follow. The road kept on to the south, down over the gentle slope, and turned aside under the jack-oaks, and led through a wooden gate into an enclosure which was used for the county fair. Down under the great shed by the side of the race-track the people swarmed in thousands.

When Bradley came near he saw that they were all standing about the rude tables under the shed, behind which were men and women busily hewing off great lumps of beef and mutton, and slicing fat slabs of bread, which were snatched and carried away in little paper plates by the hungry people. Here and there beside their wagons, families were eating a dinner of their own.

He was accustomed to gatherings of farmers, but these crowds appealed to him in a strange way.

The same sober color predominated. There was a little more life and gayety in their speech here. Their grim, harsh faces relaxed a little, and now and then broke into unwonted smiles as they stood about devouring their food and discussing the meeting, which they counted a success. Everywhere were hearty handshaking and fraternal greetings.

All about the grounds there stood feeble women in ill-fitting clothes, with tired children in their aching arms, a dull pain in their weakened loins. Bradley did nothing but absorb it all and wonder why such festivals had ever seemed mirthful and happy to him. He wondered if there used to be so many tired faces at the Grange picnics in Iowa. Were the farmers really less comfortable and happy, or had he simply grown clearsighted? He ended by believing in both causes.

Kansas as it stood there was Democratic. Poverty has few distinctions among its victims. The negro stood close beside his white brother in adversity, and there was a certain relation and resemblance in their stiffened walk, poor clothing, and dumb, imploring, empty hands. There lay in the whole scene something tremendous, something pathetic. It had the majesty, if not the volcanic energy, of the rise of the peasants of the Vendée.

After the dinner was eaten, the people gradually took their seats on the grandstand, facing a platform upon which the people were already assembled. Bradley looked about for Ida, but she had not come. The choir amused the people with a few Alliance songs, whose character may be indicated by their titles: "Join the Alliance Step," "Get off the Fence, Brother," "We're Marching Along," etc.

The people were watching eagerly for Ida's appearance; and when she came in view, escorted by the chairman and by the far-famed farmer legislator of Kansas, they broke into applause so hearty, there could be no doubt of their love for her and for the Sage of Medicine Lodge. The people on the platform swarmed about to greet them, and hid her from sight.

As Ida rose to speak now, it was in the broad light of the present day. No dapple of shadows was there, no rustle of leaves, no green, mossy trunks of trees. She stood on a platform facing five thousand faces under a shed-like roof. There was poetry here, but it was one of the modern contemporaneous sort. It was in the significance of this rebellion, in the attention of these people turned toward her.

She was changed too. She was now a mature woman. There was nothing girlish about her talk or her manner. There was decision in the tones of her voice, and a sense of power in the poise of her head and in the lofty gesture of her hand. She no longer made a speech. She talked straight at her audiences.

"I wish the whole world could see this meeting," she said, "and understand it for what it is. It is an *expression* of a movement, not the movement itself. It is a demand; but the revolt that lies back of the demand is greater than the expression of it. The demand, the expression, may change, the form of our whole movement may pass away; but the spirit that makes it great, that carries it forward, is invincible and imperishable. All the ages have contributed to this movement. It is an outgrowth of the past.

"The heart and centre of this movement is a demand for justice, not for ourselves alone, but for the toiling poor wherever found. If this movement is higher and deeper and broader than the Grange was, it is because its sympathies are broader. With me, it is no longer a question of legislating for the farmer; it is a question of the abolition of industrial slavery."

The tremendous cheer which broke forth at this point showed that the conception of the movement had widened in the minds of the people themselves; it was no longer a class movement. It stirred Bradley as if some vast electric wind had blown upon him.

"Wherever a man is robbed, wherever a man toils and the fruits of his toils are taken from him: wherever the frosty lash of winter stings or the tear of poverty scalds, there the principle of our order reaches. [Applause, and cries, "That's right!" "Justice!"]

"Yes, justice is our plea. Justice to the coal-miners, justice to the mechanics, justice to women, and justice to the negro. I tell you, my friends, we're just coming to see what our movement means. We're just coming to understand what the fundamental principle of our order means : *Equal rights to all, and special privileges to none.*

"My Democratic brother," she cried, turning to her right, as if talking to Bradley, "you're fond of stating that principle, but do you know what it means? Think of it a moment, — Equal rights to all, special privileges to none. That means no more national banks [the cheering at this point was deafening and prolonged]; no more special privileges to issue money based on the nation's indebtedness. It means money issued direct from the government and based upon the nation's resources. [Cheers and cries of "That's right!" from all over the vast audience.]

" Equal rights to all, means no more land grants to railways; no more giving away of franchises; no more monopolies of the city streets; no more charters given to railway kings and telephone magnates. It means that the monopoly of food and intelligence must cease.

"Equal rights to all! That means equal rights to the natural world, and to the value produced by the aggregation of men. It means no more lumber kings [applause], coal kings, and oil kings — we propose to dethrone them all."

The people turned to each other with shining

faces. She was thrilling them by her passionate, simple utterance of their innermost thoughts.

"Equal rights to all! That means equal rights to women, to the negro, to the Chinese, to the Irish, to everybody that to-day is hedged in by class prejudice, or by the walls of caste."

While she spoke Bradley had eyes for nothing else; but when she sat down to wild applause, and the choir rose to sing, he turned his eyes back over the audience, banked there in rows on the hard, wooden seats, and got again the same thrill of majesty and of desolation. There was the same absence of beauty, youth, color, and grace that he had noticed in the procession. Everywhere worn and weary women in sombre dresses, a wistful light in their faces, as if they felt dimly the difference between the lithe and beautiful figure of the girl and their own stiffened joints and emaciated forms.

The crowd as a whole sat silent, listening intently, their eyes fixed upon the speaker. They were there for a purpose; they were there to find out why it was that their toil, their sobriety, their rigid economy, their deprivation, left them at middle life with distorted and stiffened limbs, gray hair, and empty hands. They were terribly in earnest. Here was poverty without liquor. There was no trace of it to be seen or smelled. Never before in the history of the world had such a meeting been seen, and something of its mighty significance got hold of Bradley as his eyes rolled over the faces before him.

The music, which set them wild with enthusiasm, was of the simplest and most stirring sort. The fact that it pleased them so much showed how barren their lives were of music and color and light.

After the applause had subsided, the chairman came forward to make an announcement: "To-night we'll have with us again the famous son of the soil, *our* Jerry — Jerry Simpson, the Sockless Sage of Medicine Lodge." This brought out a round of cheers for Jerry, and the meeting rose.

The people pressed forward to speak a word to Ida; and Bradley, yielding to the pressure of the crowd, was carried forward with it. It stirred him very deeply to see the love and admiration they all felt for her. On all sides he heard words of affection which came straight from the heart. Their utter sincerity could not be doubted. He knew he ought to turn and go away before she saw him, but he could not.

Something in his face attracted a grizzly old farmer, who was moving along beside him, and he turned with a beaming look.

"How's that for a speech, eh? Did y' ever hear the like of it?"

"No, I never did. It was great."

"Ain't she a wonder, now? D' you s'pose there's another woman like her in the world?"

Bradley shook his head. He was sure of that.

A gaunt old woman, who wore a dark green-check sunbonnet hanging at the back of her head, put in a word.

"Shows what a woman can do if y' give 'er a chance."

"Hello, Sister Slocum, you're always on hand."

"Like a sore thumb, Brother Tobey, an' I don't know of any one got a bigger interest in downin' the plutes than the farmers' wives, do you?"

It was pathetic, it was unforgettable, to see these people as they stood beside the rounded, supple, splendid figure of the speaker and took her strong, smooth hand in their work-scarred, leathery palms — these women of many children and never-ending work, bent by toil above the wash-tub and the churn, shut out from all things that humanize and make living something more than a brute struggle against hunger and cold.

They clung to the girl's hand, gazing at her with wistful eyes. It seemed as if they could not bear to let her go out of their lives again. Ida greeted them smilingly, but her face was quivering with a sadness which she could hardly control. She had not yet seen Bradley's approach. He pushed on desperately toward her. At length, as the crowd began to thin out, he moved up and thrust his long arm in over the shoulders of the women.

"Won't you shake hands with me, too?" he said, and his voice trembled.

She turned quickly, and her face flashed into a smile — a smile different, somehow, from that with which she had greeted the others, and they saw it. It warmed his melancholy soul like a sudden ray of June sunlight.

Her hand met his, strong and firm in its grasp. "Ah! Mr. Talcott, I'm glad to see you."

The farmers' wives began to leave, saying good-by over and over again, clinging to her hand as if they could not let her go — as they would cling to sunlight.

"We may never see you again, dearie," one old

lady said, "but we never'll forgit yeh. You've helped us. I reckon life won't seem quite so tough now. We kind o' see a glimmer of a way out."

The tears were on her face, and Ida put her arms about the old lady's neck and kissed her, and then turned away, unable to speak. The chairman, followed by Bradley and Ida, made his way down the steps and out on the grounds, where the streams of people were setting back toward the city. The chairman placed Miss Wilbur in a carriage, and said, " I'll see you at the hotel."

" Won't you ride ? " she asked.

" No, thank you," he replied, with a jovial gleam in his eyes, and Ida said no more in protest.

"Well, Brother Talcott, what do you think of such a meeting as that?" she asked, after the carriage started, turning upon him with sudden intensity.

" It was like that first meeting of the Grange, when I heard you speak first, only this is more earnest — more desperate, I should say."

" Yes, these people *are* desperate. It is impossible for the world to realize the earnestness of these farmers. Just see the interest the women-folks take in it ! No other movement in history — not even the anti-slavery cause — appealed to the women like this movement here in Kansas. Why it's, — Sometimes I go home and walk the floor like a crazy woman — I get so wrought up over it. While our two great parties split hairs on the tariff, people starve. The time has come for rebellion."

Bradley was silent. He sympathized with her feeling, but he could not see very much hope in a revolt.

Her eyes glowed with the fire of prophecy. Bradley gazed at her with apprehensive eyes. She seemed unwholesomely excited. But she broke into a hearty laugh, and said : " You stare. Well, I won't lecture any more to you. How did you leave everything back in dear old Iowa?"

"Why aren't you back there? Don't our farmers need you there just the same as they do here ? "

"No, this is the State to work in this year. Next year in Iowa. What did you do in Washington?"

" Nothing," he replied ; and there was something silencing in his voice.

She glanced at his face sharply. She hesitated an instant, then asked :—

"Do you go back?"

"No, my political career is ended. I was knifed in the convention."

"You are young."

"I'm not young enough to outgrow such a defeat as that. I'm done."

This mood seemed singularly unlike him, as she had known him before. She seized upon the situation.

"Come with us. There is more wool and flax in the fields," she quoted.

"I can't. I don't see things as you do — I mean I don't see any cure."

She laid her hand on his arm. "I'm going to convert you. Will you attend one more meeting with me?"

"I'll go wherever you say," he answered, inconsistently.

"That's very pleasant, but it hardly becomes your character," she replied, gravely. "Call at the hotel to-morrow night, and I'll take you with me. It'll show you what the people are doing, and what I'm doing. You're to ask no questions, but just make yourself ready to go."

Bradley's mind was in a whirl. Ida seemed so different — not at all like that last letter she had written to him. He felt rather than perceived the change in her. An indefinite and unreasonable exultation filled his eyes with light. In the privacy of his room he sang a few notes before he realized what he was doing. His gloomy sky had let fall a sudden ray of dazzling sunshine.

XXXI.

IDA SHOWS BRADLEY THE WAY OUT.

HE did not see her again till the next afternoon. She came out into the ante-room in the hotel looking so lovely he could hardly believe his good fortune.

" Now you are in my hands, Mr. Talcott."

He noticed that she did not call him " Brother" Talcott. He was as boyish and timid as ever, subdued by her presence. He followed her out to the omnibus in a daze of delight. He really had nothing to say. The poverty of his mind was astounding to him. He had forgotten all his ideas, but he was very content to have it so.

She, however, did not seem at all self-conscious. She wore a large cloak and warm gloves, and under the wide rim of her black hat her face was like silver and her eyes like stars. A delicate perfume came from her dress, and reached him across the carriage. He had taken a seat opposite her, and gazed at her in speechless contentment. He could think of nothing else to do or say.

"It takes about an hour to go down," she said, as they alighted and stood waiting for the train, "and then the 'college' is some distance away from the station."

It was an unspeakable pleasure to sit beside her in the train and listen to her talk. It was one of the things he had dreamed of so many times, but had really never dared to expect.

"The reason I want you to attend this meeting is because the schoolhouse, after all, is the place where a real reform among the farmers must have its base. It is work in the schoolhouses that has prepared the way for the overturn in Kansas this year. I'd like to see you working with us," she said, turning suddenly towards him.

"I would if I felt as you do about it, but I can't."

"Why not? You're really one of us. Your letters showed me that. Why can't you work with us?"

"Because I"— he hesitated for a moment. "You see, I began by being a Republican; then I went into the Independent Republican Convention; then into the Democratic Independent Convention;

then I ran for Congress as a Democrat. I was elected to stay at home, as you know, because I was too 'radical' for Democracy. I tried to put principle above spoils. I'm a Democrat to-day, but they won't have me ; so I'm done. I can't go into your party."

"That doesn't appeal to me as a reason," she insisted. She wanted his real reason.

"Well, I'll tell you : because it looks like a last resort. It would look as though, after having been kicked out of both parties, I had gone into the third party out of revenge."

"Well, I see some force in that. But still, there isn't any other place for a man who really thinks, except in a reform party. Do you know, I think it was providential that you were defeated." She turned to him now, and there was something in the nearness of her face that awed him. "Your letters to me told me more than you knew. I read beneath the lines ; I saw how nearly the atmos- phere of Congress had ruined you. The greed of office had got hold of you, now hadn't it ?"

He dropped his eyes. "Something got hold of me," he said at length, "but I can't indorse the principles of your party, and you wouldn't have me " —

"Can't you indorse any of them?"

"Yes, I think so."

"Well, then, be with us to that extent."

"I couldn't do that. I couldn't work for a party whose principles" —

"Can you indorse *all* of the Democratic platform?"

"No," he confessed, after a pause.

"Then, it seems to me you're inconsistent. Why do you hold out against us? Now, that seems to me like the 'woman's talk' men are always flinging up at us."

Bradley was silent. His action, like his reasons, would not bear close inspection. He felt that she had driven him into a close corner.

Ida took a new direction. "Oh, it's glorious to be in such a revolution. I never was so happy in my life. Happy and sad too! I never was so sad. Now *that's* like a woman, isn't it? What I really mean is that I never saw so clearly the poverty and helplessness of the people before, and that makes me all the happier to think I can do something for them." She laid her hand on his arm. "Do you know what is the matter with you? I do. You've trusted politicians. You think all is destroyed because they've failed you. You think, even to-night, that they move things; but I tell you, brother, they're only the puppets. When the people really begin to think, they'll sweep these puppets from the boards, and rise to the stage of action themselves."

Her voice took on the touch of the orator's oratund as she spoke, but there was a look of deep sincerity of conviction that was almost prophecy on her face, which seemed to grow paler with the intensity of her utterance.

Bradley sat silently looking at her with his big brown eyes. He was wishing she wouldn't call him brother, and take that impersonal tone with him.

She colored a little, and dropped her eyes suddenly. "There I go again! I *must* keep the oratorical tone out of my voice. I don't like to hear it myself; but it's election time, you see, and we're all tense with the excitement of it. Don't mind my preaching at you, will you?"

"I like it," said Bradley, smiling. He had a beautiful smile, she noticed; and he looked so big and strong and thoughtful, she suddenly grew a little timid before him. Perhaps he had some unspoken reasons why he had not joined the movement.

The warning whistle of the engine announced they were nearing a station, and the brakeman shouted in the door, "Muddy Brook, *Muddy Brook!*"

The wind was strong and cold as they stepped out upon the platform.   It was nearly six o'clock, and quite dark.   They stood for a few moments in the lee of the one-room station, looking about in the obscurity.

"Well, what are we to do now?" Bradley inquired.

She seemed at a loss.   "Really, I don't know. Colonel Barker was to meet me here, I believe."

Bradley took her arm.   "There's a light up there in the cold," he said.   "Let's go for that; and if you'll tell me the name of the schoolhouse, I'll see that we get a team, and get out there."

She resigned herself to his custody at once, and Bradley's spirits rose.   He grew quite facetious and talkative for him.

"It seems to me that's a store up there; must be a town near by.   Perhaps *this* is a town.   Two houses on one side and three houses on the other make a town in the West.   We must get some supper, too; any provision for that?"

"No, I left the whole matter in Colonel Barker's hands."

The road ran up the huge treeless swell of prairie toward the lighted windows of a grocery store.

"Somebody alive in the store; let's go in, and ask for Colonel Barker."

They stumbled over the frozen ground to the door, and entered.

The store smelled of apples, onions, codfish, and kerosene, in the usual way, and was dimly lighted with lamps placed on brackets against the shelves. There were several farmers standing by the stove, while the salesman bustled about. Bradley asked if Colonel Barker had been in.

"Hain't seen him," replied one old farmer, eying Ida closely.

"Is there a place to get a bit of supper near?"

"Yes, sir," the salesman said, with emphasis; "right across the road at the hotel. You can't get a better meal in the State for the same amount of money."

Bradley again took Ida's arm, and they crossed the street and entered a gate on which was a sign, "Hotel; meals twenty-five cents." Bradley knocked on the door, but there was no reply.

After waiting a decent while, he said, "If it's a hotel, we might as well go right in without knocking."

They entered a bare little room whose only resemblance to a hotel bar-room was its rusty cannon stove set in the midst of a box of sawdust, and a map of Kansas hanging on the wall. Bradley knocked on the inner door, and it was opened by a faded little woman with a sad face.

"We'd like supper for two," Bradley said, in a loud voice. Someway he felt that the woman must be hard of hearing.

"All right!" she replied, and moved forward to the stove, which she rattled in order to give her time to scrutinize Ida, who sat on the lounge by the window. "Lay off your things, won't yeh?"

Bradley helped Ida to lay off her cloak. It was incredible what pleasure it gave him to do these little things for her. He left her a few minutes to go out and look up the matter of the team. When he came back, he found her listening to the old woman, who was asking her if she ever happened to know John Weldon.

"Don't s'pose you do; but you go round so much, I didn't know but what you'd come acrost him. He's my sister Ann's husband. Last I heard of him he was in Iowa, somewhere."

She talked like a clock. Each word followed the other at regular intervals, and without any special emphasis. Ida was really not hearing her. She was seeing her. After she went out, Ida turned to Bradley.

"Poor soul! Generations of toil and lonely life are in that woman's mind and body ; and look at this room ! The great majority of farmhouses I go into are like this : bare walls, with scarcely a single beautiful thing in them. Any sober, industrious person can get a home — like this !" she ended, bitterly. "When I was a girl, I didn't notice these things. I don't think farm-life was so hard; anyhow, I had no comparative ideas on the matter."

"You can come right out to supper !" announced the landlady ; and they went out into the kitchen, where the table sat. It was lighted with a kerosene lamp that threw dull-blue shadows among the dishes, and dazzled the eyes of the eaters with its horizontal rays of light. The table had a large quantity of boiled beef and potatoes and butter, which each person was evidently expected to hew off for himself. The dessert was pumpkin-pie, which they both greeted with smiles.

"Ah, that looks like the pie mother made," Ida exulted, as the landlady put it down.

"Waal, I'd know. Seems to me the crust is a

lectle too short. I've ben havin' pretty good luck lately ; but this pumpkin weren't just the very best. It was one of them thin-rinded ones, you know. Pumpkins weren't extry good ; weren't thunder enough, I guess, this summer."

After supper Bradley went out, leaving Ida with the landlady, who was delighted with her listener. Ida, however, only sat studying her work-worn frame. She could not listen.

" Here's our team," called Bradley, coming to Ida's relief a few minutes later. The mistress of the house had got launched on a description of her sister's family in Des Moines, and was apparently good for the entire evening.

" It ain't a very gay rig ; but it's the best I could do," Bradley explained, as he helped her in and tucked the quilts about her. " I had to skirmish in two or three houses to get these quilts, for the wind is sharp ; you'll need them."

" Thank you ; I'm afraid you've given me more than my share."

There was only one seat, and Bradley took his place beside Ida, while the driver crouched on the bottom of the clattering old democrat wagon. Ida was concerned for him.

" Haven't you another seat ? " she inquired.

"No m'm. I don't need any," he replied, in a slow drawl. "I tried to borrow one from Sam Smalley, but they're all usin' theirs. I'd jest as soon set here."

There was something singularly attractive in his voice — a simplicity and candor like a child's, and a suggestion of weakness that went straight to Ida's womanly heart. She could not see how he looked ; only his shapeless hat, which hung limply about his temples, could be seen.

"But you'll get cold."

"Oh, no m'm ; I'm used to it. Half the time I don't wear no gloves in winter 'less I'm handlin' things with snow on 'em," he said, to reassure her.

They moved off down the side hill to the north, the keen wind in their faces. There was no moon, and it was very dark, notwithstanding the light of the stars.

"How beautiful it is to-night!" said Ida, in a low voice.

"Magnificent!" Bradley replied ; but he meant more than the stars. The team started up, and the worn old seat swayed from side to side perilously. Bradley put his arm around, and grasped the end of the seat on the other side,

"I'm afraid you'll fall out," he hastened to explain. She said nothing, and they rode on.

The driver babbled away in his childlike fashion, telling them of his life and the work he was doing. He showed that the Alliance education had reached him, and that he had found time to attend many such meetings, though he could find little time to read.

They climbed the slope on the other side of the bridge, and entered upon the vast rolling prairie, whose dim swells rose and fell against the stars. The roads were frightful—gullied with rain, and full of bowlders on the hillside. The darkness added a sort of wild charm and mystery to it all.

"How lonesome it all is! What a terrible place to live!" said Ida with a shudder.

"Civilization hasn't made much of an impress here, that's sure. How long has this prairie been settled?" he asked the driver.

"'Bout twenty-two years."

"Twenty-two years! Good Heavens! It looks as if it hadn't been settled two years."

"And these farms are mortgaged, too?" said Ida.

"Most of 'em," said the driver. "But it

ain't s' bad here as it is out in Lane County. They're *all* mortgaged out there. I lost a farm out there; I sunk nine hundred and fifty dollars out there!"

He said this as if it were a million that he had lost, and he prattled away, telling his pitiful, tragic life — a life of incessant toil and hardship. Men cheated and trampled upon him; society and government ignored him; science and religion never knew him, and cared nothing for him — and yet he bore it all with uncomplaining heroism.

There was something in his way of telling his story that made the hearts of his hearers ache. Ida glanced up at Bradley now and then, at the most dramatic points, and they seemed to grow nearer together in their sympathy.

"There's the schoolhouse," said the driver, suddenly pointing at a dim red light ahead. It looked to be on the other side of a wide ravine. They had been riding for nearly an hour across the treeless swells of prairie, and the wind had penetrated their very blood. Ida was shivering, and Bradley was suffering with her out of sympathy. Suddenly the schoolhouse loomed upon their eyes. It was only a few rods away, but in the darkness it had seemed farther. It was a bare little box, set on the wind-swept crest of a hill, not a tree to shelter it from the winds of winter or the sun of summer. Teams were hitched about at the fences, and others could be heard on the hard ground, clattering along the lanes. Men coming across the fields on foot could be heard talking. The plain seemed cold and desolate and illimitable.

Bradley helped Ida to alight, and hurried her towards the open door, from which a dull red light streamed and the hum of talk came forth. They found the room full of men and women — the women all on one side of the room and the men mainly on the other, or standing about the huge cannon stove, that was filled with soft coal, sending out a flood of heat and gas. The people stopped talking when they saw the strangers enter, and gazed at them curiously.

Then a tall man, with a military cut of beard, pushed his way forward.

"Good-evenin', Sisto' Wilboo, I'm right glad to see you."

"I am glad to see you, Brother Barker."

"I must apologize fo' not coming myself."

"This is Mr. Talcott," Ida interrupted, introducing Bradley.

"Glad to meet you, Brotho' Talcott. As I was sayin', Sisto' Wilboo, I was late, and so I sent Brotho' Williams. I am ver' sawry " —

"Oh, no matter ; we got here."

Colonel Barker introduced them to the people who stood near. The crowded condition of the room did not allow of a general introduction, although they all looked longingly at Ida, whom they knew by reputation.

At first glance the effect was unpromising. Most of the men had their hats on — the wide wool hats of the Kansas type. Most of them were fresh from the corn-fields, and their hands were hard as leather, and cracked and seamed, and lumpy with great muscles. Everybody wore cots upon their fingers, which were worn to the quick with husking. Everywhere was a certain unkempt look, and every where color was in low tones : browns, grays, drabs ; nothing light and gay about dress or bearing. Bradley noticed a few girls in the middle seats, but only a few.

It looked like an uncouth audience for Ida to address. But he suddenly found himself seated beside a young farmer in a brown hat whose face startled him. He was in rough dress, and his hands were mere bludgeons ; but his eyes were beautiful and his face very handsome. There was a seriousness and delicacy about his face and in the tone of his low, soft voice that drew Bradley to him.

"It's a cold night to come out to a political meeting," Bradley began, by way of opening conversation.

"We don't stop f'r cold," replied the young fellow. "Some o' these people are from six or eight miles away. They'd go ten to hear Miss Wilbur, if they could get in. They won't be able to get in to-night."

He spoke with fine directness and force as he went on, showing much thought and reading. Others joined in, and Bradley soon found himself forced to do his best thinking. They were armed at all points.

Colonel Barker called the meeting to order, and made an astonishingly able and dignified speech. He then asked Brother Williams to say a word.

Brother Williams was a middle-aged farmer with unkempt hair. His clothes were faded to a russet brown, and his collarless neck was like wrinkled leather, and his fingers were covered with cots ; but he was a most impressive orator. His words were well chosen, and his gestures almost majestic.

He spoke in a conversational way, but with great power and sincerity. Bradley was astonished, and said so to Ida, who sat behind him.

"There are hundreds of farmers who can talk like that," she said. "This is one of the 'shock-headed farmers' the plutocratic press are fond of ridiculing."

Ida began to speak in a strictly conversational tone: "Brothers and sisters, this is not the first time I've driven across the Western prairies in a wagon to speak at such a meeting as this, and it isn't the last time. I expect to do so just as long as there is a wrong to be righted, just as long as it does you good to have me come."

"That will be while you live," said the colonel gallantly.

"I hope not," she replied, quickly. "I hope to see our reform established before the gray comes into my hair. It will be accomplished if we are true to ourselves ; if our leaders are true to themselves ; if they do not become spoils of office [she looked at Bradley, and the others followed her glance ; she saw her mistake, and colored a little as she went on]; if they are true to their best convictions, and speak the new thoughts that come to them."

Bradley studied their applause to see if it would not betray them. It showed that the money monopoly was nearest to them, but that any wrong received their condemnation. The expression of their applause showed nobility of purpose.

Ida closed by saying: "We have with us to-night a very distinguished young Democrat from Iowa,—the Honorable Mr. Talcott. He has something to say to you, and I will yield the floor to him."

While the people stamped and clapped hands, Ida went over to Bradley and said : " You *must* talk to them. Tell them just what you think."

Bradley rose. He would have done more had she asked it. He began by speaking of the Grange and its effect, and then passed to the Alliance and Reform party.

"I've been studying this question, Mr. Chairman, ladies, and gentlemen, more during the last few days than ever before. It is possible that a third party is necessary whenever a distinct work is to be done; but," he said, checking the applause, " I am not quite convinced the time has come for this movement. If I was, I'd join it, even though some of the planks in your platform were objectionable, for I am a farmer. My people for generations have been tillers of the soil. They have always been poor. They got nothing for their toil. All the blood in my heart goes out, therefore, towards the farmer and the farmers' movement. It seems a hopeless thing to fight the old organizations, with all their power and money. It can be done, but it can be done only by union among all the poor of every class. Since coming to your State, since day before yesterday, my mind has been changed. I suppose (to be perfectly candid) that my defeat for renomination had something to do with liberalizing me." As he paused he caught Ida's eyes shining into his, and on a sudden impulse he said, "But no matter! Now I'm with you from this time forward." He ended there, but he stood for a moment numb, and tingling with emotion. He had uttered a vast resolution.

The people seemed to realize the importance of this confession on the part of the speaker. There was a thrilling intensity in the tone of his voice, which every listener felt, and they broke out in wild applause as he sat down.

Ida, with her eyes shining and wet, reached forward over the seat, and clasped his hand, and held it. "Glorious! Now you're with us, heart and soul!" In their exaltation it did not occur to either of them what a strange place this little schoolhouse was for such a far-reaching compact.

Out under the vast skies again, into the crisp air! Bradley turned and looked back upon the little schoolhouse, packed to suffocation; it would always remain a memorable place in this wild land. His heart swelled with the pity, the significance, of it all.

"Oh, you've done them good — more than you can tell!" Ida said.

"I begin to believe it is the beginning of the greatest reform movement in history," he said, at last. "They are searching for the truth; and whenever any great body of men search for the truth, they find it, and the finding of it is tremendous. Its effect reaches every quarter of the earth." He was curiously exalted.

They mounted to their perilous seat once more, and moved out into the night. The wind seemed to have gone down. There was a deep hush in the air, as if the high stars listened in their illimitable spaces. The plain seemed as lonely and as unlighted as the Arctic Ocean. Even the barking of a dog had a wolfish and wild suggestiveness.

They rode in silence. Ida sighed deeply. At last she said: "It's only an incident with us. We go back to our pleasant and varied lives; they go back to their lonely homes, and to their bleak corn-fields."

"But the Alliance has given them something to hope for, something to think of," Bradley said, seeking comfort.

"Yes, that is the only comfort I can seem to get out of it. This movement has come into their lives like a new religion. It *is* a new religion — the religion of humanity. It does help them to forget mud and rain and cold and monotony."

Again Bradley's arm seemed necessary to her safety, but this time it closed around her, strong and resolute, yet he dared not say a word. He was not sure of her. It seemed impossible that this wonderful, beautiful, and intellectual woman should care for him; and yet, when he was speaking, her eyes had said something new to him.

The driver talked on about his experiences, but his companions were silent. Under cover of listening they were both dreaming. Bradley was forecasting his life, and wondering how much she would make up of it; wondering if she would make more of it than she had of his past life. How far off she had always seemed to him, and yet she had always been a part of his inner life. Now she sat beside him, in the circle of his arm, and yet she seemed hopelessly out of his reach. She liked him as a friend and brother reformer—that was all. Besides, he had no right to hope now, when his fortunes had all turned against him.

She was thinking of him. She was deeply gratified to think he had entered the great movement, and that she had been instrumental in converting him. Her heart warmed to him strangely for his honesty and his sincerity; and then he was so fine and clean-souled and strong-limbed! The pressure of his arm at her side stirred her, and she smiled at herself. Unlike Bradley, she was self-analytical; she knew what all these things meant.

"There's the station," the driver broke out, indicating some colored lights in the valley below them.

At his word the picture of it all, and the significance of it all, rushed over Ida — the serene majesty of the stars, the splendor and unused wealth of the prairies, the barriers to their use, the limitless robbery of the poor, in both city and country.

"Oh, the pathos, the tragedy of it all! Nature

is so good and generous, and men are so ignorant and selfish. Can it be remedied? It *must* be remedied. Every thinking, sympathizing soul must help us."

Bradley's voice touched Ida deeply as he said, slowly, " Henceforward I shall work for these people and all who suffer. My life shall be given to this work."

A great, sudden resolution flashed into Ida's eyes. She laid her hand on his and clasped it. There. was a little pause, in which, as if by some occult sense, their minds read each other.

"We'll work *together*, Bradley," she said ; and the unconscious driver did not see the light caress which Bradley put upon her lips as a sign of his unspeakable great joy.

XXXII.

CONCLUSION. — WASHINGTON AGAIN.

BRADLEY and Ida went down the hills together on the way to the theatre. It was the fourth week of the short session of Bradley's term, and the tenth week since their marriage. Ida had returned with him to stay the winter. They paused in the midst of the grounds where the shrubbery was the thickest; where, to Bradley's mind, it conveyed a faint suggestion of mid-forest. His love for nature had intensified during his city life. They turned, as they always did, to look at the dome. The untracked snow swept in shadowless white to the Capitol, which rose out of it hardly less white and seamless. The yellow flare of the lamps only flung the snow and the marble walls into more cold and glittering relief.

They gazed at it in silence, listening to the jingle of bells, the soft voices of the negro drivers, the laughter of children coasting on the winding mall, and the roll of carettes.

"Beautiful! Beautiful!" said Ida.

"Yes, but I can't think of it without its antithesis, the home of the working-man and the hut of the poor negro."

They moved on in silence, arm in arm. The darky newsboys, shivering with cold, met them on every corner, holding out in their stiffened hands their evening papers. "Styah papah?"

"We hear a great deal about the indolence and shiftlessness of the negro," said Bradley, "but I have never met a people more pathetically eager to earn a living than these same negroes."

Swarms of people loitered along the store fronts. Negroes in ragged, faded garments, and men with chin beards, in Western or Southern hats, went streaming past. The old man with the cough medicine met them again. They could repeat his sing-song cry: "*Doc-ter Fergusson's double-ex selly-brated, Philadelphia cough drops, for coughs or colds, sore throat or hoarseness; five cents a package.*"

They soon struck into the gayer streams of people making their way towards the theatre; and when they took their seats on the crowded balcony, poverty was lost sight of.

"There! who says this is not a bright and gay world?" said Ida, looking about. "No poor, no aged, no infirm, no cold or hungry people here."

"This is the bright side of the moon," replied Bradley gravely. They looked around, and studied it with a mental comparison with other crowds they had seen on the fair prairies of Kansas and Iowa. There were girls with eyes full of liquid light, with dainty bonnets nestling on their soft hair; their faces were like petals of flowers; the curves of their chins were more beautiful than chalices of lilies; their dresses, soft, shapely, of exquisite tones and texture, draped their perfect bodies. Their dainty fingers held gold-and-pearl opera glasses. The young men who sat beside them wore the latest fashions in clothing and of the finest texture. Heavy men with brutal faces slouched beside their dainty daughters, the purple blotches on their bloated and lumpy faces showing how politics or business had debauched and undermined them. Everywhere was the rustle of drapery and soft, musical speech.

The curtain rose upon the fair at Nottingham-shire; and with the sweet imaginative music as solvent and setting, the gay lads and lassies of far romance sang and danced under the trees in garments upon which the rain had never fallen, and unflecked with dust. Knights in splendid dress of silver and green, with graceful swords and sashes, came and went, while the merry peasant youths circled and flourished their gay scarfs and sang task-free and sin-free.

The scene changed to Sherwood Forest; and there, in the land of Robin Hood, where snow never falls, where rains never slant through the shuddering leaves, the jocund foresters met to sing and drink October ale. There came Little John and Will Scarlet and Alan-a-Dale in glittering garments, with care-free brows and tuneful voices, to circle and sing. Fadeless and untarnished was each magnificent cloak and doublet, slashed with green or purple; straight and fair and supple was every back and limb. No marks of toil anywhere, no lines of care, no hopeless hunger, no threatening task; nothing to do but to sing and dance and drink after the hunt among the delightfully dry and commodious forest wilds — a glorious, free life! A beautiful, child-like dream-like, pagan-like life!

As they looked, and while the music, imaginative, sweet, and persuasive, called to them, a shadow fell upon Ida and Bradley.   That world of care-free, changeless youth, that world of love and comradeship, threw into painful relief the actual world from which they came.   It brought up with terrible force the low cottage in the lonely forest of Wisconsin, or the equally lonely cabin on the Kansas plain.

When the curtain fell, they rose and went sombrely out.   When they reached the street, Ida pressed Bradley's arm.

"Oh, it was beautiful, *painfully* beautiful!   Do you know what I mean?"

"Yes," replied Bradley simply.

"O Bradley! if we only could discover a land like that, to which all the poor could go at once and be happy — a land of song and plenty, with no greed and no grinding need!"

"Yes," Bradley sighed, "I am afraid you and I will never taste anything again that will be perfectly sweet.   There will always be a dash of bitter in it."

"Yes, we are born to feel others' cares.   The worst of it is, we could have that land in America if we only would.   Our forefathers thought it was coming, but instead of it" — she did not finish, and they walked on in deep thought.

" Yes," said Bradley, " we could have it ; but the way is long and weary, and thousands and millions of us must die on the road, I am afraid."

As they walked on, Bradley could hear the occasional deep-sighing breath of the heart-burdened woman beside him. Again they passed by the cold and stately palace of the government, lifting its dome against the glittering sky. The moon had swung high into the air, giving a whiter tinge to the blue, and dimming the brilliancy of the stars ; but it was still beautiful. The crusted snow sparkled like a cloth of diamonds, and each snow-burdened branch took on unearthly charm. It was very still and peaceful and remote, as if no city were near. They stood in silence until Ida shivered with cold ; then without a word Bradley touched her arm, and they walked on.

When they arrived at their room, Ida sat down in a chair by the fire without removing her things ; and when Bradley came in from the hall she still sat there, her eyes shaded by her hat, her chin resting on her palm, her gloves in her lap. He knew her too well to interrupt her, and sat down near her, waiting for her to speak.

At last she turned abruptly, and said, " Bradley, I'm going home."

It made him catch his breath. "Oh, no, I can't let you do that, Ida."

"But you must; I can't stay here. That play to-night has wakened my sleeping conscience. I must go back to the West."

"But, Ida, you've only been here four weeks; I don't see why" —

"Because my people need me. I am cursed. I can't enjoy this life any more, because I can't forget those poor souls on the lonely farm grinding out their lives in gloomy toil ; I must go back and help them ; I feel like a thief to be enjoying this beautiful room, and these plays and concerts, when *they* are shut out from them."   .

Bradley had a sudden impulse of rebellion. "But we have done our best, haven't we ?"

"Yes, but we must continue to do our best right along, and I am of no use here ; there's nothing I can do here ; the battle is only half won yet, and I've enlisted to the end ; besides," she said, looking up at him with a faint smile, "I've got to go right into your district and pave the way for your re-election by the people's party, you know. If you expect to do your part here, I must do my part in electing you. We've had our vacation, and **you've got** work to do which I hinder. I'll leave you here, and go back. You know how much good it does the poor wives and mothers to meet me and to hear me. Now, we mustn't be selfish, dear; you've got your work to do here, and I've got my work to do there."

They sat in silence again. Bradley looked at the fire; there was a burning pain in his staring eyes; his throat hurt him. To be left alone in this way was hard, and yet he saw it was consistent. When he spoke again, it was in his apparently passionless way. "All right, Ida; we enlisted for the whole war." He was able to smile a little as he looked up at her.

She rose and came to him, and put her arm about his neck. "As a matter of fact, you'll fight better here without me, and then at the end of your term, when you come home, there will be two years that we can work together."

THE END.